# *What the Heart Wants*

Judith Paolercio

2026, TWB Press
https://www.twbpress.com

What the Heart Wants


Edited by Terry Wright

Cover Art by Terry Wright

ISBN: 978-1-967888-18-4

# DEDICATION

For Theresa. Who gives more than she receives,
and finds joy in the happiness of those around her.

## ACKNOWLEDGEMENTS

Books are not completed without the assistance of editors, beta readers and publishing experts, who work behind the scenes to bring the vision of the author to life, transforming a raw manuscript into a polished, engaging and professional story, ready for the world.

Ben has been, and continues to be, my trusted beta reader since 2013. A talented writer in his own right, I'm fortunate to have his critique as a guide to move my stories forward.

My thanks to TWB Press for giving this book a home.

Special gratitude to Jeannie and her knowledge of New England.

# Chapter 1

During the height of the busy summer season, the small town of Wellfleet found itself mourning one of its own.

Vivienne stood out in a subdued gray t-shirt and jeans, among tourists who crowded the streets in their shorts and tops of lemon, lavender, pink, green and white. The colors reminded her, *I could use some of Howie's saltwater taffy before going to Magda's shop.*

Howie's taffy and sundries store was stocked for the summer and already crowded with tourists browsing for t-shirts, flip flops, visors, hats and other Cape novelties. Standing behind the counter, the sound of his old cash register rang like the bell at the end of a boxing round.

"Morning, Howie." Vivienne maneuvered her way through the tourists and narrow aisles. Sand from the beach dusted the old, uneven wood floor and crackled under her sandals. After taking one of the small bags, she filled it with every flavor he had. Waiting patiently behind several people, she then handed Howie the bag. "I could use this today."

His frown was one of many in the town, saddened by Vivienne's loss. "It's on me."

Magda's shop was on the opposite side of the street and toward the middle of town, so Vivienne went to the corner and waited with the others to cross. Directing traffic was Jack Higgins. He was new on the Wellfleet Police Department, and Vivienne could feel his calm demeanor simmering in the rising heat, having landed this duty no one wanted. Sweat lines appeared on his short-sleeve khaki uniform.

"Stay hydrated, Jack," Vivienne said.

"Got plenty of water, Mrs. Callane, thank you. Steve is replacing me in a few hours, so I'm good."

Before she entered Magda's shop, Vivienne paused outside, admiring the two window displays that Magda changed every day. On the right, she had coordinated cotton and linen tops with patterned shorts and leisure pants, for daywear. The other window showed the transition to evening. Magda chose long flowy dresses in jeweled colors that would graze sandaled ankles, and pashminas to cover sun-kissed shoulders. Needing nothing more than a delicate velvet hanger, a little black dress shared the spotlight for eveningwear. In Vivienne's eyes, it stole the show. A row of tiny black sequins around the neckline, added a stunning elegance to this classic dress. Vivienne's sigh was deep. For an instant, she closed her eyes and wished for that time again, when life was simple, and beautiful dresses like this one hung freely in her closet.

Magda was ready for Vivienne's visit to her shop. Having been widowed herself, five years ago, she would never forget how Vivienne helped her shoulder her grief and find a way to live without her husband. Magda knew Vivienne needed the same support now. "Morning, Viv. I got a coffee for the both of us."

Vivienne held up the bag of taffy. "I stopped at Howie's on the way."

Magda reached for the bag. "The coffee can wait. I love the white ones."

"I know you do, so I bought extra. They're all yours." Vivienne opened the wax paper and popped a pink taffy in her mouth. She admired the seafoam green cotton top Magda wore, paired with white cropped pants and sandals. "I love that you always choose something to wear from the store every day."

"It shows customers the fit and look of the clothes. I picked out a dress for you. It's hanging in front of the changing room, but there are more on the racks against the wall, if you want another option."

"Thank you." Vivienne's gaze went to the store window again. With sad resignation, she glanced down at her not-so-slender hips then picked one other dress from the *conservative* section to try on.

As Vivienne came out of the changing room, modeling the first dress, Magda examined her from head to toe. "You look lovely."

"I don't need to look lovely."

"Why? There's nothing overstated about this simple black dress. I'm sure Nate would want you to wear something nice, Viv."

With a twist of her body to the right and left, Vivienne eyed herself in the mirror. "My mother would approve. It falls below my knee."

"And sleeveless will be perfect. They're predicting record heat tomorrow."

"Now that you mentioned it, is the air on in here?" Vivienne fanned herself with her hand.

Magda walked to the control panel on the wall. "I'll turn the temperature down a bit."

Vivienne sighed. "Menopause. It robbed me of my hormones, left me with the flashes from Hades, and obsessing with a tweezer over every stray hair that pops up on my chin. And the days of wearing that little black dress in the window are long gone."

"They're gone for me, too, but the young women who vacation here may need something that makes a statement at a party. You'd do more justice to those hips in a pair of fitted jeans." Magda pointed to the table in the middle of the store. "These just arrived." She rummaged for Vivienne's size and picked out a pair in a dark-blue wash.

Behind the changing room curtain, Vivienne put the other dress aside and pulled on the jeans, which slipped easily over her legs and hips. She took more than the few seconds to admire the woman looking back at her in the mirror. The jeans sat just below her waist and hugged her hips, tapering down to her slender ankles. She opened the clip keeping her hair off her shoulders and shook her head, releasing the thick, unruly brown curls that hadn't been touched by a stylist in months. Her fingers tugged on a ringlet that fell below her shoulders, and she asked the woman in the mirror, "Where have you been?"

Magda was waiting when Vivienne pulled aside the dressing room curtain. Pushing her glasses up the bridge of her nose with her index finger, she scrutinized the fit and overall appearance, as she would for any customer. "They're a perfect fit and just what you needed today." She held out a pair of sandals. "Give me your old jeans, I'll get rid of them. Out with the old, in with the new."

Vivienne swapped her jeans for the simple pair of black sandals.

"You know, it's okay to be angry, Viv."

She sighed and let the gentle permission of Magda's words settle in her heart.

"Why didn't he tell me he was ill? Did he think I wasn't strong enough to walk that road with him?"

"I wish I had an answer for you. You'll never know what was in his mind, but what I do know, is that those rough years have ended. You can breathe now, Vivienne, and tell him what's in your heart, at the cemetery tomorrow."

Vivienne had pushed the cemetery from her mind, like the throbbing pain of a bad tooth, until Magda mentioned it. "Tomorrow."

***

The next morning, Vivienne hung the *Closed* sign on the door of the restaurant, as did the whole town of Wellfleet. Tourists showed their disappointed frowns as they peeked in the darkened windows of stores and restaurants, having nowhere to spend their money except the crappy little store on Route 6 that sold only floats and seashell trinkets that would break after a couple of hours.

Town folk gathered at the Wellfleet Rural Cemetery to pay their respects around the casket of local fisherman, Nate Callane. Father Caspian stood at the head of the casket with a Bible in hand.

When he began to recite The Fisherman's Prayer, Vivienne squeezed Evan's hand and leaned to him. "Thank you for being here."

"Mom, where else would I be?" Evan whispered. "Everything, I mean everything I am, I owe to Dad." His glance strayed past his wife Grace and their son, Tory, to his sister, Audrey. She was standing on the other side of Vivienne, with an impeccably dressed older man at her side. "I can't say Dad would approve of *that*."

Vivienne followed his glance. "She told me she was bringing someone."

"Don't tell me she needs another father figure now."

"Keep your voice down. We'll find out who he is soon enough."

Father Caspian glanced at Vivienne before he continued. "With just one boat, Nate Callane built a fishing business that continues to thrive to this day. He devoted his life to his family, and his son, Evan, will continue to keep the Callane fishing boats full. Nate touched all our lives in some way. Let us reflect on those times with his wife, Vivienne, and their children, Evan and Audrey."

Vivienne knew Juliet Gardner from the church choir. Her twenty-something angelic voice sang *Be Not Afraid,* bringing some of those gathered to tears, and solace to the souls who occupied the cemetery. Yet, Vivienne couldn't imagine that Nate would be smiling, if he could read her mind from wherever he was. He would remember the familiar slur in his voice, and the glassy stare in his steel-gray eyes that would make her tremble when he stumbled in the door after a night's worth of beer and bourbon chasers.

It was the warm hand of Audrey, touching hers, that brought her back. "Mom, are you okay? Father Caspian finished his prayers."

Through dark sunglasses, Vivienne saw her daughter's concern in her frown and pensive eyes. "I'm fine." She nodded to Father Caspian to make the announcement.

"The Callane family invites everyone to their restaurant."

With Evan and Audrey by her side, Vivienne watched people place roses and carnations on Nate's casket as a parting gesture, before walking away in quiet procession.

"Go on ahead," Vivienne said to Evan and Audrey.

"Are you sure you don't want us to stay?" Evan asked.

Even if she did, the presence of Audrey's mysterious man felt out-of-place there. "No. Head over to the restaurant. Gram is there, and I'm sure she'll need help with all these people arriving. I just need some time alone."

With no one else around, Vivienne removed her sunglasses to reveal her tired and dry eyes to Nate. She could feel her emotions rising from deep within her, and her breathing began to escalate. In a one-sided altercation, with no chance of interruptions or challenges, a resentful string of pent-up rage burst from her, that was sure to wake Nate's sleeping neighbors. "Damn it! I'm so angry with you! Now you're stuck in that casket with no choice but to listen to me. What were you trying to spare me and the kids from? What? The pain of knowing we were going to lose you, or was it knowing you were going to lose your family? Either one was a sellout, Nate. In sickness and in health. Do you remember those words? I do, and I would have never left your side, but you took that from me and chose to brave your illness at the *Fore and Aft*. Dying alone at home, for me to find you, wasn't heroic. It was a coward's way out. I'll never tell Audry and Evan why you denied me that precious time with you."

She placed the rose she'd been holding, among the other flowers on his casket. Suddenly, her hands balled up, her fingers squeezing her anger into tight fists. "Why, Nate? For God's sake, why didn't you tell me? I thought we shared everything, but now you left me with this question that will always linger six feet between us."

Vivienne had never walked away from Nate, even in the heat of an argument. Tears began to slip down her cheeks. "Goodbye, Nate." She turned and left him for the first and only time.

# Chapter 2

Vivienne had only taken a few steps, when she turned and looked back to where Nate was. The words she said to him lightened the weight on her shoulders, but the emptiness she felt left her feeling hollow and drained inside. It was her friend Magda, waiting with patience for her, that brought her some relief.

"I thought I was the last one to leave the cemetery."

"You are, but I didn't want you walking alone. Are you okay?"

"I'm not sure yet. I'm kind of numb inside, but I know that will wear off soon."

Magda slipped her arm inside Vivienne's. "And I'll be here when it does."

"You've done enough already. All those nights you lost sleep, while I sat in your living room."

"Griffin's chair has your name on it," Magda said. "I'm sure he wouldn't mind me sharing it with you. He loved you as much as I do."

"I remember when Griffin passed; how hard it was for you."

"I was alone for the first time in 42 years. I would close my eyes at night and pray that I would breathe my last breath, so I could be with him. But Griff had other plans. Selling his boats to Nate, paid the remaining mortgage on our house."

"And purchased the storefront for your business. They were good friends, as are we."

Magda gave Vivienne's hand a comforting squeeze. "You have Evan and Audrey. You'll get through this, Viv."

"Audrey." Vivienne released her name with a sigh.

"At least it will give you something else to think about. Come on, Viv. Aren't you the least bit curious to know who her *new man* is?"

"She told me she was bringing someone from the office. It surprised me, because she had just broken up with a guy she'd been seeing for quite a while. I have to admit, this man wasn't who I was expecting."

"Someone our age?"

"This is so unlike her. All the guys she's dated were her age, good jobs, successful."

"Then maybe she's not dating him, but you'll find out soon enough. I bet Camille and Stella are dying to know. They were making my blood boil. Did you notice them at the cemetery? If looks could kill..."

"How could I not? Thank goodness for these dark sunglasses. I could see them giving Audrey the scrutinizing evil eye. God only knows what they were thinking."

"God's not the only one who knows. I'll tell you. They're probably running home right now to change out of those homely house dresses. Can you see them rummaging through their bathroom cabinets in a panic, looking for makeup that hasn't been opened since their last high school dance?"

The visual brought a much-needed smile and chuckle from Vivienne. "Magda, you're terrible."

"Come on, Viv, you know it's the truth. Those two have been like this for years. It's always been about what other people have, and the way they were checking out Audrey's escort..."

The scenario Magda painted changed Vivienne's expression to one of utter disbelief. "No! You honestly believe..."

Magda drove her point home. "Men like that rarely make an appearance in a small fishing town. That tailored suit he's wearing didn't come off the rack. I know clothes. It was made for him and shows he takes care of his body. He's of a certain age, and Camille and Stella are of a certain age. Need I say more?"

Their conversation was put on hold when they entered the restaurant. As Vivienne's eyes adjusted from the bright sun, the one person she needed the most came into view: Estelle, her mother, affectionately known as Esty to friends and family. Mom's arms were the comforting solace Vivienne could find in no one else.

"Mom, I finally told Nate what I needed to say."

With a gentle, calming touch, Esty ran her hand over her daughter's hair. "I'm glad you did, Vivienne. He heard you, even if you think he didn't."

Vivienne whispered, "I'm not so sure it was what he wanted to hear. Thank you for staying behind to help Auggie and the staff."

"I just want to be where you need me the most."

"How is everyone in the kitchen doing?"

"Working quietly. This hit them hard too."

"I'll talk to them."

When Vivienne entered the kitchen, she could feel the reflective sadness of the chefs as they scurried to put the menu she had chosen onto plates for the servers.

She turned to head chef, Auggie. "I want to see how everyone is doing."

"We're all so very sorry for you and your family, Vivienne." Auggie's voice carried the softness of his sympathetic words.

She looked at the chefs, some of whom rubbed tears from their cheeks. She paused for a moment, barely able to speak the words that caught in her throat. "Thank you, everyone. Some of you have been with us since we opened. Chance and Marty. I see you in the back. Crystal and Devon, our new chefs who joined the Callane family. My heartfelt thanks to you all. You've made my life a little easier today."

With a quick sniff and a couple of blinks, Auggie turned to his staff. "Okay, people, we've got a job to do."

The first thing Vivienne saw when she pushed open the kitchen door was Audrey holding out a glass of wine. "You're going to need this."

It was a leadup to what Vivienne suspected at the cemetery. The glass exchanged hands and went right to her lips. She sipped the wine while her eyes slowly settled on Audrey's mystery man speaking with Magda, Camille, and Stella. Magda was right. His lean and muscular body would have challenged men half his age. Silver strands dominated the waves of his brown hair and neatly trimmed beard. His casual smile and relaxed stance exuded a confidence that hadn't passed through this town in years. His presence was like a shot of seduction, obvious in Camille and Stella's awkward body language. Vivienne had to know. "Who's your friend?"

"His name is Hugo Lawson. He's the managing editor at the Boston Tribune."

Vivienne's eyes widened. "He works with you? Don't play with me, Audrey. Why is he here?"

"We've been dating for six months now."

The remaining wine in Vivienne's glass went down in the next big swallow, hitting her empty stomach and going straight to her head.

"I didn't tell you...because I wasn't sure where this was going. When I decided to tell you, this happened with Dad."

Vivienne glanced at the striking man, who now had a name and a place in Audrey's life. "He's not even close to the other men you've dated."

"You deliberately left out two words in the sentence, Mom," Audrey whispered with a roll of her eyes. "Just say it. *In age.*"

"I'm glad you noticed. What are you doing, Audrey?"

"We can talk about this later. Can I at least introduce you to him? Magda, Camille, and Stella have already met him."

"Magda? Since when, have you stopped calling her Mrs. Winslow?"

"Since she just told me I'm old enough to call her Magda. How is this important?"

As they made their way toward Mr. Lawson, Vivienne homed in on the subtle and quick flare of Magda's eyes that was the unmistakable code for *I told you so.*

"Mom, this is Hugo Lawson."

When Vivienne placed her hand in his, he didn't shake it but gently held it. "Mrs. Callane, I'm so sorry for your loss, and for your family, Audrey, Evan, and your mother."

Empathy, sincerity. For someone she had just met, they rang true in the softness of his brown eyes and tender words. "Thank you, Mr. Lawson."

"Please, call me Hugo. I wish we could have met in happier times."

"Some things can't be helped, but I'm happy to meet you. Audrey tells me you're the managing editor for the Boston Tribune."

"It's a busy place."

"We've been hearing all about what Audrey does there," Stella cut in. "Editing articles, doing research for other staff writers."

"Has she neglected to tell you that she also writes promotional materials, fact-checks stories, copy edits, and proofreads text?" He shot Audrey a quick glance. "While these various roles overlap, they are crucial in the running of the paper. As managing editor, I rely heavily on her skills and contributions."

Vivienne saw it instantly. How the eyes project the heart's feelings. She'd seen it in Nate's, when their love was new, and now it was Audrey who was the object of Hugo's affections. He may have been talking about her valued contributions to the success of the paper, but his eyes glistened with the declaration of his love for her.

Meanwhile, Stella's jealousy of Audrey made its first smug appearance. "That's all very impressive, although, it sounds like Audrey doesn't have much time to socialize after hours." While she basked in highlighting the negative aspect of Audrey's job, it put her in an embarrassing spotlight of which she was unaware. The tight constraints of the dress she chose made it difficult to stand naturally. Likely she had pulled it from deep within her closet where it hadn't seen the light of day in years. Tiny white peonies were stretched into full bloom on the deep red material that strained to cover her body.

"How is the Boston nightlife, Audrey?" Camille asked.

Audrey tried not to focus on what looked like two pink racing stripes on either side of Camille's face, and lashes clumped together from mascara that had long since lost its expiration date. "Not much different than any big city."

Camille then turned to Hugo. "What are your interests outside the office, Mr. Lawson?"

"Hugo, please. I left Mr. Lawson at the office. I enjoy the arts, reading—"

"He's a big Red Sox and Celtics fan," Audrey cut in. "I wasn't as much, but it's easy to get hooked when you're sitting behind home plate or courtside."

Stella's feigned interest couldn't mask her envy of Audrey. She studied her through unscrupulous and resentful eyes. Audrey's familiarity of Hugo, and his tastes, balled up like a sailor's knot in her stomach. "It all sounds very fast-paced," Stella blurted before Camille could respond. "But there's something to be said for watching the sun come up on the bay from your back porch with a good cup of coffee."

"The image you painted is very serene," Hugo said.

Everything about Hugo took hold of Stella. The sensuous pinch of titillation tweaked pleasure deep within her as she indulged in her own secret, private moment with him. She imagined his voice, light as the wings of a butterfly, beating soft seduction into her ear and giving in to the helpless rapture in his strong arms. The wine lowered her inhibitions and set the tone for her reply. "Wellfleet isn't far from Boston. There are lovely bed and breakfasts that overlook the bay."

"Actually, I'm staying at the Bayview Inn. Audrey took care of the arrangements."

His reply caught Stella off-guard, stalling her in a brow-raising moment of silence. "Oh!" Turning to Audrey, she rallied back. "Did you check the Sandpiper House? It's closer to the bay."

*Closer to the bay or closer to your house?* The thought made Magda's blood boil. Stella's insinuation may have passed by Hugo, but it only served to infuriate Magda, whose dander had been prickling since the cemetery. "You know the Sandpiper is geared to tourists staying for the summer." She countered. "It's loud, and the rooms haven't been updated in years. That's why the rate is low." She then turned to Hugo. "Audrey chose The Bayview, because it's the finest Inn in Wellfleet. The rooms have private balconies overlooking the gardens. It's quiet and perfect for a *morning cup of coffee.*"

Caught with her proverbial *pants down,* Stella puffed her already overflowing breasts. She lifted her chin and looked down her pinched nose at Magda to deliver a curt response. "Well...I only thought..."

Magda fixed her eyes on Stella. "I *know* what you thought."

Letting out an exasperated breath, Stella turned to Vivienne. "I'm very sorry for your loss. Nate was a good man."

"Thank you, Stella. I appreciate your support today."

"You should rethink your friends, Vivienne." Stella pointed a shaking index finger at Magda.

Camille's words were quick and uncaring, like a waitress with too many tables, instead of someone Vivienne had shared coffee with on occasion. "If there's anything I can do..." She left on the heels of Stella's hasty departure.

"I really didn't need those two today," Vivienne grumped.

"I know, Viv," Magda said. "But they're gone now."

After Stella's failed attempt at her not-so-subtle seduction, it put Vivienne's focus on the one thing she couldn't ignore: Audrey, at thirty-seven, had the affections of a man Vivienne suspected was around sixty, Nate's age. So, she looked away. "I'm sorry, everyone, but if you'll excuse me, I still have some people I need to talk to."

Without waiting for a response from anyone, she made her way farther into the restaurant. She was speaking to some of Nate's fishing crew, when her grandson, Tory, bolted from his parents.

"Grandma!"

Her son Evan ran after him. "Tory!"

But Vivienne caught him in her arms. "It's okay, Evan." She closed her eyes, reveling in her grandson's hug around her neck. "How's my big boy?"

He pulled back, and Vivienne smiled at the puffy cheeks of this inquisitive four-year-old. His brown eyes were wide with questions waiting to be asked. "Mommy and Daddy were crying because Grandpa died. They said he was sick."

"Yes, sweetheart, the doctors couldn't fix him."

"Did you see him die, Grandma?"

"No. Grandpa died when everyone was sleeping."

"Grandpa isn't coming back?"

"No, Tory, but you can talk to him whenever you want, and he will hear you."

"I want to be a fisherman like him and Daddy."

One of Nate's crew was standing close enough to hear. "Your grandpa will like that".

Vivienne kissed Tory's cheek. "That will make him very happy."

"I'm sorry to interrupt," Evan said. "Mom, can I speak with you for a moment?"

When Vivienne excused herself, Evan brought Tory to his wife. "Grace, please take him over to the dessert table for some ice cream."

After Evan's remark at the cemetery, Vivienne knew what was coming.

He glanced across the room at Magda, Audrey, and Hugo, and spoke quietly. "Mom, have you talked to Audrey? Who is that guy?"

"His name is Hugo Lawson. He's Audrey's boss, and she's been seeing him for six months now."

Evan's eyes widened. "She's dating her boss?"

"Evan, keep your voice down."

"I'll admit, he's not a bad looking guy for someone his age, but has she lost her mind? What happens if this *thing* she has with him goes south? She'll have to look for another job."

Vivienne took in a huge breath and released it with a roll of her eyes. "It's my tolerance that's going south. I don't have answers for any of this, and it's the last thing I want to think about today. I'm going to talk to a few more people and then head home."

"I'm sorry, Mom. I'll take you when you're ready."

"It's alright, Evan. The walk will do me good. I just need to be by myself. I'll be fine."

Given that Vivienne had been up since dawn, the short time she spent speaking to people was her limit. Before she left, she grabbed a container of chowder and stopped to see her mother sitting next to her great grandson while he shared some of his ice cream with her. "I'm going to head home, Mom."

Despite the brief distraction Tory brought, it couldn't dissipate the sorrow Esty carried for her daughter. Her heart swelled, pushing her grief to the surface as she looked up at her daughter through teary eyes. "Have you eaten anything Vivienne?"

"I'm fine, Mom. I'm taking home some chowder."

"I'll call you later."

She was almost at the door, when the gentle touch of a hand on her arm stopped her.

"Mom, where are you going?" Audrey asked.

"Home. I'm exhausted."

"I have no doubt you are, but you shouldn't be alone."

Vivienne touched Audrey's cheek. "I'd better get used to it."

"No, Mom. Just give me a minute. I'll tell Hugo I'm taking you home."

She took Audrey's hand and, with a soft but decisive grip, left no room for argument. "You'll tell him nothing, Audrey. Please, just let me go."

Even with her sunglasses, Vivienne squinted as her eyes adjusted from the dim restaurant light to the bright sun. Her palms felt the warmth of the container of chowder that food critics raved as the best on the Cape.

She stopped a block away from the house to look at the saltbox that she and Nate called home. Years of New England weather had turned the clapboard to a beautiful gray. Pink and white petunias flourished in window boxes, while hydrangeas blossomed into perfect round balls of tiny blue petals. As she approached the red wood door, she bit her lip and placed her shaking hand on the handle. Taking in a breath, she let it out as she pushed, and the door swung open. She had never heard a silence so loud but felt compelled to step into it. Her eyes closed, and she let it cover her as she breathed in the emptiness.

This was home, where she belonged, where her life would never be the same.

# Chapter 3

Mist slowly creeped in from the bay, draining the morning of color. Millions of minute drops sparkled under the gray clouds as they settled on every blade of grass and flower petal in the garden. With a shawl covering her shoulders, Vivienne stood on the deck, holding a mug of coffee. Too soon for her heart to reminisce, she just listened to the silence. Hearing movement behind her, she turned to find Audrey in her old Boston U sweatshirt and a pair of plaid pajama bottoms.

"Why are you still wearing your dress?" Audrey asked.

"I fell asleep on the couch. I'm surprised to see you home. Your manfriend is going to miss you."

The sting of her mother's sarcasm was obvious, and Audrey felt defensive. "His name is Hugo, Mom, and it's not just about the physical stuff. I told you I didn't want you to be alone. Please give me a little more credit."

It was the first time Audrey had ever taken a stand for herself. "I'm sorry, Audrey. Let me rephrase that. I'm glad to see you home."

"I couldn't sleep last night, knowing Dad wasn't in the house."

"That makes two of us. I couldn't bring myself to sleep in our bed." Vivienne flinched as she rubbed the knot in her shoulder. "The couch has always been uncomfortable."

"Maybe it's time to buy a new one."

"We can talk about couches inside. My coffee is getting cold, and so are my old bones. I'll make you some breakfast."

"I miss your pancakes."

Vivienne smiled. "Then I'll make some."

In the small confines of the kitchen, conversation suddenly came to an awkward halt. Vivienne mixed the pancake batter more than she needed while stealing quick glances at Audrey who sat at the counter. Her eyes were lowered, as she slowly stirred her sugarless black coffee. Both of them were aware of the pink bulbous animal floating between them.

"It just happened," Audrey blurted. "Neither of us were looking for it."

Vivienne was waiting for this door to open. "What happened with Oliver? You were seeing him for a while."

Audrey sat back in the chair and huffed. "Not after we were having drinks after work and I came back from the bathroom to find another woman handing him her number. Do I really have to go over this again? It's the same thing that happens with all these guys, Mom. They're full of themselves. They're confident, have good jobs, lots of money, and roaming eyes. Hugo isn't like that."

"So, tell me what he's like."

"He's a one-woman man. He lost his wife, Emily, a few years ago. They met in college and have a son my age. His name is William. She was his whole world, and he was devastated when she died."

"I can relate to that. And now he's moving on to younger women? Sounds to me like he's into the *love em and leave em* thing."

"You'd be surprised to know that he hasn't been with anyone since his wife passed."

Vivienne cocked her head, and a bit of skepticism drizzled onto her words. "He told you that? Audrey, really?"

Audrey stood up, taking a defensive stand for herself and Hugo. "Haven't you ever felt it in your heart? When Dad would whisper something to you, that you just knew was sincere?"

"My heart is not made of stone, Audrey." In an instant, Vivienne was transported back to the night Nate proposed. Beside a blazing bonfire on the beach, he'd scattered rose petals on the sand and knelt before her. *I was born for you. To live my life with you. Marry me, Vivienne.*

She turned her back to wipe her eyes, remembering that moment, and knowing how her life with him had changed so drastically in the years before his death. A life she took great pains to shield from Audrey and Evan, even now, as she masked the relief she felt with the sorrow in her voice.

"I didn't mean to upset you, Mom, but if we're going to have this conversation, then you need to be open to what I'm saying. I've never felt that sincerity with anyone, until Hugo."

Vivienne wasn't usually skeptical, but she had been fired up about this since yesterday. She took the bait Audrey threw and turned to her. "Okay. Tell me why he's not interested in women his own age?"

"Why are you stuck on this *age thing?* If he had met someone his own age, I wouldn't be in the picture. If two people are compatible, why should age matter?"

"I'm going to play devil's advocate, so hear me out, young lady. What if one person wants a family and the other doesn't?"

"You have a point. It's true. Most women my age, or younger, are looking for a guy to settle down with, and have a family, but you have to admit that there are women out there who don't want that...and neither do I."

It was a blow that took Vivienne's breath away. Her dream for Audrey died as suddenly and unexpectedly as her husband. She reached for the chair to steady her legs and sat opposite her daughter. "You can't be serious, Audrey. Do you realize what you just said? Being a mother, raising your children. You're giving that up for him?"

"No, Mom, I'm not."

"Then for God's sake, what made you come to this decision?"

"I'm thirty-seven years old. I can't do this dating thing anymore. Every year gets harder. You take a chance and open your heart, only to be left for someone younger or better looking. Hugo and I have talked about where both of us are in our lives, and the things that we want."

"I'm not interested in what Hugo wants. What do you want, Audrey?"

"What everybody wants, Mom. To be loved and cherished."

"And that doesn't include a family and children?"

"Hugo has never been anything but honest and upfront with me. We were dating about a month when he decided it would be better if we didn't see each other. I said, 'better for who?' He knew that I was okay with him not wanting children but was sure I'd have a chance to have a family with someone my own age. I cried and pleaded with him, but he wouldn't listen. When he left me, the future I wanted with him was gone. I had nothing."

Vivienne's eyes glistened, as Audrey shared this heartbreaking time in her life. "What brought you both together again?"

"I guess you could call it divine intervention. We were apart for several weeks and only saw each other at work. I couldn't concentrate because I wasn't sleeping. Seeing him every day, knowing I couldn't be with him, was too much for me to bear. I thought he would have been relieved when I gave him my resignation but, sometimes, life has an empathetic heart. He confessed that the time we were apart brought back the pain of losing someone he loved, and it made him realize that he was being offered another chance at love."

"You're giving up a lot, Audrey. Are you sure this is what you want?"

"There are no guarantees in life, Mom, but I know in my soul that Hugo is the first person to truly open my heart and show me love I never thought was possible. I would rather take this chance at happiness and lose than regret this time in my life that I let slip away. I know your dream for me was to have a family. My decision has nothing to do with settling. It's a chance to live my life with the man I love. And, by the way, he ripped up my resignation letter."

"I want you to be happy, Audrey, but you've just hit me with a life-altering decision you made for a man you've haven't known long and I just met yesterday. I'm more than a little reluctant to take what you have told me about him at face value."

"You have doubts, I understand. For some people, it takes a year or more to know if they are compatible, while for others, six months is enough. Try to keep an open mind and get to know him while he's here with me. Please, Mom, do this for me." Audrey rose from her chair and stepped into the comfort of her mother's open arms.

"I've never heard you say you were in love before, so I guess I'd better pay attention."

"Thank you, Mom." She began to cry.

Vivienne ran her hand over Audrey's hair. "There's no need for tears."

"I'm not crying for me. My heart is breaking for you."

Vivienne hugged her a little tighter. "Everything will be okay, Audrey. I'll have my days, like you and Evan will, but life will keep moving us along." She stepped back and, with a gentle hand, wiped Audrey's cheeks. "You know, instead of using this over-stirred pancake batter, you should head over to the Bayview. I'll get ready to help Gram at the restaurant."

"You're going to work the day after the funeral?"

"It's better than sitting here with my thoughts." Vivienne took Audrey's hand, and together, they walked out onto the deck. The sun's rays began to dissolve the mist as it broke through the clouds.

"Looks like it's going to be a good beach day. Tourists will be lined up outside the restaurant, waiting for a table or a seat at the counter."

"I'm surprised Gram still puts in the hours there. Shouldn't she be doing something more relaxing, like crochet or needlepoint?"

Vivienne chuckled. "Not while she's still alive. She likes the interaction with people and helping Auggie in the kitchen. She says it makes her feel young."

"I was planning on having lunch there with Hugo today."

"If you text me when you're close to the restaurant, I'll have a table for you."

"No, Mom. We'll stand in line like everyone else."

"Suit yourself, but you may want to wait until after 2:00. Most of the tourists will be back at the beach, and the line won't be as long. You better get going. I'm sure Hugo will be hungry, and the Bayview chef offers a delicious breakfast for their guests."

Audrey kissed Vivienne's cheek. "I'm glad we talked. Thank you for understanding."

"I'm not just going to bow down and accept this. He's in for some interrogating."

"He knows. He's a parent, too. I'm taking a shower, and I'll be by the restaurant later."

Vivienne remained on the deck. The shock of Nate, and now Audrey, had her thoughts less than optimistic. *I'm on rough seas. What's waiting for me when the waves subside?*

***

Audrey gave Hugo's door a couple of light taps. It was still early, and she thought he may be sleeping. She knew what he wore when he went to bed. The thought of stripping off his boxers, and feeling his body against hers, tingled intimate places she loved his hands to touch. She was surprised to see him in a towel when he opened the door. His hair was still wet and slicked back.

"You're up early," she said. "I thought I was going to wake you."

"I'm not used to sleeping without you. Come here."

Audrey stepped inside and into his arms. She pressed herself against his chest and lifted her eyes to his. They verified the obvious language his body spoke to her.

"God, you smell so sexy," she said, breathing in the light scent of sandalwood and balsam. "You're making me weak in the knees."

He pressed his lips against hers. The towel fell from his waist.

# Chapter 4

On a restaurant critique assignment for the paper, William Lawson was greeted by a stunning brunette, poised at the mahogany hostess stand. A deep-blue silk sheath flowed like liquid sapphire over her silhouette. Her dark chestnut-brown hair was styled in soft waves that brushed her shoulders, and locks tucked behind one ear revealed a delicate gold earring. First impression: elegance.

Her eyes were a delectable dark chocolate, accented with smokey hues of brown and taupe.

"Good evening, sir. Welcome to *On the Bone.* Do you have a reservation?"

"Lawson, table for two."

She smiled as she looked at the reservation book. "Yes, Mr. Lawson. Nina, your personal server, will be right with you."

Nina's blond hair was a striking contrast to the hostess's brunette. Pink-polished toes peeked out from her jeweled stilettos. The square diamond ear studs were a classic pairing for her sleeveless black dress.

"I'm Nina, and I'll be your personal server tonight. If you and your guest will follow me, we have your table ready."

She walked ahead of them with confidence, like she owned the place. Stopping at a table on the perimeter of the room, she said, "I hope you and your guest will be comfortable here. The owner is on his way to welcome you."

Passing by her as she left, the owner approached. "Welcome, Mr. Lawson. I'm Vincent Carter, and I'm happy to have you and your guest dining with us. Our sommelier, Anthony, will be out shortly."

Will kept a mental note of the professionalism so far and scanned the dining area to assess the number of occupied tables.

The sommelier arrived, wine bottle in hand. "May I suggest this Shiraz tonight? It will be an excellent paring with the special menu the chefs have prepared for you." He popped the cork and poured a small amount for Will's approval. "Of course, Nina will be happy to assist you, if you have something else in mind that appeals to your pallet."

Will gave the wine a swirl and took a sip. "The Shiraz will be fine."

Anthony then poured the wine into their glasses. "Nina will be out shortly with your first course."

Will looked across the table at the red pouting lips of his companion, Alexandra Kalahani, and rolled his eyes. "What now, Alex?"

"*Nina?*" she said.

"You don't like her name?"

"I don't like the way she looked at you. Couldn't we have one of the male waiters?"

"So *you* can flirt with him? Do I have to remind you that I'm working?"

Nina approached, carrying a tray of six colossal shrimp surrounding a well of cocktail sauce. "Enjoy." She shot Will a quick, enticing glance before leaving.

"I would have stayed home, but you still won't give me a key to your place. Seeing *Nina,* I'm glad I joined you. She doesn't seem the type that's into man buns."

"You can't possibly know what she's into and stop referring to my place as *home.* You have your own apartment." He dipped the tip of a shrimp in the sauce. *If the chef chickened out on the heat, this is going to be a long dinner and a short review, and neither will be pleasant.* When the fire rose in his mouth, he mentally gave the chef his first thumbs up.

Alex, on the other hand, threw her shrimp on the plate. "Ugh! This is way too spicy." She cooled her mouth with the ice water on the table, but didn't miss a beat. "My apartment is not like yours, Will. It's a walkup and too small."

His annoyance was growing. He scowled under his breath and reached across the table for her discarded shrimp. "Give me that!" Covering the shrimp with the sauce, he added, "I'm not going to let this go to waste. Do you have any idea how much a shrimp this size costs? You can afford a better apartment, Alex, but you choose to spend your money on Prada and Manolos."

Out of their line of sight, Nina kept a watchful eye on the progression of the meal, approaching only to prepare the table for the next course...and steal a quick look at Will.

Alex stared her down while she picked up the empty tray and

walked away. "She's always interrupting us. Doesn't she see we're talking?"

"It's her job to wait on us, Alex. She doesn't care if we're talking."

She then changed the subject as carefully as she chose the dress she wore, Will's favorite, emerald-green satin, strapless and short. "Why don't we take a trip to Maui? My parents would love to meet you. You know, I was taught hula when I was young." She took another sip of wine and leaned over the table. Her voice became soft and provocative. "I'll dance for you, Will."

He showed his exasperation with a huff and a roll of his eyes. "I know where you're trying to steer me, Alex. When are you going to stop with these hints and suggestions? I'm sure your parents are nice people, but meeting them implies something serious, and we're not serious."

"Six months of no one but each other isn't serious?"

"Not when I have no intention of tying the knot."

It was then that Nina approached with another waiter, each carrying a main course dish. The chef had fanned porterhouse strips on each plate, drizzled them with peppercorn jus, as an artist would create his masterpiece on a canvas. A small mound of roast potatoes shared the plate, and a wash creamed spinach was drawn around the perimeter, for color.

Nina and the other waiter had just set the plates down, when Alex pushed hers away. "This steak is too rare."

Immediately, Nina and the other waiter picked up the plates. "May I tell the chef how you would like your steaks?"

Will jumped in. "Mine looked medium-rare, which is fine."

She turned to Alex. "And for you?"

It was Nina's calm professionalism, more than the rare steak, that provoked Alex's brash reply. "So it won't walk off the plate, *please.*"

Unfazed by Alex's outburst, Nina shot Will a sympathetic glance before she walked toward the kitchen, along with the other waiter.

Will took a healthy swallow of wine. "This is effing great, Alex. You're lucky the chefs are trying to impress us and won't mess with our food."

"What are you saying?"

"Chefs have a way of dealing with customers who are rude to the wait staff. I'm sure they were informed that you complained about your steak. If you were here on your own, your dish would likely be coming back with some well-hidden, creative additions."

It wasn't long before Will saw, out of the corner of his eye, two waiters approaching. One had accompanied Nina earlier, and the other one now replaced her. "I'm Xavier and this is Ramon. We'll be your servers for the rest of the evening. The owner apologizes, and had the chef prepare another porterhouse for both of you." They then set Will and Alex's plates before them.

"Mr. Lawson, your steak is cooked as requested, medium-rare," Xavier said.

Ramon said to Alex, "The chef prepared yours medium-well."

Xavier asked Will, "Would you like another bottle of the Shiraz?".

"Yes, and please thank the owner and chef."

They began to eat in silence, but the tension between them bubbled like a cauldron. Xavier returned and filled their glasses from a new bottle. "Is there anything else I can get you?"

"No, thank you, Xavier."

"Enjoy." He then walked toward the kitchen.

Will couldn't hold his tongue any longer. "What is it now, Alex? It wasn't enough that you hit the owner's pocket for another steak? Don't even tell me it's Nina again."

"She sent those two waiters to get under my skin."

"You mean the two *male* waiters you wanted instead of her? I shouldn't have brought you here tonight."

Alex didn't utter another word, even through the dessert course. It was a reminder to Will that his impending breakup with her, when he took her home, would result in words between them as molten and messy as the warm dark chocolate oozing from the cake.

The owner came by as Xavier and Ramon were removing their dessert plates. "I hope you and your guest enjoyed the dinner we prepared for you, and I apologize for the inconvenience."

"Apologies are not necessary." Will stood and extended his hand in gratitude. "Excellent dining experience."

Alex walked ahead of him, but Will could see Nina standing at the front desk next to the hostess. Her dress plunged at the back, drawing Will's eye to her narrow waist. He wanted to stand behind her, close his eyes as he breathed in her perfume, and press his lips against her skin.

"It was a pleasure having you here, Mr. Lawson." Nina passed the restaurant's business card across the desk. "We'd love to have you dine with us again."

Before he took it, she turned it over. There, in her brown eyes, was the promise of her body loving him, if he called her.

Half an hour later, at Alex's apartment, Will's violation of his creed, never to get involved with someone in the office, came back to bite him in an explosive end.

"I want to wring your fucking neck, Will! You told me—"

"I told you what, Alex? What?"

"That we had a good thing."

"We did, until you started all this jealousy shit."

"I'm sorry. Please, Will, I won't bring it up again."

"You won't for a while, but you'll just go back to pushing me." Will's nostrils flared, and anger flushed his face. "I was upfront with you from the beginning, Alex. I told you I wanted no strings, and what did you do? You tried to corral me with a lasso! You can have your pick of men in the office. I suggest you go back there and try again."

Her rage was doused with tears that turned her perfect cat-eye eyeliner into black streaks down her cheeks. Hiding behind all her jealous tantrums, and efforts to get him to settle down, was the simple truth. "I just want *you*, Will."

With a deep sigh, he let go of his anger. "Baby, you're entitled to the things you want in your life, marriage and children, but it's not something I see for myself. You and I would never work."

He was hoping, but not hopeful, that she wouldn't make a scene at the office tomorrow. "It's better this way."

He didn't kiss her and just closed the door between them and their rollercoaster relationship. The push and pull that began six long months ago, was over.

Back at his apartment, he tossed his jacket over the back of the couch and headed to the shower. The steamy water warmed his skin...and his thoughts about Nina. He pictured her attending to guests, checking her phone when she could, hoping he would call. Nina's soft, silky voice beckoned to him from the restaurant card, tucked away in his jacket pocket. It would be an easy hookup, but what he needed was a little distance from intimacy. He opted for a scotch and sat down to begin writing his review.

*Restaurants are reviewed for their excellence in food preparation and presentation. They are, at times, reviewed for their ability to adapt to unforeseen circumstances, while still being able to provide the highest quality food in taste and display. Tonight, On the Bone rose to the occasion with finesse and professionalism.*

It was a good start to the five-star review he would give, but his mind had enough stimulation for one night. Tomorrow was another day.

***

The next day, Will was on edge, anticipating another run-in with Alex. It was early afternoon, when he began to think he was off the hook, until he heard the click of her stilettos approaching in a crescendo. He could feel her presence standing in front of his desk, yet he continued to work, focused on his computer, knowing he was getting her goat. When he finally looked at her, he was met with her angry, narrow eyes and the defensive jut of her hip.

"Looks like you recovered from last night," he said.

"What's going on with you and Audrey? I was at Sonny's desk and overheard you talking to her on the phone."

He shot her a resentful look. Her accusatory tone dug into his skin like her nails on his back. "You're spying on me now?" He lowered his voice. "It's over, Alex. When the guys in the office get wind of this, you'll have a date by the end of the day."

"I don't care. So, now you're moving on to Audrey?"

"Her father just passed away. Did you read the email that was sent to everyone?"

"As a matter of fact, I did, and I sent her my condolences. Why was it so important for you to call her?"

"That's none of your business, Alex. Why don't you focus on making your deadline instead of interrogating me like some undercover CIA officer, or are you bucking for a new career?"

"Say what you want. I know you're up to something."

"What I'm up to is finishing this review, but there'll be hell to pay for you if you don't meet your deadline. You won't be so fond of the color pink when you're handed a slip instead of a paycheck. Your shopping sprees at Prada will be over."

Her stilettos clicked on the floor as she stormed down the hall toward her desk. Turning to his computer, he put the finishing touches on his review and put it to bed by emailing it to the editors. He glanced at his watch and decided to call it a day. Facing a rainy Boston weekend holed up in his apartment, Audrey's suggestion to try the best chowder on the Cape was a mouthwatering alternative.

***

The day began as most days. Vivienne tended to customers at the counter as a bartender would, catching up with locals, getting to know new clientele, while jotting down their orders and placing the ticket on the wheel for Auggie to grab. "I need another chowder," she called, and within minutes, a piping hot bowl was placed before the customer.

"Triton would rise from the ocean for this," he announced.

His enthusiastic praise roused responses from others at the counter as they lifted their beverages. "Best darn chowder on the Cape!"

Vivienne couldn't help but smile. "You keep coming in, we'll keep making it."

She was clearing a couple of places at the counter, when she glanced at the door. Audrey waved, while Hugo, behind her, flashed a broad smile as they were being escorted to a table.

Behind the counter was like sitting behind home plate, having a full view of the stadium. While she took the next customer's order, she couldn't help stealing quick glances where Audrey and Hugo were sitting. In a short-sleeve summer-yellow shirt, Hugo's biceps were evidence that he wasn't enrolled at any classes for *seniors* at the gym. Somehow, seeing him out of his suit made him seem more approachable. She watched his interaction with their server, Brendan, standing by their table, smiling, and pointing to the menu while he wrote on his pad.

Moving between the tables, Brendan stopped at the counter and handed Vivienne their lunch ticket. "Can I also have two iced teas, please?"

Vivienne poured two glasses, then turned and clipped the ticket on the wheel for Auggie.

"One cup and one bowl of chowder, one small cob salad and one clam roll," he barked.

Brendan set the glasses down for Audrey and Hugo and moved to his next table.

Vivienne felt her gaze being pulled toward them. They leaned toward each other and, like a scene in a movie, began sharing words and smiles just for each other, as if no one else were in the room. The moment that Vivienne knew they were in love, what convinced her of their feelings, was seeing Hugo's index finger gently touch Audrey's lips. Vivienne quickly shifted her eyes away, feeling as if she were a voyeur, and focused on the next customer at the counter. It was the distraction she needed, until they stopped by before leaving.

"You've officially won me over," Hugo said. "Audrey was right. This is the best chowdah, I ever had. It's not like anything I've tasted before."

It was a compliment worthy of Vivienne's proud, broad smile. "Well, thank you, Hugo. I'm sure Audrey also mentioned that it's a guarded family recipe."

"She did," he replied, and then turned to Audrey. "I should call Will."

"You don't have to. He already knows," she replied, and then addressed her mother. "Mom, remember I mentioned that William is Hugo's son? What I didn't tell you, is that he's a food critic and works for the paper."

"Who is?" Esty asked, shuffling out from the kitchen while she wiped her hands with a towel.

"Hugo's son William, Gram." Audrey carefully wrapped her arms around her frail grandmother, in a delicate, loving hug.

"We've had critics here before." Esty pointed to the wall behind the counter lined with signed and framed pictures.

"He thanked me for the heads up," Audrey said. "He had a deadline to meet, and said he'd try to make it here before we left."

"Thank you, again for a great lunch, Vivienne," Hugo said.

"You're welcome. That's what we like to hear from all our customers."

"Would you like to join Hugo and I for dinner?" Audrey asked.

"I appreciate you asking, but I can't leave Gram by herself. Enjoy the day with Hugo."

Esty waited until they were gone and turned to Vivienne. "What does she see in him? He's old enough to be her father."

"It's not what she sees, Mom, it's what she's found. Love."

***

People trickled in after the lunch crowd had headed back to the beach. Vivienne knew a resurgence would come around 5:00, so she began rolling forks, spoons, and knives in cloth napkins and stockpiling them for the servers to place on the tables. Auggie had the kitchen running like a well-oiled machine. Vivienne helped herself to a bowl of the best-selling item on the menu, along with some oyster crackers. "I haven't had lunch yet, but this will hold me over until we close."

"Eat, Vivienne." Esty removed her apron. "I'll take care of the customers out front."

She sat in the back corner of the kitchen, scooped a spoonful of chowder, and blew on the dripping mound before her lips gingerly touched it. Nate suddenly entered her thoughts, stirring melancholy and a longing for the restaurant's early days, branching out from the fish market. She smiled, remembering the bustling opening night, and their quiet celebration later in bed, careful not to wake Audrey and Evan. All their time and energy were put into the market, restaurant, and raising kids. *If I could go back, I would have seduced Nate on those nights when he gave in to exhaustion.* Her pensive reflection made her sigh. *No use pining for things I should have done.* When she was finished, she washed the bowl and put it on the shelf, along with her memories.

***

Heidi, the hostess, cradled the phone on her shoulder while looking at the seating chart. "*Callane's.*"

"May I speak to Vivienne, please?"

"Vivienne!" she called, as she raised the phone up.

Vivienne picked it up behind the counter. "This is Vivienne Callane."

"This is your daughter. I wanted to check if you changed your mind about dinner, but it sounds like things are hopping over there."

"You waited tables during the dinner rush, Audrey. Gram had to come out from the kitchen to help serve. I appreciate you asking, though."

"I can let myself in tonight."

"I'm sure I'll be sleeping. Where are you going for dinner?"

"P-town."

"Try Vorelli's. I gotta run, Audrey."

"Bye, Mom."

If Vivienne was proud of anything, it was her staff, especially during the dinner rush. In the kitchen, or out on the floor, they worked together like the crew on a ship, making *Callane's* a staple for locals, and a go-to on the tourist maps.

The restaurant was at its peak during dinner. Families always arrived early, eager to get the kids fed, tucked in bed, and rested for another day at the beach. Locals and tourists filled the remaining hours, until the dining area had only a few tables to serve. Vivienne felt herself winding down and went into the kitchen to check on her mother. She found her at the sink, her hands deep in a pot, scrubbing with vigor. "Mom, Brendan's about to leave. He'll drive you home."

Esty stepped up to any place that needed her, whether it was helping to cook, serve, or wash pots. Vivienne pressed her hands to her cheeks.

"You know, you can stagger working here with other things. When was the last time you played bridge with your group?"

"I'd rather be here than parking my backside on a chair playing cards with the ladies. They understand."

"They may, but I'm worried about you, Mom. Auggie and the cooks are younger and can handle this pace."

"They take care of me. While you're out front, they make sure I take breaks, and they feed me well."

"It's still tiring work."

"I'm fine, Vivienne. Brendan will take me home, I'll get a good night's sleep and be bright-eyed and bushy-tailed tomorrow."

Vivienne sighed. "You're as stubborn as barnacles on a ship's hull."

"Ready, Esty?" Brendan asked.

Her small brown purse swung from side to side on her wrist, as she waddled to the door with Brendan.

As Vivienne cleared the counter, she caught sight of someone talking to Heidi at the front desk, forcing an immediate doubletake. She found herself watching him as they spoke. The sheer *rightness* of him hit her first: the perfect, careless scruff that framed his face and the sharp contour of his jaw, a reckless pile of honeyed curls pulled up in a small, messy bun, a few curls escaping to brush his neck. Her eyes tracked the easy slide of muscle beneath a worn t-shirt, down to narrow hips covered in relaxed denim. And then it came. It wasn't a flutter she felt, but a jolt, a physical shock to the system. The sudden return of pure, unadulterated yearning. It took over her mind and heart like a tidal wave, drowning out everything, a pull she hadn't felt since Nate.

When Heidi pointed to the counter, his eyes met Vivienne's for an instant, before she lowered hers. She tried to keep herself busy, but any hope of suppressing the butterflies in her stomach, or her heart, pounding like a gavel against her chest, flew out the window.

His brown eyes made a genuine, friendly connection with hers as he stood in front of her, unaware of the unexpected feeling he had created, which hit her broadside. "Excuse me, is this seat vacant?"

"Let me guess, you're a comedian?" His chuckle in response tickled her insides.

"No. Just here visiting some friends, but I didn't get a chance to eat before I left home."

She reached under the counter for a menu and placed it in front of him. "Can I get you something to drink?"

He sat down and picked up the menu. "An iced tea, if you have it."

She poured a glass. "I'll give you some time to look at the menu."

Retreating to the kitchen, she began to silently chastise herself. *Get a grip, Vivienne, what's wrong with you? Are you insane? You could be his mother.* But her silent browbeating wasn't enough to stop her, being driven by the last bit of estrogen she had left. Tossing her dirty apron in the laundry, she went to the back of the kitchen to check her hair in the small mirror. Whispering to herself, she rummaged through the drawer under the cabinet. "Where's that tube of lip gloss or mascara when I need it? What am I talking about? When was the last time I used either?"

It was a rude awakening, to find herself in the same position as Stella and Camille, who had rushed home after the funeral to resurrect some dried-up makeup buried deep in their dresser drawers.

"You!" She pointed to herself in the mirror. "Pathetic." After taking a moment to compose herself, she opened the kitchen door and was met with his waiting smile. "So, have you decided?"

"The drive gave me an appetite. I'll have a bowl of the chowdah, and a lobstah roll."

His unique pronunciation raised her brows. "Where did you drive from?"

"Bawstin."

She smiled and lowered her eyes as she wrote his dinner ticket for Auggie. "Say no more."

"You want me to stop talking?"

His quick-witted, clever reply was like a left hook she didn't see coming. Embarrassment flushed her cheeks, and she scrambled to reply with a string of nervous, run-on words. "No, no, no, that's not what I meant. I'm so sorry, it's just a figure of speech."

"I know. It's okay. I was just joking."

A half-smile was all she could muster, longing to crawl in one of the holes her son Evan used to dig in the sand when he was a small boy. She placed his order on the wheel, which was quickly picked up by the chefs.

"One chowder." Auggie's voice rang out like a dinner bell. He set the piping-hot bowl on a saucer, and Vivienne placed it on the counter with some oyster crackers.

"Be careful, it's very hot."

"This looks good. Thank you."

A couple of locals walked in and sat at the end of the counter.

"Be right with you," she called. She retreated to the kitchen to catch her breath. The kitchen door was the wall between the handsome man and her mortified self. She poured a glass of ice water and drank it down with purpose. Feeling renewed, she steeled herself and pushed open the kitchen door.

Relieved to find the young man intently focused on his phone while eating, she took out her pad, ready to take Aiden, Caleb, and now, Liam's order. "Poker night, guys?"

"Not me." Liam pointed to the other two.

"I lost my shirt," Aiden said, "but Caleb here was the big winner, so he's buyin'. What's the special?"

"Crabcake hoagie."

"We'll take two, and a couple of beers," Caleb added.

"What can I get you, Liam?"

"I'll make it easy on the chefs. The same for me."

"Lobster roll waiting," Auggie called.

Not only was the man's bowl empty, but it looked like it had been licked clean. "Hungry?" She placed the lobster roll in front of the handsome stranger.

"I've never had anything quite like it."

"You won't," she replied. Raising her finger to her lips, she handed him another napkin to wipe a bit of the cream from his top lip and mustache.

"Thanks."

"Would you like another iced tea?"

He bit into the tender lobster roll and nodded with a full mouth, his cheeks puffed.

Instead of putting Aiden, Caleb and Liam's dinner tickets on

Auggie's wheel, she took them to the kitchen. While the chefs went to work, she wrote out the new customer's bill, while her mind was on the bit of cream he wiped from his lip. *Don't even go there, Vivienne.* She placed the locals' dinners on a tray and pushed the kitchen door open with her back.

"That's a big tray you've got there," he said.

Vivienne gave him a quick smile, as she placed his iced tea down, focused on keeping the tray level. As she walked to the other end of the counter, her heart thumped in her chest. *Is he watching me?*

"Enjoy," she said to the three men.

With the empty tray in hand, she asked the heartthrob, who was waiting patiently for her, "Any coffee or dessert?"

"No thanks. The desserts sound delicious though, but I can feel my stomach stretching my t-shirt. And I don't usually drink coffee this late."

"It is pretty strong. I'll get your check."

Behind the kitchen door, she held his check in her hands. She envisioned him scrolling casually through social media on his phone while he waited for her, yet she found herself hesitating, to keep him there just a little longer. He had shifted her thoughts, and she found herself *wanting* again. Wanting a man's naked body against hers, seduction, foreplay, sex. She sighed and reluctantly pulled herself back to reality. *These thoughts will do you no good. Clear your mind. He'll be gone soon.*

Vivienne returned to the counter and handed him the check.

He stood up and gave her fifty dollars.

"I'll be right back with your change."

"No, please. The rest is for you."

"This is a generous tip. Thank you very much." She hoped her eyes wouldn't give away the emotions she struggled to hide.

"And thank you for a great dinner."

"Enjoy your visit with your friends."

He just smiled. Vivienne watched the casual sway of his hips and closed the curtain on the useless thoughts that had no place in her life.

Caleb and Aiden had left, but Liam seemed disinterested in his dessert.

"Did you not like the Pecan pie?" Vivienne always kept a sharp eye on her customers. "I can bring you a warm apple crisp."

"What I would like...is to take you to dinner, Viv. I know you may think it's too soon, and I don't want to disrespect Nate, but—"

"It's okay, Liam. Life has put me on a road I'm not quite sure about yet."

"I know how that feels. Being alone is a hard transition from death or divorce, and we share one of each."

Vivienne empathized with his attempt to form a connection from these two depressing events. "We do, but it wouldn't make for an uplifting conversation."

He chuckled. "You have a point. You only know me with Charlotte. There's more to my life that I want to share with you. I never thought I'd get the chance to tell you that, Viv."

Vivienne had never looked closely at Liam's face. She imagined it as a map of his life. Etched into the corners of his brown eyes were the lines from years on the water, squinting at the sun. Weathered from the salt and ocean mist, the face of this once-young fisherman was now the rugged, handsome face of an older man before her. His eyes held so much hope of a future to share, waiting for her to say yes.

"I'll think about it, Liam. I promise."

Her response lit up his face. Like a conquest attained, he found renewed confidence. "Take all the time you need. I'm not moving anytime soon."

It was 10:00 pm when she flipped the lights off and locked the door. She never thought, as she walked home, that when the door to her life with Nate closed, another one would open. She had to call Magda. "Are you in the mood for a drink, or two, or three?"

"Where's this coming from?" Magda asked.

"The last hour before closing."

"If you need a drink, or two, or three, it may as well be here. I'll leave the door unlocked."

Vivienne tapped the door a couple of times before cracking it open. "Magda?"

"In the kitchen," she called.

She knew about Magda's *relaxed* relationships with men, but wasn't expecting to see Owen McCarthy, Wellfleet Fire Chief, fully dressed, and Magda in her robe, a clear indication they had just spent time together privately. It was an intimate intrusion Vivienne hoped never to repeat, leaving her in an awkward position. "Hi, Owen."

"Hey, Viv." He turned to Magda, his voice low and tender. "I'll call you." He kissed her quickly.

Vivienne was quiet, watching Magda wash a couple of coffee cups, until she heard the front door close. "You could have told me it wasn't a good time."

"I would have, if it wasn't."

Vivienne pointed toward the front door while unable to hide her curious stare. "Wasn't he seeing Stella?"

"Yes, but not for long. He had ended it with her before Nate's funeral."

"So, that's why she rushed home to primp up, when she saw Hugo. What happened?"

"She led Owen to believe she was okay with no commitments."

"I bet that didn't last long."

"You know Stella. Eventually, her jealousy wouldn't allow her to share him with another woman."

"What did she expect from a bachelor?"

"She knew he was retiring soon and thought she could sway him into finally settling down."

"I can see how that went over," Vivienne said.

"He knows I want no strings or commitments. He called today and asked to take me to dinner. I told him I'd cook. When Stella finds out, it'll be just another reason for her to dislike me, but enough of this. I'll get the bottle of wine in the fridge. We'll talk in the living room."

Magda watched Vivienne take two healthy swallows of wine. "Feel better?"

"I'm a mortified mess! Brendan had just left to drive mom home, and I was cleaning the counter, when this guy walked into the restaurant and threw me for a loop."

Magda sat on the edge of her chair, intrigued, and took a sip of wine. "Hundreds of people come into the restaurant, Viv. Those are words I haven't heard from you since you began dating Nate. What was it about this guy?"

Vivienne's mind saw him sitting at the counter, his chest hair peeking out from the V-neck of his faded blue T-shirt.

"Are you okay?" Magda asked, noticing red blotches on Vivienne's neck.

She rose from the chair and stood at the open window, letting the evening breeze cool her down. "I don't know if I can repeat it, Magda." Finishing the last of the wine in her glass, she turned to her.

"Beside the fact that he's probably Audrey's age, I was walking here and thought about putting my hands in his hair and releasing that messy man bun he had. It gave me a hot flash that hit me between my legs."

"Man buns are all the rage now," Magda added.

She held out her glass for Magda to fill. "He had a bit of chowder on his top lip and mustache. I began thinking about kissing it off. I handed him a napkin and had to compose myself in the kitchen. What's wrong with me? I'm supposed to be mourning, not fantasizing."

Magda finished her glass and laughed. "It's not what's wrong with you, it's what's *right* with you. You and Nate hadn't been intimate in a long time, and keeping his illness from you did nothing to help the situation. This guy, whoever he is, triggered feelings that you've suppressed for years, but they're obviously not dead, Viv. He may be younger than you, but sometimes life reminds us that fulfillment can be found in any age."

"What am I supposed to do with these feelings now? I'm a 55-year-old menopausal widow with a schoolgirl crush."

"Be happy those feelings haven't died. Keep an open mind. It took a while for me to feel comfortable being with other men and knowing it wasn't a betrayal of my love for Griff. If I wasn't open to Owen's advance, I would have missed getting to know him. Someone else can come into the restaurant, the same way this guy did."

"Someone else did. Liam."

"This is nothing new, Viv." Magda shrugged. "You said he's been eating at the restaurant a lot. We both know, since his divorce from Charlotte, he's had his eyes on you. He asked you out, didn't he?"

The wine was like a shot of truth serum. "He did. That handsome man wants to take me to dinner, and by the look in his eyes, I suspect to bed."

"I have to agree with you, he is attractive. How do you feel about that?"

"I don't know, Magda. I told Liam I'd think about dinner, but I can't get that young guy out of my head. I just wish I knew his name, instead of remembering him as some random guy I'll never see again. Between him and Liam, my emotions are all over the place."

"No one is setting a clock or putting a time limit on when you should be ready. The only one who can tell you that is you."

Vivienne finished her glass, and Magda split the last of the bottle between them.

"How does it feel to be in a place where you're comfortable with other men?" Vivienne asked.

"Griff didn't want me to spend the rest of my life alone. I keep his name out of my relationships, but he'll always be a part of my life."

"I hope I can remember that, if I ever get to that place."

"You will, Viv. It just takes time."

"Speaking of time..." Vivienne stood. "I took up too much of yours tonight. Thanks for letting me barge in on you and Owen."

Magda tightened the sash on her robe. "You didn't. We're just getting to know each other."

At the door, Magda hugged Vivienne. "Everything will be okay, I promise."

Vivienne was wary and pulled back. Her worry and uncertain thoughts showed in her eyes, as plain as wearing her heart on her sleeve. "Will it? I'm not so sure."

"You won't have the answers to everything. No one's expecting you to. What you *can* do, is tackle one day at a time."

Vivienne listened to the hypnotic serenade of the crickets as she walked home. It slowed her breathing and opened her mind to what Magda had said. But she couldn't quiet her thoughts. *I wish the evening would have turned out differently.* She could see the hurricane lamps shining on either side of the front door in the distance. *Audrey must have left them on.* The house was quiet. She removed her sneakers, but the wood floors still let out a creak here and there as she headed upstairs and past Audrey's door. She grimaced and squeezed her eyes tight while she kneaded the muscles in her lower back, which reminded her she'd been on her feet too much all day. Her bed offered a better night's sleep than the couch she had slept on last night. Sleeping alone was not unfamiliar to Vivienne. She reached over, touched Nate's pillow, and began to cry for what she lost...and what she couldn't have.

***

Will tossed his duffle on the floor and scanned the no-frills room at *The Sandpiper Hotel.* It smelled of the beach, and sand crackled under his sneakers on the wood floor. He eyed the piece of driftwood hanging precariously over the double bed. Likely put there by the owner...or some wannabe designer, unaware of a possible lawsuit, or worse, should it fall on the head of a sleeping guest. Not wanting to think of it hovering above him, he carefully removed it and placed it in the corner.

From the open window, he heard the faint sound of laughter and music. *Probably kids at a beach bonfire, sneaking a few beers. If only their parents knew...* A warm night breeze drifted through the window. After a shower, Will sat in the middle of the bed with his legs crossed, opened his laptop, and began to write the first few words about his experience at *Callane's.*

*Tucked between a novelty shop and taffy store, in the town of Wellfleet, is a small, inconspicuous restaurant. There's no awning or savvy marketing that would catch your attention, just the name Callane's on the front door. Having driven from Bawstin to meet some friends, I arrived in Wellfleet with my duffle and an appetite. A teenager with hometown hospitality greeted me at the door and directed me to the counter.* He paused for a moment, smiled at his thoughts, and opened a new blank page.

*You're going to keep me awake tonight. Whoever you are, you're the cream in the best chowdah this guy from Bawstin ever had.*

# Chapter 5

Vivienne was lying on her side when she opened her eyes. The picture on her night table, of Nate holding up a five-pound lobster, bid her good morning. After finishing a bottle of wine with Magda, and crying herself to sleep last night, she rubbed the stabbing pain in her head. The morning looked anything but good.

The aroma of coffee made its way from the kitchen and enticed Vivienne to slip on her robe. It was barely 8:00AM, but she knew Auggie and the chefs were already at the restaurant, prepping for the day. A generous increase in their pay showed her appreciation for their loyalty and keeping the restaurant running smoothly.

Audrey was sitting at the table, nursing a steaming cup. "Morning, Mom."

Vivienne desperately needed some caffeine and went straight for the coffeemaker. "You're up early."

"Hugo and I wanted to get an early start today. His son, Will, drove in from Boston. Remember, I told you he's a food critic? Anyway, we're picking him up at The Sandpiper and heading to P-town. Then we're stopping by the restaurant later for lunch. I know you'll be working, but I would really like you to join us, Mom."

Vivienne stood frozen, holding the coffee pot. *That guy drove in from Boston.*

"Mom? Are you okay? Did you hear anything I said?"

She was glad she had the headache to blame, and it was the perfect excuse to do a little digging. "I'm sorry, Audrey. My mind is on the coffee I need for this headache. I had a little too much wine at Magda's last night. So, you were saying Hugo's son is here?"

"Yeah. I've been telling him for a while that he needed to check out the best chowder on the Cape."

*He said it was the best he ever had.* "I guess he'll find out when he has lunch with you."

"Mom, did you forget already? I asked you to join us for lunch. Oh, and I want to warn you. I know they turn you off, but he has one of those man buns."

It wasn't the caffeine that was giving her palpitations. *Oh my God, it's him! Turned off? I've never seen anything sexier.* At that moment, there was nothing worse in Vivienne's mind than the fear of discovery. With a roll of her eyes, she put a lock on her feelings. "Ugh! I'm glad you reminded me, Audrey."

Vivienne was in emotional turmoil. Saying his name in her mind made her heart thump like she had a schoolgirl's first crush, but her thoughts were far more seductive and hands-on.

"I'm meeting Hugo in an hour, so I guess we'll see you later."

Vivienne waited at the stairs, listening for the water and Audrey's music playing in the bathroom, before she called Magda.

"Are you sitting down?"

"I am. Having coffee."

"My crush has a name."

"You've got my attention."

"Audrey just mentioned that *Hugo's son* drove in from Boston. *That guy* drove in from Boston. She told *Hugo's son* he had to try the best chowder on the Cape. *That guy* said it was the best he ever had."

"Oh God, Viv!"

"Then she warned me *Hugo's son* had one of those man buns I used to hate. I'm using the words *used to* here."

"Like the one you wanted to loosen on *that guy* that gave you the hot flash?"

"Yes! When Audrey said that, I damn near dropped my coffee cup. That guy is Will, Hugo's son, and Audrey asked me to join them for lunch."

"This could get complicated, Viv."

"I know, and why is my heart telling me I haven't felt this excited since Nate?"

"Keep this in mind," Magda said. "You don't know if that short interaction had the same impact on him. Just let the conversation go where it wants. If he's interested, or not, you'll know."

"He's staying at The Sandpiper, and they're picking him up soon, so I can rummage through my closet for one of those nice tops I bought from you."

"Choose something between understated and flashy, if that makes sense."

"I'll just stay away from flashy. I'm glad you made me buy those jeans."

"I'm happy for you, Viv. You could use a break from stress."

Standing at the coffeemaker, Vivienne hoped a second cup would soothe the remaining throbbing at her temples. She heard the flip-flop of Audrey's sandals on the stairs.

Vivienne sighed, looking at Audrey's hair. "You waste so much time straightening those beautiful curls you were born with."

"It's not a waste of time if I want my hair straight." She kissed Vivienne's cheek and grabbed the cup from her for a quick sip of coffee. "I don't know what Hugo has planned, but we'll probably be at the restaurant around 3:00PM."

Vivienne knew that was the time of day when locals had already stopped for lunch, and most tourists were at the beach. "Okay, have fun."

After a quick shower, she followed Magda's advice and chose a sunny yellow top. The color, and swirl of gold in the cotton, was perfect and just a bit more than a plain t-shirt. The last check in the mirror before she left showed her a woman she hadn't seen in a long time. All it took was the smile from a man she couldn't wait to see again.

***

The line for breakfast was already halfway down the street, when Vivienne arrived. Heidi was at the door, greeting people. "Good morning, Vivienne."

"Morning, Heidi. What does the wait-time look like?"

"Fifteen minutes. We'll get everyone seated."

"That's what I like to hear." Vivienne stopped at the kitchen door and spoke to Brendan, who was working the counter until she arrived. "You can switch to the dining area, but I'll need you to work the counter again this afternoon, for a while."

"Sure, Vivienne."

She loved this time of the day. The smell and sound of breakfast cooking filled the kitchen. "Morning, everyone." She pulled a clean apron from the shelf.

A *'morning'* here and there, were like lyrics to the clanging of pots. She glanced at the clock and silently told herself, *keep your eyes off the time and on the customers.* Easier said than done. When the line outside was only two deep, she caved in. Eleven-thirty. She began wrapping utensils for the waiters to place on the tables for the lunch crowd and checked on her mom in the kitchen.

Esty held up half a sandwich to Vivienne. "See? I'm having lunch."

"You can't fault me for looking out for you. I still think there are better things you could be doing."

"Don't bring up the *cards and crochet group* again," Esty warned. "Honestly, they couldn't have put two, more boring things together, if they tried. I bet any one of those ladies would love to trade places with me, instead of sitting on their keisters, playing Bridge and crocheting blankets, and scarves, and hats."

It was the same effective argument Esty had been using for years, to keep her from the dreaded *cards and crochet* group, and she was winning the argument. Vivienne silently agreed. *She does have a point.* "Okay, Mom. Just remember to take the breaks that Auggie gives you."

"That's what I'm doing now, and I have to say, you look especially nice today. And your face has such a nice glow."

*If she only knew.* "Thanks, Mom, but it's all Magda. This top is from her store, and I used one of the facial masks she carries. I wanted to wear something a little different today. Audrey is having lunch here with Hugo, and they invited me to join them."

Esty tugged on Vivienne's apron, urging her to squat down next to her chair. "You should get to know this man Audrey says she loves," she whispered.

"That's my plan, Mom, but it's gonna take more than this lunch."

"Whatever it takes."

When Vivienne pushed open the kitchen door, she was thrown completely off-guard. Audrey had arrived ahead of schedule and was speaking to Heidi. Hugo and Will stood behind her. Will's eyes went right to that familiar place at the counter. Seeing Vivienne made his smile impossible to hide.

She thought she would never see him again, but there he was, smiling at her from across the room, and she wondered, *is he thinking about last night, too?* She walked from behind the counter to greet them.

"Will, this is my mom, Vivienne," Audrey said.

"It's nice to meet you, again."

"Will told us he had dinner here last night," Hugo said.

"He did. Heidi will show you to your table, and I'll join you all in a minute."

In the back of the kitchen, Vivienne took a minute to look in the mirror. Her hands shook as she applied some blush to give her cheeks a bit of color. She tossed her apron in the laundry bin and stopped at the kitchen door. On the other side was what she never thought she'd get, another chance to see him. Without wasting another second, she pushed the door open and rushed past Brendan, at the counter, to their table. Hugo and Will both rose.

"Please, sit next to your daughter," Hugo said, stepping aside.

It had nothing to do with Audrey, but Vivienne wasn't going to let chivalry get in the way. "Thank you, Hugo, but that's not necessary, though it's nice to see that some gestures haven't gone by the wayside."

"I guess you'll have to sit next to me then." Will pulled the chair out for her.

Her eyes met his and she smiled. "I think I can manage that."

Hannah approached, her serving skills in the spotlight, to be waiting a table that included her boss. She was on pins and needles, terrified of making a single mistake. "Can I get you something to drink while you look at the menu?" Quickly scribbling 4 beverages onto her pad, she then presented the specials with confidence and was rewarded with Vivienne's smile.

Hugo said, "You can imagine Will's surprise when he discovered the engaging conversation he had with a very witty waitress was Audrey's mother."

"Since we didn't exchange names, I have to say in his defense, there was no way for him to know."

When Hannah returned, she scribbled their orders on her pad and gathered the menus.

"I'm glad my chefs don't know there's a food critic sitting in the dining arca."

"I'm not working today," Will said. "But what I ate last night blew me away. Audrey wasn't kidding when she told me it was the best chowdah anywhere."

After Hannah returned with their lunch, everyone settled into the business of eating. "Hugo and I will be leaving tomorrow," Audrey said, "but we would like you to join us and Will for dinner tonight."

Her mind was already thinking of what to wear. "I'd like that."

"I was thinking about *The Wicked Seashell* in Chatham."

"They have a nice outdoor terrace for drinks before dinner," Vivienne added.

"Good. I'll make a reservation for 8:00PM."

Vivienne couldn't ask for anything more, but she wouldn't have to.

"Great," Will said. "I'll pick up Vivienne in my car, and we'll meet you there at 8:00PM."

"That's fine," Hugo replied.

"Is it okay with you?" he whispered to Vivienne.

"I was hoping you'd say that," she said quietly and tapped her address into his phone.

Hannah returned to clear their plates. "I hope everyone enjoyed lunch."

"We did, thank you." Hugo handed her his credit card.

"Lunch is on the house, sir," she said.

Vivienne's eyes met Hugo's. She saw it, a genuine appreciation for her gesture of hospitality, even before he spoke those three simple words.

"Thank you, Vivienne." He then handed Hannah a hefty tip.

"My pleasure, and I look forward to dinner tonight."

"If you get there before us," Audrey added, "The reservation will be under Lawson."

"We'll just wait for you on the terrace," Will replied. With a slight lean toward Vivienne, he whispered, "I'll pick you up at seven."

Magda's voice was a subtle whisper in Vivienne's mind. *'Watch for the signals.'* Vivienne knew the drive from Wellfleet to Chatham was about 30 minutes, which would give Will a little time to spend with her...alone.

What seemed to be a casual dinner was turning into a full-blown date, right in front of Audrey and Hugo's unsuspecting eyes. A knot of anticipation tightened in Vivienne's stomach, the lunch suddenly feeling less like a polite gathering and more like the beginning of something she hadn't dared to hope for. Will smiled at her before he left the restaurant, but it wasn't the same as yesterday. This time he wasn't walking out of her life. He was giving her a chance to walk into his.

# Chapter 6

As the sun set, drab gray clouds moved in from the bay. All the excitement swirling around Vivienne's life had taken her thoughts away from where they should be...with Nate. She could see her house up ahead as she walked home, but she knew at the dead end was the entrance to the cemetery. And her feet took her there.

It was a place of lonely repose for the residents who had nothing but endless time on their hands to wait for their next visitor. Vivienne's appearance was a welcome change from the boredom of eternal sleep.

She stood for a moment at Nate's headstone, before she began to speak. "I know what I say will not be for your ears only," she began. "I'm standing among people who, I imagine, will be eavesdropping on my conversation. But how far can gossip travel six feet under anyway? I'm sure you were rolling in your casket, seeing the man your daughter brought to your funeral. I'm more than a little skeptical myself, but Audrey asked me to keep an open mind. Your son, Evan, on the other hand, is having none of it. He's sure it's one of those *father-figure* things. She says she loves him, and Audrey's never said that about anyone. Hugo may love her too, but he's going to have to walk barefoot on hot coals for her before I'm convinced. Mom's anxiety has gotten worse since you passed away. She's spending more time at the restaurant to be with me, and seeing Audrey with Hugo didn't help. Audrey brought him to the restaurant for lunch today. Given his age, I got the feeling it was important to Hugo to make me feel at ease, and I appreciated that. They asked me to have dinner with them, and Hugo's son, Will, tonight before they go back to Boston tomorrow."

As she paused to gather her thoughts, she could almost sense Nate's impatience with her hesitation. "There's something else and, if you were here, you'd be telling me to, 'Just spit it out, Viv.' Remembering your jealous inclinations, and what I'm going to say, I have to admit I'm relieved that this is a one-way conversation. Nothing can come of it because he's Hugo's son, Audrey's age, and I'm 55. It's just a crush. I know it's crazy. I haven't lost my mind, but why do I feel like I've lost my heart?"

The only sound breaking the silence were the crickets. Vivienne listened as their tiny wings beat their own morse code, speaking to each other in the darkness, and it brought her a little peace.

***

Vivienne stood in her robe, staring in awe at her closet. She hadn't noticed the slow accumulation of clothes that crept up on her, making her closet a personal advertisement for Magda's store. With Audrey getting ready at the hotel with Hugo, Vivienne had the house to herself.

She pushed the hangers back and forth, her nervous indecision growing as the clock ticked away. Finally, she threw in the proverbial towel and called Magda.

Without coming up for air, Vivienne rattled off her plea into the phone. "I hope you're not busy and, if you are, could you spare your panicked friend a little time?"

Magda had her suspicions and masked it well. "Owen was just leaving with a container of leftovers from dinner. I'd love a cup of tea."

"The door will be open."

Magda couldn't hide the expression of shock on her face as she stood at the entrance to Vivienne's bedroom. Covering every inch of her bed was evidence of Magda's favorite customer. "Viv, I must have lost track of the clothes you were buying."

"When it's a dress one day and a blouse the next, who has time to count? I'm having dinner with Audrey, Hugo...and Will. He's picking me up at seven."

"You better hurry, Viv."

Vivienne's panicked voice rose an octave. "That's why I called you. Pick something while I get ready."

When Vivienne returned, Magda had put away all the clothes on the bed, leaving Vivienne with two options. "These are perfect for tonight. You can pair a classic white tee and your new jeans. The air is a little cool, so this light lemon-color shawl over your shoulders will keep you warm and adds a pop of color. You've worn this bohemian maxi dress before, and it looked amazing on you. The same shawl will go well with the brown and gold in the dress."

"I don't feel amazing," she replied.

Magda's eyes softened. "You are, Viv, and someone else thinks so, too." Magda then picked up the t-shirt and jeans. "Wear the dress tonight."

Vivienne's kiss on Magda's cheek was quick. "Thank you. What can I do to repay you?"

A glint of mischief shown in Magda's eyes. "Let me know how your *date* goes."

***

Vivienne was swiping a bit of red on her lips when the bell rang. Her heart began to race, but she kept her feelings in check. With her clutch in hand, a couple of deep breaths was all she could manage before she opened the door.

There he was, but this time it wasn't his man bun that caught her attention, nor his sexy scruff. In a crisp white shirt and jeans, it could have resulted in a mortifying matching outfit disaster, had she gone with Magda's other choice. There was no restaurant counter to separate them, yet Will kept a reasonable distance and seemed as relaxed as if he were calling on a friend. Vivienne set the tone with the first greeting. "Right on time. I'm a fan of punctuality."

"When you work for a paper, it's all about being on time."

"I guess we can go, then."

Vivienne didn't know too much about him, but his car said he appreciated classics. A Karmann Ghia, in a beautiful light gray, was parked and waiting for her. "Wow, these cars were popular during the Woodstock era. You don't see many of them around. It looks brand new."

"I picked it up at an auction. It took me several years to renovate it."

Sticking out like a sore thumb, with nowhere to hide, was her rusted little Civic, parked in her driveway.

"I was going to do the same thing, but then I thought the reddish-brown rust wearing away at the blue, gives it a special two-tone vintage touch."

Will chuckled at her bit of playful sarcasm as he opened the car door for her. "It makes it unique." She breathed in the smell of leather. The rich cognac color covered the seats and felt as comfortable on her skin as a soft, worn-in jacket.

In the small confines, Will shifted the gear stick, thinking nothing of it when his hand brushed her leg. He made his way slowly through town and picked up speed on the outskirts toward 6W.

"I was sorry to hear about Audrey's father passing," he began. "If I had known you were Audrey's mom—"

"There was no way for you to know."

"But I know now, and I'm sorry, Vivienne."

"Thank you." If nothing else, she didn't want to be thought of as the grieving widow. Not tonight. A quick switch of the conversation turned the focus to Will. "So, what got you started as a restaurant critic?"

He chuckled. "I'm a graduate of the Culinary Institute of America, but decided I wanted to review food, more than cook it. It was just the honesty of my palate that was outspoken but believe me, I have never sent anything back to the kitchen."

"If I remember correctly, you practically licked clean your bowl of chowder."

He smiled as if the memory moved him. "And I said I never had anything quite like it."

"My guess is you won't be writing about it, as it would look biased."

"I did write something in my hotel room that first night, based on an *anonymous* tip."

It raised her brows as she looked at him. "Can I read it?"

"It's only a line or two. Maybe when I've got more."

Vivienne wasn't going to push against his reluctance and moved on. "Do you like living in Boston?"

"The paper keeps me there, and the sports. I've been to the Cape a few times."

It was the spark of interest she needed. "Really? Where did you stay?"

"Here and there, Falmouth, Barnstable, Chatham, Truro, P-town. Some friends and I pulled together a weekend at Woods Hole and took the ferry over to Martha's Vineyard for the day. All the women wanted to do was shop, so we settled in to wait at a restaurant near the wahtah."

Vivienne had just received a stark reality check. Sitting next to a man, whose looks could rival the celebrities on Page Six, she didn't need visual proof that the women in his circle of friends were in their prime, beautiful and full of promise. She was lacking all three. Short of making her escape from a moving vehicle, she had no choice but to slip her disheartenment under the front seat and toss her empathizing hat in the ring.

"I can relate to that. A good friend of mine owns a boutique in town. Most of my clothes are from her store."

Will took his eyes off the road for an instant and looked at her. If they were the windows to his soul, Vivienne saw a glimpse of herself in that instant.

"If you bought that dress from her store, I need to thank her."

Renewed hope began to flutter in her stomach and made her smile. "I'll be sure to tell her."

Taking the exit off the traffic circle, Will drove slowly through the town then parked a block away from the restaurant. Vivienne took his hand and stepped out of the car. Her shawl dropped from one of her shoulders, but Will was quick to grab it before the thin material hit the walkway.

On a shelf above the maître d's head, nestled in a cloud of fisherman's netting, lay a giant horse conch. Every bit of two feet, its flaming-red color was an eye opener that greeted the guests as they entered the foyer. The young man's alert blue eyes, framed by delicate wire-rimmed glasses, greeted Will and Vivienne. "Good evening. Welcome to *The Wicked Seashell.* Do you have a reservation?"

"Eight o'clock, for Lawson." He then gave Vivienne a quick glance, before he added, "We're early, but I hear the outdoor terrace is nice."

She caught her breath, never imagining that Will would remember, let alone repeat, her casual comment about the terrace.

"It is," the maître d' said, "and the weather is perfect if you wish to wait there. I'll let you know when the other guests have arrived."

Tiki torches gave a soft ambiance to the terrace, while two bartenders kept an attentive eye on the guests, as well as those who were just arriving. "Are you dining with us, or just enjoying the terrace this evening?"

"Both," Will replied. "We're early for our reservation."

"Great. What can I get you to start your evening?"

It was *ladies first,* as Will's eyes settled on Vivienne. "I'll have a Pinot Noire."

"And for you, sir?"

"I'll make it easy. Budweiser."

With their drinks in hand, Will then led Vivienne to the railing.

In a moment of silence, they looked up at the evening sky, showcasing a mass of brilliant stars, while the sound of waves gently lapped at the shore.

"I wasn't expecting such a beautiful sky tonight," Vivienne said. "It was so cloudy this afternoon."

Lifting his beer bottle, he carefully tapped Vivienne's wine glass. "Here's to the unexpected, beautiful sky."

On the first sip, she could taste the zingy tartness of the wine.

"Being right on the wahtah, this must be a popular place for wedding proposals."

"And receptions, too."

"Have you attended any weddings here?"

"No, but I've had some *I'm sorry* dinners here, and Magda and I have shared some soul-bearing sessions at the bar."

"I'm guessing you weren't the one who was sorry."

Vivienne began to feel the wine's pleasant, stimulating effect, and replied with a bit of playful sarcasm. "You men are *so* perceptive."

Will chuckled. "Yeah, I've been in the *I'm sorry* seat myself a few times, but soul-bearing sessions?" He took a moment to scratch his bearded chin. "Hmm...I'm not gonna go there."

"Wise choice."

"Magda. She's the one who has the clothing store?"

"The one you need to thank."

His eyes focused on her dress before they settled on her eyes. "More like, pay homage to."

A pass was the same at that moment as it was thirty years ago, and it wasn't the wine that was heating Vivienne's skin.

Attending to the guests, the bartender noticed Vivienne's empty glass. "Would you like another Pinot Noir?"

"Sure." After placing the glass on his tray, she slipped her shawl down to cool her shoulders.

"And for you, sir, another Budweiser?"

"No. I'm driving tonight."

"Audrey mentioned you're returning to Boston tomorrow."

"He has a little wiggle room," Hugo said as he and Audrey joined them. "His review made the deadline."

"How long have you been waiting?" Audrey asked her mom.

Vivienne shrugged. "Not long, just enough time for small talk."

"Mr. Lawson," the maître d' announced. "Your table is ready."

Vivienne's witty comment didn't go unnoticed by Will. Walking behind Audrey and Hugo gave him a chance to whisper his *anything but subtle* response in Vivienne's ear. "Not long *enough*. I was just getting warmed up."

Vivienne's eyes widened, sending a sharp, warning glance at Will. She feared his whispered seduction was close enough to Audrey to rouse suspicion and questions she wasn't ready to answer. Will's advances, however flippant, aroused her forgotten sensuality and excited her libido with heady thoughts of him. Would Audrey understand? Worry brought her back to her senses, and thoughts of romance came to a halt as they sat down for dinner.

***

On the drive back to Wellfleet, Vivienne stewed in silence.

It was Will who finally caved in, speaking to the back of her head as she looked out the window. "I'm sensing that you're upset about something." Receiving only continued silence from her, he added, "I'm going to apologize, but I don't know why."

His provoking felt like the first instigating push in a schoolyard fight. Vivienne turned to him and pushed back. "Audrey and your father are trying to make me feel comfortable about their decision to be together."

"I was trying to do the same thing."

"Us flirting on the terrace was one thing, but—"

"Did you enjoy it?"

"Imagine their shock if they overheard you?"

"But they didn't. Did you enjoy it, Vivienne?"

"But what if they had? Dinner would have been a catastrophe."

Will's frustration raised his voice. "But they didn't. You want me to say I shouldn't have said that to you, with Audrey and my dad right in front of us? Okay. But I won't apologize for saying it."

"Why are you doing this?" she demanded.

"I can be a little more direct if you want."

"The last thing I want is to become the focus of your flirting."

"I wouldn't call it flirting. I'm just a bit hung up on you."

"Hung up? You don't even know me."

"Then why not give me a chance to know you?"

"For what? So you and your friends can have a laugh at my expense?"

Will took his eyes off the road for an instant, to return his anger. "I would never do that!"

Her chuckle added a condescending bite to her response. "Oh, right. And you're the *one guy* who actually means that pathetic line?"

"Would you just give me a break, Vivienne, and meet me halfway? I'm attracted to you."

Her answer was looking out the window until he stopped in front of her house. Tired and disillusioned, Vivienne knew she had to say something to Will, who walked her to the front door.

"Thanks for the ride. I had a good time tonight."

It surprised Will, whose brows rose at her comment. "Good time? You chewed me out and then cut me off for the remainder of the ride home."

Vivienne sighed when she realized there was nothing to even fight for. "Tonight was about Audrey and your father. I lost my focus and may have overreacted a bit."

His soft gaze was like a rose he was offering her. "So, you forgive me, Vivienne?"

"Why is my forgiveness so important to you?"

"Because I want to see you again. You never answered me. Did you enjoy tonight?"

She wanted him, dreamt about him, but her dreams were safe and held no consequences. Vivienne looked away, knowing that in the real world, what he was offering her would eventually break her heart. "You don't know what you're asking. My life is something you can't relate to."

"Why don't you let me decide that?"

"I can't. I won't let anyone make decisions for me again. I'll decide who I let in my life." She paused for a moment, wrestling with her urge to release his hair and let it fall on his shoulders. "I'll tell Magda you liked the dress."

"I loved the dress."

"Good night, Will. Have a safe trip back to Boston." Tears filled her eyes as she fumbled with her key to open the door. Once safe on the other side, her back rested against the wood, and she listened to the rumbling motor fade in the distance until there was nothing but quiet and her thoughts.

***

Seashells crackled under Will's tires as he pulled into the parking spot in front of his hotel room. Despite the late hour, there was no curfew for kids on vacation, whose loud voices bellowed from the neighboring rooms, not that he could sleep with Vivienne on his mind. The name of the local bar had caught his eye as he was driving toward the hotel. Standing at his door, he did an about-face and walked the few blocks toward the green neon lights above the weathered, cedar building, blinking *Fore and Aft.*

It smelled of the ocean, with a hint of the fish being served. A burly man was hunched over the bar, nursing a half-finished glass of ale and a plate of steamed crabs, that his knotted fingers methodically picked apart. Ocean winds had pelted the sea salt into his beard and hair, giving them the illusion of gray. Will took the barstool two down from him.

"What can I get you?" the bartender asked, wiping the area in front of Will.

"You have Budweiser?"

"Yes, and Bud Light, too."

"I don't drink that swill," he replied, wrinkling his nose. "A regular Bud please and hold the glass."

"You vacationing here?" the bartender asked.

After the disastrous dinner, Will wasn't sure his answer was true. "No, just visiting some friends for the weekend."

Above the bar, he noticed a framed picture draped in black, of a fisherman standing on a boat. His broad smile and pride were obvious as he held up, what looked like, at least a five-pound lobster in each hand.

"Who's that?" Will asked, pointing to the picture.

The man next to him looked up and replied before the bartender. "That'd be Nate Callane. He owned *Callane's* restaurant in town with his wife, Vivienne. They also own the fish market. Best damn chowder on the Cape. His son, Evan, took over the fishing business."

The bartender said to Will, "I still have three or four crabs if you've got an appetite."

"No thanks." Will's focus sharpened as he looked at Vivienne's husband for the first time. He was rugged and built for the ocean, with muscular arms to hold up the heavy lobsters. A twinge of jealousy made him gulp a mouthful of beer while staring at the man who was no longer a contender for Vivienne's affections, but he definitely stood in the way. He was the kind of man that attracted Vivienne, and everything Will wasn't. More than that, Nate had Vivienne's heart and had shared her bed.

"Can I get you another beer, young fellow?"

"Nah." Will put cash on the bar. "Keep the change."

When Will approached the hotel, the lights were out, except for one above each door. More important, the place was quiet. He brushed the sand from the bottom of his feet before climbing into bed. Lying in the darkness, he knew Vivienne wouldn't let him sleep, so he settled to see her face in his mind, smiling at him on the terrace under the beautiful night sky.

# Chapter 7

*Her hands released Will's hair, and she wove her fingers into his waves. The simple act sent shivers through her. It excited her. Her breath hitched, quickening, and a soft moan escaped her as she urgently drew his mouth to hers, but something kept her from kissing him.* Her eyes opened as she heard him ask in the lingering end of her dream, "What are you afraid of?"

Vivienne turned over and buried her face in the pillow. "A lot more now than last night." Raising her head, she saw the digital clock read 5:00AM and scurried out of bed. Getting to the restaurant took precedence over her pointless dreams. She knew where Audrey was when she passed her room and empty bed. She was sleeping next to someone she loved, but it was Hugo's commitment that still had Vivienne on the fence.

The morning sights and sounds at the restaurant had become part of Vivienne's life. When Vivienne arrived at 6:00AM, the early wait staff rushed past each other, preparing the tables.

"Morning," she said, raising her hand on the way to the kitchen. The teenagers could have been sleeping in, and enjoying their time on the beach, but decided to work during the summer.

When she pushed open the kitchen door, Vivienne was hit with a flurry of activity. "Morning, everyone."

"Those aren't nearly enough blueberries for the muffins and pancakes, Devon," Auggie shouted. "We need another batch. Chance, get the big pots of chowder from the fridge. Put them on the stove under a low flame for Esty."

As if on cue, Brendan held the kitchen door open for Esty. "I'm here," she announced.

"I appreciate you picking her up," Vivienne said, kissing Brendan's cheek.

"It's no trouble. I'm happy to do it."

At the back of the kitchen, Vivienne took a clean apron from the shelf and placed her bag underneath the small cabinet. As she was tying the apron, she happened to glance in the mirror. Leaning closer, she inspected the strands of gray at her hairline and rolled her eyes. "I could swear they weren't here yesterday, and I know who to blame for putting them in my head." Pulling her thick, unruly curls off her neck and into a bun, she headed out to the counter. Seeing Caleb waiting to order his early-bird breakfast, Vivienne knew to go to the coffee urn first.

"Morning." Vivienne placed a steaming mug of Auggie's coffee on the counter, along with a menu.

"Mornin', Vivienne," Caleb replied and moved the menu toward her. "Just my usual."

She smiled. "Two sunny side eggs and corned beef hash."

She was placing the order on the wheel when Magda walked in for her morning coffee. Vivienne urgently waved her toward the last seat at the counter.

"I wanted to call you this morning," Vivienne said quietly, "but wasn't sure if you had company."

"I was thinking the same thing," Magda whispered.

"Seriously, Magda?"

"Okay. I know you're not ready for that. So, what happened?"

"Plenty, but for the sake of time, I'll break it down in one sentence. He was coming on to me, I was enjoying it until he whispered something to me within earshot of Audrey and Hugo, I gave him the look of death, and the night ended in a huge argument on the way home."

"How did you leave off?" Magda asked.

"Sunnyside eggs, corned beef hash," Auggie shouted.

"Hold that thought." She picked up Caleb's order and then walked two stools down to Liam. After taking his order and leaving it with the kitchen, she was about to continue when she saw Will speaking with Heidi at the front desk.

"Do you have time for another coffee, Magda? Will just walked in."

Magda pushed her mug toward Vivienne, who was refilling it, when Will took the empty stool next to Magda. His still-damp hair had left tiny drops of water on his t-shirt. Vivienne could see the waves forming as his hair dried.

"Morning, Vivienne," he said.

"Scrambled eggs and wheat toast coming out," Auggie shouted.

"Morning, Will. Excuse me." She served Liam with a cool exterior, hiding her turbulent heart. The intimate dream she had just hours ago, still lingered in her mind. Her hands breaking Will's hair free from its tie, her heart hammering in her chest as she drew his lips to hers, emotions she learned to live without, until that fateful night Will walked into her restaurant. "You're up early."

"It was the bed. I couldn't sleep, so I thought I'd get on the road now to beat the traffic."

But there in his eyes, Vivienne saw what he meant. *It was you.* Without asking, she filled a mug with coffee. "You'll need this to stay awake."

He pushed the mug away. "I don't *need* you to be my mother."

Liam lifted his eyes toward the man's condescending voice.

"That's not what I meant, Will." His sarcasm stung her still fragile, unsure feelings for him.

"Then, tell me what you meant."

Magda sat quietly amid the rising tension, looking into her now empty coffee cup.

"You can't just back me into a corner," Vivienne snapped. "I have a business to run."

Hoping to interrupt what sounded like an argument-in-progress, Liam raised his hand to get her attention. "Viv, can I have the check, please?"

Vivienne left Will and Magda, each with their own part in the argument, one the instigator and one the innocent bystander. She quickly tabulated Liam's check. "Was your breakfast okay?"

"Take a guess." He inched his empty plate toward her. "You can tell Auggie I didn't like the eggs." He glanced at the receipt then handed Vivienne enough cash to cover the meal and a generous tip. "Always good to see you, Viv."

She smiled. "Thank you, Liam. I appreciate it...and Auggie will, too."

When she returned to Will, he was reaching into the pocket of his jeans for his wallet. No smile, no frown. His lips were an unwavering, unreadable line. "Since you poured the coffee, I'll take it to go," he said, putting cash on top of the check.

The alternative to attracting attention was to avoid it.

Will headed to the door with a travel mug, while Vivienne began to clean the counter in silence.

"That's it?" Magda whispered. "You're going to let him leave?"

"What do you expect me to do in front of these people? This whole thing with Will is just crazy. It's better this way."

"For whom, Viv? When you close tonight, have dinner at my place."

***

The restaurant continued to fill with morning customers, giving Vivienne no time to dwell. She was picking up two orders, when she spotted Audrey and Hugo at the front desk. Her quick scan of the room showed only one table open for four and waved to get Heidi's attention. "Heidi, give them table 12."

Heidi pointed them to two empty places at the counter.

"It's not Heidi's fault, Mom," Audrey quickly said. "I told her to give the table to four people. You know I always liked sitting at the counter."

"Thank you. I appreciate that."

As she followed her path into journalism, over the years, Audrey hadn't lost her keen eye, always checking the tables to accommodate another customer or two when she could. Vivienne's wish to see Audrey running the business, someday, became an unfulfilled dream she had learned to live with.

"We wanted to stop in before we got on the road," Hugo said. "We drove to The Sandpiper to see if Will wanted to join us, but he'd already left."

"He was here and took a coffee to go." Turning to Audrey, Vivienne said, "Let me get your grandmother. I'm sure she'll want to see you before you leave." She held the kitchen door open for Esty, who's beaming smile distracted from her slow steps.

Audrey rose and went around the counter to Esty's open arms. "You know I wouldn't leave without saying goodbye."

"Did you see your brother?"

"He's already out on the boat, but we stopped at the fish market to see Grace and left a little something for Tory."

Esty embraced Audrey's cheeks between the palms of her hands. "Stay close to your family."

"Of course I will, Gram. Boston isn't far."

"I'll make sure she does," Hugo added.

"Take care of my granddaughter."

Hugo may have been head and shoulders above her, but he stooped down and nodded like a schoolboy. "I have every intention of doing that."

"Now, I'll go back to my chowder."

"Best I've ever had," Hugo said.

It pulled at Vivienne's heart to see them leave after a quick coffee and bagel. Diving into the busy lunch and dinner crowd kept her from facing, even for a brief time, her feelings for Will.

***

She stood at the front door with her hand on the light switch and glanced around. The kitchen was dark. The counter was gleaming, tables were clean, and Esty was on the way home, courtesy of Brendan. She turned off the lights.

After putting the restaurant to bed for the night, she arrived at Magda's with her arms full. "I stopped for two bottles of wine and a box of sinfully delicious dessert."

Magda quickly wiped her hands on her apron and reached for the wine. "Let me take those. Dinner's almost ready."

Vivienne followed her to the kitchen, the place that was the silent gatekeeper for each other's lives, where they sat, and laughed, and cried through the years. "What was I thinking, Magda? I'm officially delusional and, by the way, this roasted chicken is delicious."

Magda smiled and placed another helping on her plate. "You're not delusional, Viv. There are many couples now who have age gaps. It isn't a big deal anymore."

"Five years is a big deal in this town. It's stuck in the past."

Magda's hand brushed the air, as if swatting an offending bug. "Oh, who cares about this town."

"Are you forgetting about Audrey and Evan? They'd hang me out to dry if they found out their mother was attracted to someone their age."

"Or maybe not, but you won't know if you continue to push him away."

"I know you're talking about this morning, but I wasn't going to let him force me into discussing my feelings in a room full of people, so I pushed back. Not to mention, I think Liam may have overheard us."

"He may have, but if you're not interested in him, let it go.

Between last night's argument and this morning, Will's gotten a dose of your feisty side, but it doesn't look like he's backing down. I could tell in his voice that he feels something for you, so why don't you tell that handsome guy how you feel?"

"Because he went back to Boston and that's it. He'll have no reason to come back here."

"But he does, Viv. You."

"Oh, and you!" Vivienne added. "He wants to, and I quote, *pay homage,* to the woman who sold me the dress I wore last night."

"I think that can be arranged. Tell him you mentioned the dress to me, and *I'm* inviting him to dinner."

Vivienne's head cocked to the side, and she looked at her through skeptical eyes. "What are you scheming in that head of yours?"

"Making sure your life doesn't fall through the cracks."

***

After dinner, they moved to the living room, where Vivienne relaxed in a lazy sprawl on the couch, while Magda sat across from her, cuddled in Griffin's favorite chair.

"Promise me you'll call him," Magda said, while reaching for a tiny éclair. "The good thing about being our age is there are no rules, just what feels right."

"Before I went to dinner last night, I paid Nate a visit. I talked about Evan, Audrey, Hugo...and Will, and how nothing would come of it."

"Who were you trying to convince? Nate or yourself?"

She closed her eyes, tilted her head back and whined. "Oh, I don't know, maybe both."

"Nate can't change the outcome of this, but you can. Sleep on it. Somehow, everything always seems clearer in the morning."

Arriving home, Vivienne slipped out of her sandals and sat on the couch, mulling over Magda's words. But one thing was certain. The thoughts in her head were not conducive to sleep.

# Chapter 8

Will was back at his desk Monday morning, with a cup of joe from the local shop at the corner. He stared at the list of restaurant invitations, but none sparked his interest, nor could they deflect his thoughts from Vivienne. *What if I asked her if she'd like to join me for a restaurant review?* He was grabbing at straws, but the prospect excited him. When he reached for his phone, their last prickly exchange at her restaurant paid an unwelcome visit in his mind. *She won't answer,* he convinced himself and put the phone down.

With no more last-minute tricks up his sleeve, he got to the business of narrowing the list of prospective restaurants to a handful. The familiar sound coming down the hall made him close his eyes. Alex's stilettos hit the linoleum floor, their clacking like the steady tick of a timebomb heading right for his desk. Will leaned back in his chair and raised his eyes to meet the scowl on her face.

"So, you were too busy to call or text me this weekend?"

"You could say that. And why are you asking?"

"Because I wanted to talk about us. Where were you?"

"There is no *us,* and it's none of your business."

With her hand placed on the defiant jut of her hip, her words were as accusatory as a detective pressing for a confession. "I know you were with Audrey this weekend."

It wasn't Audrey, but Vivienne that Alex sparked in his mind, standing on the restaurant terrace, wearing that dress he hoped to see her wearing again. He couldn't hold back the amusing smirk that pulled at the corner of his mouth, as he watched her anger squeeze her perfect brows together.

*If you only knew how far off base you are.*

"Don't bother denying it," she said. "You've got that guilty grin on your face."

"I don't have time for this, Alex." He stood abruptly and brushed past her.

His father opened his office door. "Will, you got a minute?"

"Sure."

"Will," Alex called to his back. Infuriated by his obstinance, she raised her voice like a petulant child. "Will, turn around. I won't be ignored." She followed him until she stood at Hugo's office door. The last thing Will saw were Alex's eyes, seething and staring him down with the glare of Medusa, until he closed the door on her.

***

"What's up, Dad?"

"Did you enjoy the weekend?"

"I did, actually." Will took a seat in front of his desk. "Audrey was right about *Callane's*. Best chowdah I've ever had. Too bad I can't review it."

"She knows you can't. She's just proud of her family's restaurant. I want to talk to you about Audrey and I."

"You want to propose to her?"

"Why...yes."

"I was wondering when you would."

Hugo's brows rose, staring at his son's calm demeanor. "You're okay with this?"

Will had his own agenda. *What's good for the goose...* "You and Mom were married a long time. I can't imagine that she would want you to spend these years without her, alone. I wouldn't either, Dad. Audrey may be younger than you, but the heart doesn't know age."

"I'm glad to hear you say that, Will," Hugo replied, while unable to hold back his curious but happy skepticism. "Since when have you gotten so philosophical?"

*You'd fall off the chair if I told you.* Will shrugged. "I don't know. Maybe seeing you and Audrey together this weekend, and spending time at her mom's restaurant. The heart wants, what the heart wants."

"I think Alex would tell you the same thing." Hugo grumped.

Will stood. "She's used to getting what she wants. Don't let her fool you. It's more her pride than her heart. So, when will you propose to her?"

"Not before I ask Vivienne and her son, Evan, for her hand. I hope they don't rake me over the coals."

Will had sensed Vivienne's stubbornness to admit her own feelings but couldn't imagine that she would hold back her empathy for his father and Audrey. "You may be surprised."

"You'll be the first to know how it went."

Will smiled. "Thanks, Dad." But he knew he wouldn't be the first to know. *Vivienne would.*

***

*Somehow, everything always seems clearer in the morning.* One thing clear to Vivienne this morning was that her sleep was fitful the night before. Groggy and irritable, her pace was slow as she was dressing for work, until the buzz of an incoming text on her phone spurred an eye-waking shot of adrenaline. A feeling of dread hit her stomach. It was a message from Hugo.

*Vivienne, Please don't panic. Everything's okay and Audrey's fine. There's something I would like to discuss with you and Evan. Audrey will be out this evening. If we can talk when you both end your day just text YES, with the time that's good.*

A quick scroll on her phone took her to Evan's number.

*Evan, Hugo would like to speak with us this evening about Audrey. There's nothing to worry about; Audrey's fine. Text YES if you can. My house. 7:00.*

Vivienne knew Evan was irked. Despite being out on the boat, his text came back just minutes after she sent the message.

*Fuck, yes, I'll be there. If he breaks Audrey's heart, you'll have to bail me out of jail.*

*Let's just hear the man out.* Vivienne sent back. *You have a family. Remember?*

Another few taps of her trembling fingers took her back to Hugo's number, where she left her reply.

*Hugo, yes, my house. 7:00.*

Hugo's upcoming visit left her with no choice but to end her procrastination of overdue housework.

Two hours later, and a sweaty mess, she was satisfied that he wouldn't trip over her shoes, sandals, and sneakers in the foyer, or have to share the couch with a basket of unfolded laundry. After another quick shower, she left the house in a huff and walked into the restaurant in desperate need of Auggie's morning coffee.

Auggie looked at the kitchen door, his pinched brows showing his concern. "Is everything okay, Vivienne? You're never this late."

"I'm fine, Auggie. I had some things to take care of at home, but I knew I could count on my second in command."

Auggie accepted her compliment with a prideful jut of his chest.

"Okay, chefs, we have people to feed."

She grabbed a porcelain mug from the shelf and held it under the large coffee urn, sending a stream of Auggie's coffee to the brim.

She sipped it gingerly, watching Brendan tend to the counter crowd while she went over the lunch and dinner specials. When Magda arrived for her morning coffee before opening her store, Vivienne looked at the time, surprised at how the hours had passed.

Magda stirred cream into her coffee while waiting for Vivienne to get a free moment.

"I didn't sleep a minute last night," Vivienne said.

"No one else will tell you, but you know I will. It shows, Viv."

"Do I really look that bad?" she asked.

"Nothing that a little concealer and blush won't fix, but what happened between the time you left my house and this morning?"

"A lot." She placed one of Auggie's blueberry muffins in front of Magda. "Eat. I'll be back in a minute."

After clipping a customer's order on the wheel, "Are you free for lunch?" Vivienne asked Magda.

"You don't have to ask."

"Good. I'll stop by at noon."

Before Magda left, she pointed to Vivienne's face. "Concealer and blush. Now."

***

A few hours later, Vivienne left the restaurant in the capable hands of Auggie and her staff. When she arrived with Esty's chowder, Magda let her in and promptly flipped the sign on her door.

"I can see you listened to me," Magda commented, as they sat at a small table in her office. "You look much better."

"Hugo texted me this morning. He wants to speak to me and Evan after work tonight. I'm getting a bad feeling about this."

Magda's eyes lit up. "Wait a minute, Viv, maybe he wants to propose to Audrey."

"That would've been my guess, except that Audrey mentioned Hugo doesn't want to get married again, or father more children, so my thoughts aren't on the positive side. And, to add to this, when I told Evan, his reply included an *F bomb*. You think he's mad? Just a bit?"

"There's not much you can do but wait to hear what Hugo has

to say."

"You forgot trying to keep Evan from going off the deep end." Vivienne put her spoon down and sat in quiet contemplation for a moment, then: "You know, when I heard my phone buzz, my first thought was Will. My heart began to race like it did when I was young, waiting by the phone for Nate to call."

"Viv, we were talking about Audrey."

Vivienne lowered her head to the table, groaning in utter confusion. "Ugh...I can't think straight."

"You're surprised? You're running on no sleep. You won't be able to respond with a clear head to anything Hugo has to say, if you're like this. Take a nap. Auggie and the staff have managed the restaurant in the past."

Vivienne felt herself losing the battle to stay awake. "You're right. Auggie will make sure the place doesn't burn to the ground." With that, she stood and took the empty containers to the trash. "I've taken enough time away from your business."

Magda grabbed her by the shoulders, her eyes holding Vivienne's as she pressed her words home. "Viv, you *are* my business. Go home and get some sleep."

Auggie was already in *boss* mode when Vivienne left him in charge for the rest of the day. With her mind at ease and a house ready for Hugo, she stepped out of her sandals, pulled the sheet over her, and didn't remember falling asleep until the alarm rang.

***

She knew Hugo wouldn't announce his arrival with the aggressive knocks on her door.

"You look nice, Evan," she said.

His sharp retort was like a valve, slowly releasing the pressure of anger. "Don't try to pacify me. This guy better not say what I'm thinking." He kissed Vivienne's cheek and walked past her to the living room. "What time will he be here?"

"I said 7:00PM, so any minute, Evan."

He stood with his arms crossed, his biceps bulging under his short-sleeve shirt. He was Audrey's ever-defensive brother, whose nostrils flared with every angered breath, ready to take on a battle for his sister.

"Evan, please try to stay off your emotional high-horse." But

Vivienne's pleading only served to open the valve a notch.

"Oh, come on, Mom. The minute I saw him at the cemetery, I knew this wasn't going to work. What could they possibly have in common, except sex? He's too old for her and she's too young for him."

His steadfast condemnation threw an ice-cold dose of reality right in Vivienne's face.

When the hum of the car motor ceased, the uncertainty of the coming moments felt like the start of a boxing round, beginning with Hugo's knock on the door. Vivienne was surprised to see him holding a bouquet of white peonies.

"Thank you for seeing me on such short notice. These are for you."

"They're beautiful, Hugo, thank you. Please, come on in. You remember Evan."

Evan's unwavering stare wasn't a deterrent for Hugo, who stepped toward him with the confidence of his age. "I appreciate you being here."

Vivienne released the breath she was holding, when Evan uncrossed his arms to accept Hugo's outstretched hand.

"Are those *I'm sorry* flowers?" Evan asked.

"Just appreciation."

"You mentioned to my mother, that you wanted to talk to us," Evan began. "Funny thing about last minute visits or phone calls. They almost always turn out to be bad."

"That will depend on you and your mother."

Vivienne cut in with a quick interruption. "Let's all sit. Can I get you something to drink?"

"Watah, please."

Evan raised his palm. "I'm fine, thank you."

Hugo sighed. "I know you've had some reservations about me."

"*Serious* reservations," Evan added.

"I don't blame either of you."

Vivienne handed him a chilled glass of water. "Audrey's told me that marriage and children aren't in your future."

Blindsided with this news, Evan glared at Vivienne before he stood to confront Hugo. "Wait a minute. You don't want to get married, *and* you don't want children, so if you're here to tell us you have nothing to offer my Audrey—"

Evan's flushed face was a red flag that Hugo had to quickly dodge. "No, Evan. That's not why I asked to see both of you. Please give me a chance to explain."

"This better be good," Evan growled out, "because that's all you're getting. *One chance.*"

"Yes, children aren't in my future, but Audrey is. I want her to have what she was willing to give up for me. I asked you to be here, Evan, for your father. I want to marry her, but I won't offer her this ring without both of your blessings." Hugo reached into his jacket, placed the ring box on the coffee table, and opened it.

In the silence, Hugo's eyes toggled between Evan and Vivienne, hoping to see some reaction.

It was Evan who spoke first, his mistrust evident as he stared through narrow, skeptic eyes at the brilliant, pear-shaped diamond. "I'm not impressed by material things. You're asking us to place Audrey's life in your hands. You have to give us more reassurance other than this ring."

"You're looking out for your sister, and I wouldn't want it any other way." Hugo nodded. "Your reservations about the age difference are understandable."

"Then, change our minds," Evan said.

"I struggled with it. We were only seeing each other for about a month, but we both knew it was serious. It was hard for me, but I had to tell her that we couldn't see each other anymore. I tried to reason with her, telling her I wanted to see her with someone her own age, but Audrey was inconsolable."

"She told me about your breakup," Vivienne said.

"Have you ever seen your wife cry, Evan? Tell me you didn't feel the pain in her tears and how you would have done anything to spare her that. I felt the tears Audrey shed for me in the core of my soul. I was in love with her, but I couldn't put my happiness before hers. I was trying to spare her a life with an older man, but all I did was break her heart."

Vivienne's own struggles found a way to shed light on Will's feelings, without fear of suspicion. "And how does Will feel about this? Does he see Audrey replacing his mother?"

"It was hard for me after my wife, Emily, passed. I didn't know if I had the capacity to love on that level again. I have to say, Will surprised me. 'Mom wouldn't want you to waste the life you have,' he said. 'I've always liked Audrey. Yes, she's younger than you but the heart doesn't know age.'"

Vivienne's heart skipped and her stomach fluttered, imagining for an instant that Will wasn't talking about Audrey and Hugo. "She asked me to keep an open mind, but it's an open heart that she needs." She reached for the box and looked at the simple three-carat diamond that would grace her daughter's hand. Turning to Evan, she wiped her eyes. "It's not our dream for Audrey that's important, but Audrey's dream for herself."

"I promise you both, Audrey will be in loving and devoted hands."

Hearing Hugo's words sparked a memory that flashed in Evan's mind. A moment in his life he hadn't thought about until now, laying his own vulnerable heart, and the same promise, before Grace's parents. His last bit of apprehension was replaced with empathy, as he extended his hand to Hugo. "I won't deny Audrey the happiness she wants and deserves."

When Hugo sighed, a smile of relief replaced the tension in his pinched brows. "Thank you, Evan."

"I can see that asking for a woman's hand doesn't get any easier with age."

"I knew I was in for a hard time when I saw you seething in the living room," Hugo said.

"Oh, believe me. The outcome would have been far worse if my father were here."

"You wouldn't have gotten in the door," Vivienne added.

"Not to mention the screaming that would have followed, but I know my sister. She would have found a way around him. As for me, I must admit I wasn't a fan when I saw you with Audrey at the cemetery."

"You certainly stirred the pot of gossip among the town talkers, Hugo," Vivienne added.

"Are you referring to the ladies I was introduced to at the restaurant?"

"Stella and Camille. No one's escaped the whispers of gossip they plant in the ears of anyone who will listen."

"I guess every town has them," Hugo replied. "The Tribune has the *breakroom gang*. They'll have a lot to talk about when Audrey comes in wearing this ring."

Vivienne never expected Hugo to leave something for her to consider as they shared in a celebratory hug. "We've both experienced loss. Life surprised me, Vivienne. I hope it does the same for you."

***

After Hugo and Evan had gone, Vivienne took a glass of wine on the terrace. The evening breeze was cool, but the shawl warmed her shoulders as she relaxed on the chaise. The crickets' incessant chirping and the throaty notes of bulbous frogs were the familiar songs that Vivienne could rely on to lull her to sleep, but not tonight. They couldn't silence her thoughts of Audrey and the somewhat unconventional path her life would take. There in the darkness, she realized her path wasn't far from Audrey's. She took the last sip of wine and closed her eyes. What Audrey wouldn't give up, and everything Vivienne was pushing away, was pulling them both to what they couldn't ignore. What the heart wants.

# Chapter 9

Vivienne slipped into the halter dress that she chose with Magda for Audrey's engagement party. There, in the full-length mirror, was a woman who had disappeared in the years that passed by, in the blink of an eye. Shoulders that had been covered in t-shirts were toned from years of balancing trays of food. She put on the pearl-drop earrings Nate had given to her on their wedding day and took a step back. Tiers of alabaster chiffon skimmed her ankles and complimented the cherry-red polish on her toes that peeked out from her jeweled sandals. For the first time in a long time, she felt beautiful, and she wanted to be, especially tonight.

Two taps on the door took Vivienne's attention to Magda's voice carrying up the stairs.

"Viv? Are you ready?"

As Vivienne made her way down the stairs, she was met with Magda's satisfying smile. "You look gorgeous."

"I have you to thank. It's the dress."

"And everything else. Lynette did an amazing job on your hair."

"Do you like it?" Vivienne asked. "She convinced me to go with the deep burgundy."

"Lynette's talent is color. It's perfect for your fair skin." With a tilt of her head, her eyes took on an impish glint. "I see you pulled some curls down from your chignon. Feeling a little sexy?"

"I'm not even sure why it did it."

"Yes, you do. Admit it. I haven't seen you pay this much attention to yourself in years."

"The last time we were at *The Wicked Seashell*, things went from bad to worse with Will, and the next morning at the restaurant...well, you were there."

"He was trying to get you to tell him how you felt."

"In front of everyone, Magda?"

"Okay, I'll give you that, but what about tonight?"

Vivienne locked the front door and turned to Magda. "What if tonight is more of the same, or worse, what if he put the whole mess behind him and moved on?"

"A lot of *what ifs*, Viv, but you won't know until Owen gets us there."

Although talk in the car centered around Audrey and Hugo, tucked between the conversation was the unmistakable inflection in Magda and Owen's voices when they spoke to each other. As Magda leaned toward Owen, smoothing his hair with the gentle touch of her hand, Vivienne realized she was witnessing more between them than she had before. *Had Magda finally found someone to share her life with again?* Vivienne's thoughts mirrored the wishes she held in her heart for Magda.

When Owen pulled up in front of *The Wicked Seashell*, guests were already mingling in small groups. Through the backseat passenger window, Vivienne saw Auggie speaking with Will. It was as if her heart finally found the rhythm it had been waiting for when he turned toward the car and smiled.

She took Owen's hand as she stepped out and kept a tight control on her emotions when she approached Auggie and Will.

"Auggie!" she said, wrapping her arms around his broad shoulders. "I'm so glad to see you." Taking a step back, she took in his transformation with widened eyes. "You look so stylish."

"I thought Audrey would appreciate me trading my apron for a jacket and tie."

After all the conversations Vivienne had with Magda about Will, she knew Magda was as eager to meet him, as she was to introduce him. "Magda and Owen, this is Will Lawson."

"I heard about your anonymous late-night appearance at my friend's restaurant," Magda said.

"Audrey knew I was driving from Bawstin to see her and my dad," Will replied, "and suggested I try *Callane's*. I had no idea the beautiful woman serving me at the counter was her mom."

Vivienne remembered everything about that night. But her confusion was obvious, tilting her head with a clearly baffled stare at Will. "Beautiful? I guess you don't remember my white apron covered in cocktail and tartar sauce, or the mess of hair I piled on top of my head that could have been a nest for any bird looking for a home. Beautiful is definitely the wrong word."

Will held up his hand. "Never argue with a woman."

"Good advice," Owen said.

"While we were talking, Will mentioned he's a food critic for The Tribune," Auggie added. "I would have come out from the kitchen that night to talk."

"I was just a customer that night," Will replied.

Vivienne said, "You know, Auggie, some of Audrey and Hugo's female colleagues at The Tribune will be here."

"I know them all personally," Will added. "Trust me. Women love when men cook for them, and you being a chef? You just may be their *cup of tea.*"

Auggie was pumped by Will's encouragement and straightened his shoulders. "I guess it's never too late to dip my toes in the water again."

"I know a chef's kitchen is sacred ground," Will put in, "but do you think I'll have a shot at seeing you prepare the menu items *Callane's* is famous for?"

"As long as you're willing to get your hands dirty."

With a confirming grip, he shook Auggie's hand. "I'm all in."

Magda then reached for Vivienne's hands. "Viv, we're going to head inside to see Audrey and Hugo." Vivienne felt her gentle squeeze, and the amused glint in her eyes, produced a knowing smile from Vivienne.

"I'll catch up with you and Owen later," Vivienne replied. Turning to Auggie and Will, she added, "Well, gentlemen, let's join the party."

***

Vivienne felt as if all eyes were on her, the mother of the bride, announcing her arrival on the arms of two men, equally handsome despite the significance in age. She saw Audrey up ahead and took in a breath. She stood with confidence next to Hugo, holding his hand, talking to guests, and her smile exuded happiness that Vivienne hadn't seen before. Esty sat beside them.

"Mom," Audrey said, kissing her cheek, "You look beautiful, your dress, your hair. Don't tell me. Magda and Lynnette."

"Even small-town shops can rival the big cities."

"Obviously. I never noticed how toned your shoulders and arms are."

"I guess there's a benefit to lifting heavy trays for years, and no gym fees."

"I remember balancing those trays, and my gym rates just went up."

"You're always welcome to pick up a shift or two and learn the business."

"I think I'll stick with journalism, Mom."

Audrey's blunt response wasn't a surprise to Vivienne who, nonetheless, got the last word in. "Just a thought."

Moving past that subject, Audrey stepped toward Auggie, hugging him as if he were her father. "Auggie! I'm so glad you're here. Tonight wouldn't be the same without you."

"I shared in every major event in your life. You couldn't keep me away."

"And look at you, Will," Audrey said, her brows rising in apparent surprise. "I'm in shock."

"You should be. I put this tie on just for you."

"And no man bun. Don't I feel special?" Audrey always had the kind of infectious laugh he couldn't help laughing with. Her broad smile would be followed by a wave of laughter that squinched her eyes and shook her shoulders. Vivienne couldn't remember the last time Audrey laughed with such carefree abandon.

Esty said, "I recognize this young man from the restaurant."

"This is my son, William," Hugo told her. "He was with Audrey and I when we had lunch at the restaurant."

Will took a step toward her and extended his hand. "It's an honor to know the woman who makes the best chowdah I've ever had."

Esty smiled as she rested her hand in his. Raising her eyes, she looked into the clear and open honesty of his. "Thank you, William. I remember Audrey saying you're a food critic."

"Yes. I work with her at The Tribune."

"He won't be able to write a review, Gram," Audrey added.

"He enjoyed it," Esty said. "That's enough."

Auggie caught sight of the staff from *Callane's*. Marty held up his hand and waved him over. "It looks like I'm being summoned by the *Callane's* crowd."

"They're a tight, loyal bunch," Audrey said, hearing them roar when he joined them.

"Hey, Dad," Will said. "Would you introduce Auggie to the women from the office? I think they would enjoy a conversation with a chef."

"I'd be happy to, Will."

Vivienne smiled at him. "I appreciate that, Hugo."

"It's good to see you smiling again, Mom," Audrey said.

Vivienne had more than one reason to smile. It was the perfect time to take that first step. "I'll let you greet the rest of your guests. Will, would you like to accompany me on the terrace for a drink?"

He offered her his arm. "I'd love to."

She slipped her hand inside Will's arm, and they sauntered off.

***

Vivienne spotted Magda's arm stretched high, waving her over to the railing.

One of the servers approached Vivienne and Will. "Can I get you something to drink from the bar?"

"Cosmopolitan," Vivienne replied.

"And you, sir?"

"Water, thank you."

"This is a great party, Viv," Magda said. "Owen and I have been enjoying the perfect weather and sampling the amazing hors d'oeuvres.

"Audrey made it easy. A simple menu, a few of her and Hugo's friends, the family, and our family at the restaurant."

Will's shift was a seamless whisper of motion woven into his reply, for no one to notice...except Vivienne, who felt the soft brush of his body barely touching hers. "Speaking of parties, I guess it's on me to plan one for my dad," he said, with a side glance to Vivienne.

"Don't look at me," Vivienne replied, chuckling at the thought. "I don't do bachelor parties."

"Oh, come on," Will pleaded. "You just said how easy this was."

Owen laughed. "Doesn't look like you're gonna get anywhere with this."

Looking to Magda, Will gave his last-ditch effort to her amused smirk. "Anything I can do to change her mind?"

"Yes. Don't try to."

Feeling playful and aroused by his valiant efforts to win her over, Vivienne's words were like a soft, flirtatious breath in his ear. "Don't listen to Magda."

He responded by taking her hand. The connection lasted but a mere second when they heard Audrey's voice.

"Mom. I thought I'd find you out here."

"We were enjoying the terrace and talking about the restaurant."

"I know you and Magda are thick as thieves, but can I pull you away for a bit? I have some friends I want you to meet."

"I'd love to, Audrey." She turned to her friends. "I'll catch up with you all later."

As a server was passing, Will took Vivienne's empty glass from her and placed it on the tray. "I'm having water tonight," he said, "so you can enjoy another Cosmo or two. I can take you home, if you want."

"Thank you, Will," Audrey replied. "I appreciate you taking care of my mom."

***

Having Will drive her home would be the perfect end to the evening, and it was all Vivienne could think about. In the back of her mind, Will was somewhere among the guests. As she talked to Audrey's friends, she sipped her Cosmo and stole a glance here and there, trying to spot him. *Could he be on the terrace with someone?* A silent storm brewed inside her at the thought of him with another woman. A *younger* woman. Any of Audrey's attractive friends would make the possibility highly likely. The urge to know, and the conversation to end, began in the slight shift of Vivienne's feet and tapping the stem of her glass.

Emma crinkled her nose and flinched, unable to stop the urge to gingerly scratch her red, itchy shoulders. "What do you think of Audrey's decision to have a beach wedding, Vivienne?"

"I used to call her my little beach bunny, so I'm not surprised. But I would advise you ladies to use more sunscreen and take care of those sunburned shoulders, Emma."

She huffed. "Boy, did I learn my lesson."

Vivienne felt it was a natural end to their conversation. "Audrey, if you don't mind, there are still guests I need to speak to."

Her mind turned to Will again, until the sight before her made her brows jump. Evan had given Hugo a hard time on their first meeting, but the smiles of these two men, who barely knew each other, looked as if they were sharing time together as old friends would do.

"I have to admit," Vivienne commented, "I was hoping, but not hopeful."

Evan glowed. "Sports. It's a tried-and-true icebreaker."

"I was glad to hear Evan is a Red Sox fan," Hugo added. "Audrey will be busy with the wedding, and I know she'd be happy to give her season tickets to her brother."

"Are you talking about my Sox tickets?" Audrey cut in. "They're a hot commodity...right behind home plate." Stepping up to her brother, she kissed him on the cheek. "It's one of the perks when you give the bride away. I'm happy that you're doing this for Dad."

Evan took Audrey's hand and gazed again at the simplistic beauty of the ring. "You know he would have barked for a bit about your decision, but your happiness would have mattered more. No one deserves this more than you, Sis."

Vivienne covered her mouth; they loved him and missed him as much as she did. Despite the stormy and turbulent last years of her marriage to Nate, he had been a good provider for them.

It was then that she realized these moments with her family had pushed Will from her mind. She began to scan the room but didn't have to look long, when her eyes settled on him speaking to a friend of Audrey who she hadn't met yet. Unlike Emma's sunburned shoulders, this young woman's skin had a subtle glow that showed a sprinkling of freckles.

Will was attentive as she spoke and picked up the conversation when she stopped occasionally to sip her glass of wine. The playful flirting Vivienne shared with him earlier, now seemed flippant and nonsensical. When the woman's baby pink manicured fingers reached to straighten his tie, Vivienne had to hide any evidence of the sharp bite of jealousy.

"It seems like your friend is interested in Will," she said. "I haven't met her yet."

Audrey rolled her eyes. "That's Sivila. I was trying to spare you. Unfortunately, she's in the group of friends I'm close with. We all know how she operates. She's currently dating someone, but he couldn't make the party tonight. Don't think for a minute that she's upset. She's been complaining that the *energy* between them is stalling. It's the same line she uses with all the guys she dates. We know it's her excuse to start *looking*, and Will is right up her alley.

Audrey had taken Vivienne inside her circle for a couple of precious minutes. "You've never spoken about your friends like this before."

"Friend, singular. She's one of a kind, Mom."

*Is she Will's one of a kind?* Vivienne had to know. "Will seems interested."

Audrey began to chuckle. "Will would never date Sivila. You don't know Will like I do, but as he's going to be family, I'll give you a peek."

She knew she would remember every word Audrey said as she shed a new light on Vivienne's understanding of Will.

"Will's a bachelor and has clear boundaries in his relationships. No strings attached. He's not looking for anything serious. He likes to hang with his friends, dates casually, and keeps the two separate."

That wasn't the way with Nate. After their first week together, love had hit him hard. Vivienne knew it and so did half the town. Looking back, she couldn't remember a time when her life wasn't bound by strong ties. *Can my heart handle the fickle inclinations of a man who may want to love me with no strings attached?*

***

When the last guest had left, Vivienne was in the bar, settling the bill, when Will wandered in.

"I was wondering where you were."

Had Audrey not given her an inside glimpse into his life, she may have thrown caution to the wind tonight. Seeing him with Sivila put his lifestyle in her face. Realizing how foolish and naïve she must have looked to him, she chose to focus instead on signing the bill and handing it to the owner. "Thank you, Cane. Everything was perfect."

"Anything for you, Vivienne. I wish Audrey and Hugo the best."

With a copy of the bill in her hand, she turned to Will.

"For a minute, I thought you'd skipped out on me," he said.

Annoyed with herself, more than him, Vivienne was ready with her answer. "For a minute, I was thinking you had done the same thing."

"Why would you say that? You know I'm taking you home."

"Are we taking anyone else with us?"

"No. I'm only interested in being alone with you."

They stood in silence until the valet drove up with his car. As Vivienne got in, their last disastrous drive home from this restaurant was no longer a memory. She was reliving it.

"What about Sivila? She seemed awfully handsy."

Will groaned. "Handsy is the right word. I don't know why Audrey is friends with her. She jumps from one guy to the next before the bed is..." Will stopped mid-sentence. "Sorry."

"Oh, please, don't stop on my account. From what I saw, it looked like she had you pegged for next in line."

For an instant, Will took his eyes off the road. "You were busy talking to guests. I was trying to be polite, but all I could think about was you, seeing me with her."

Vivienne turned to him. "Why? I have no ties to you, but I've heard you're a *no-strings attached* bachelor."

"Maybe I've been looking but haven't found anyone who could hold my interest. You're the first woman I've offered to give a ride to twice, who tried to pick a fight with me each time."

A bit of playfulness slipped into her voice. "Maybe it's you."

"Or maybe I've found someone worth the fight." Will shifted gears. "When she made that pass and straightened my tie, I told her I was interested in someone else."

Vivienne's skepticism showed as she peered at him. "You did?"

Will reached for her hand. "I have been since the night I walked into your restaurant."

It felt like a lifetime since she had heard words so endearing.

Will pulled up in front of her house.

"We need to talk. Would you like to come in?" Vivienne was glad the house wasn't in the usual state of untidiness. "I'm going to change into some comfortable clothes. There's a bottle of wine in the fridge. The bottle opener is in one of the small drawers in the kitchen, and the glasses are above the stove."

Her hands trembled as she slipped out of her dress and into a t-shirt, and the skinny jeans she bought in Magda's store. Her sandals announced her descent down the stairs, making that flipping noise, as they hit each wooden step. Will seemed to be the opposite of how she felt, relaxed and waiting for her on the couch, with two glasses of wine ready on the coffee table. What caught her attention more than his missing tie, and the top button of his shirt open, was his hair, which he had pulled up off his neck.

He sat up when Vivienne sat next to him. "I've been wanting to do this for a long time. We keep getting off on the wrong foot."

"I think we can fix that." She kicked off her sandals. Will followed, reaching down to untie his shoes and pull off his socks.

They reached for their glasses of wine and held them for a moment before Will broke the silence. "To our first barefoot discussion."

After the clink of their glasses and their first sip, Will began, "You know, after I dropped you off on the night we had dinner with Audrey and my dad, I walked over to the Fore and Aft in the hopes of drowning my thoughts of you in a few beers. Above the bar was a framed picture of a fisherman. A black drape hung around the top of the frame."

"That's Nate," Vivienne said. "He would stop there occasionally after he pulled his boat in for the day."

"One of the patrons told me who he was."

She felt the words inside, pushing for her to release them. If there was a time to let him in, it was now. "My marriage to Nate began the same as most. He fished and kept the restaurant and fish market going. I ran the restaurant with my mom, and raised Audrey and Evan. When the kids were grown, and out of the house, I noticed a change in him. He began spending more time at the bar. Weeks turned into months and years, until I couldn't see that far back in my mind. Trying to talk to him about it only pushed him further away. Before long, there wasn't a night that I wouldn't dread him stumbling in the door, with the smell of beer and bourbon following him through the house. When he'd collapsed on the bed, or any other place in the house, I knew his ranting and temper were over, and I could finally relax."

Will's face was an open book, frowning at the difficult situations Vivienne described, but not once did he take his eyes from her. "I'm sorry you had to go through that."

"All that ended when I found him lifeless on the floor. His doctors told me he had been ill for some time, and gave explicit instructions not to tell me, Audrey, or Evan. I believe he used the bar as a shield, finding it easier to hide the truth of his illness behind his stupor, than to face me with a clear head. I'll never know why he denied me the right to stand by him in the most difficult time of his life, and I'm not sure if I'll ever be able to let go of the anger I carry."

"You've lived through a war, Vivienne," Will replied. "What you're feeling is understandable."

Wanting to take the attention from herself, she said. "I don't dwell on that time too much. So, tell me who Will Lawson is. Being a food critic must have the ladies swarming around you. Is there someone in your life?"

"Correction: there was. We had absolutely nothing in common. Alex wanted to get married. I didn't. The more she pushed me, the more I dug my heels in."

"So, you want to be free to do whatever you want?"

"Some people may see it that way, but decisions under pressure rarely end well. That's why I avoid them. Case in point...Alex."

Will reached for her hand, but she pulled it back. Putting her still-full glass on the coffee table, she rose from the couch. "I don't know if I can do this." She walked to the sliding door and stepped out onto the terrace.

Everything she had learned about Will tonight told her it would never work, yet a part of her struggled to suppress her growing feelings. Suddenly, she felt him behind her. He slipped his arms around her waist, and she moved hers down to cover his, holding him close to her. She knew then, as she closed her eyes, that it was more than any man's touch she needed. It was Will's.

His voice felt like a shot of smooth scotch, warming her as his lips brushed against her ear. "I didn't think I would get this close to you tonight."

"You're right."

"Because of tonight? Because of Sivila?"

It was easier to admit it, without looking into his eyes. "Sivila, Alex, your lifestyle."

"I was just someone to fill Sivila's night without her boyfriend. I wasn't going to be that guy."

Vivienne faced him, the honest concern evident in her voice. "I've been with one man for a long time. My heart isn't wired to be a temporary fixture in someone's life."

"I don't want us to be temporary. There's something between us. A connection neither of us can ignore. We argue, but you've showed me your soft side, that tells me you feel it, too. I had too many reasons to avoid commitment, until now. I'm holding in my arms what I can't avoid. If you want me to leave, I will."

Vivienne let him see a flicker of wanting in her eyes. "You're exactly where I want you to be."

"Will you let me kiss you?" he whispered.

"Only if you let me kiss you back."

"I'm all yours."

Vivienne knew this moment by heart, having dreamt it so often. A subtle tingle would rouse her from sleep, feeling as if his lips had touched hers, but this wasn't a dream. He leaned in to kiss her, and the soft hair of his mustache brushed against her lip. She felt her body wakening by this alluring pleasure. Slowly, his lips parted, getting to know her with the light touch of his tongue.

His lips broke from hers. "You're the reason I can't concentrate, I can't sleep," he whispered. "I want you so much, baby."

Her hands released his hair, letting the curls fall on his shoulders. Fueled by her body's rising arousal, her lips pressed against his, enticing his tongue to dance with hers. She pulled back, her breath hitching. "It's been a long time since I've been with a man."

"I'll bring you back slow," he whispered. "Tonight, it's just us. I want you to know every part of the man who wants to adore every inch of you."

She had learned to live without the sensuality of a man's touch. Now, Vivienne tilted her head back and closed her eyes, reveling in the ecstasy of his fingers playing with the tips of her breasts. Just as natural as a breath, a soft moan came from a place inside her, that she had deserted and forgotten.

Without another word, she led him inside.

***

Vivienne lay still as she opened her eyes. As her mind woke, she glanced at the clock on her nightstand and realized how little sleep she had gotten, and how alive she felt. Turning to the other side of the bed, she saw a note on the pillow, scribbled hastily with the pen Will must have picked up on her nightstand while she was sleeping. *I'm downstairs.*

His relaxed smile met her from the kitchen stove. "Mornin', baby. You hungry?"

"Sure," she replied, but seeing him barefoot and bare-chested, she rethought her decision about food and stood behind him. Her hands reached around and dove into the soft hairs on his chest. "Your boxers don't seem to be serving any purpose."

He chuckled while stirring the eggs into a fluffy mound. "I'll be more than happy to remove them for you, but it would be to my benefit if I did, *after* I step away from the stove." Moving the skillet to the back burner, he turned the flame off and faced her. "I didn't think you could be more beautiful." He pulled her close and kissed her. "I guess you can tell what I want," he said, ending his kiss with a gentle peck, "but eggs get cold fast."

Vivienne knew it was a breakfast disaster that Auggie and the chefs avoided at all costs. "I can't argue with that."

Settled at the counter for their first breakfast together, Will put his coffee down. "Would you like to join me when I review my next restaurant? It's Slow Hand Luke. Southern cooking, and it's opening Saturday evening. We can blend in with the crowd."

Vivienne's face it up. "I'd love that, Will."

"I'll understand if you're a little apprehensive about being with me in public."

"I own a restaurant, you're a food critic. I don't see anything wrong with you asking me to join you."

Will glanced at the kitchen clock. "Who will open the restaurant if you're late?"

Vivienne couldn't help her half-smile of amusement, as she tilted her head. "Auggie. Do you anticipate me being late?"

Looking at their clean plates, he stood and took her hand. "No more eggs left to get cold, and I can't leave without a proper goodbye."

With her bedroom door closed, Will snuggled up to her in bed. When she began to love him, she remembered why she had gotten so little sleep.

# *Chapter 10*

Vivienne left the house late but savored those couple of hours with Will. Her outward cheerfulness and bright smile greeted everyone.

"Morning! The line is to the end of the street."

In full breakfast swing, their collective voices were like lyrics to the clink of utensils on customer's plates and music to Vivienne's ears.

The kitchen was in its usual chaotic rush.

"We have a long line of hungry people to feed," Vivienne said.

Esty was well ahead of breakfast, keeping a close eye on the flames that were slowly heating the large pots of chowder the chefs placed on the stove for her.

Suddenly, the loud clang of aluminum hitting the tile floor echoed through the kitchen. Everyone turned toward the sound and to Devon, whose face had paled with fear, as he looked at the muffin batter sprawled on the floor. "I'm sorry, Chef. I'll clean this up and make another batch fast."

"You bet your ass you will!"

"It's okay, Devon," Vivienne said then ran to the back of the kitchen for the mop and bucket.

As Auggie watched him working quickly to clean up the mess, a cheeky smile turned his lips upward, remembering that same feeling he had when he looked into Devon's distraught eyes. "This isn't half as bad as my first disaster in a kitchen," Auggie said. "I spilled cooking oil on the floor. Can you guess where head chef's ass landed?"

Relief washed over Devon's face, as a burst of laughter from everyone defused the tension.

"I'll make the muffins." Auggie placed another bowl on the counter. "Prep the clams for the clam rolls."

"Yes, Chef," Devon replied.

Vivienne shared a questioning glance with Esty, both witnessing the obvious shift in Auggie's temperament. *Could it be Ellen, the woman Hugo introduced him to, at the engagement party?* With everyone back on track, she grabbed an apron from the shelf and took her place at the counter.

The long line outside was quickly filling the dining area and counter. The wait staff was on their *A game.* Everything was the same as it was yesterday, but Vivienne wasn't. In the hours she and Will had spent together, he slowly brought her back to life. As she filled customer's mugs with coffee and walked the counter, taking orders and delivering piping hot breakfasts, she remembered how he took his time in the peaks and sensual valleys of her body. Their unrestrained satisfaction echoed in her bedroom, where Vivienne had thought love would never return.

Next in line to be seated, Magda pulled her from her thoughts. "Viv," she called.

She held up her index finger, letting Heidi at the hostess station know that a customer would be leaving soon.

"I hope you enjoyed your breakfast, Charlie," Vivienne said as she wrote out his check.

"Never had a complaint in fifteen years, breakfast, lunch or dinner." He handed her cash.

"I'll get your change," Vivienne said.

But Charlie insisted, "That's for you, Vivienne. For keeping this old geezer well fed."

"There'll always be a stool here for you, Charlie. It's going to be hot today. Stay out of the sun."

Vivienne waved Magda over and began to wipe the counter in front of her. "We have blueberry, cranberry and apple spice muffins today."

"Never mind the muffins. There's no moisturizer on the market that can produce the glow you have on your face."

"It shows?"

"If you're thinking about him, Viv, you're blushing."

Vivienne leaned toward her and whispered, "I've never been made love to like this."

"I can only imagine."

"It's the things he did, *and I did*, that are making me blush."

"Blame it on the heat. No one would suspect anything else."

Vivienne placed Magda's coffee in front of her. "He wants me to join him on his next restaurant review."

"That sounds like so much fun, Viv."

"And it's perfect. I own a restaurant, and he's a food critic."

"Perfect...for a first *official* date." Magda's brows rose above her wire-rimmed glasses. "So, Apple spice? Auggie hasn't made these in a while. I better take one before they're all gone."

Vivienne came back with one, still warm. "It's his mood. I haven't seen him this amenable in years. Devon dropped a big bowl of muffin batter on the floor and, instead of his usual *taking your head off,* he admitted to Devon that he dropped cooking oil on the floor of the first kitchen he worked in, and the head chef landed on his ass."

Magda smiled, imagining the scene. "That must have eased the tension."

"Eggs over easy, hashbrowns, hold the toast, children's silver dollars, yogurt and fresh fruit," Auggie announced, sliding the orders on the ledge behind Vivienne.

"That's my table, Vivienne," Dylan said. Placing them with precision on the tray, he moved quickly into the dining area.

"Owen and I saw Auggie talking to a woman at the party," Magda continued. "Attractive. Pretty floral sundress, and sandals."

"That was Ellen. Audrey and Hugo introduced me to her and his other female colleagues at the Tribune. Will knew they had an interest in cooking and suggested that his father introduce them to Auggie."

"I don't think I've ever seen that many of Auggie's teeth when he smiled." Magda imitated a Cheshire Cat grin. "It certainly looked as if he was enjoying himself." As soon as Magda put a piece of the muffin in her mouth her eyes closed as she tasted the warm apples tossed with nutmeg and cinnamon, and a perfect touch of allspice. "Give that man a raise."

"I already did...a hefty one after Nate passed away."

Auggie announced, "I got a short stack off the griddle."

Vivienne turned and quickly reached for the plate. "Thank you, Auggie."

"Hot off the griddle, Liam," she said.

"It's a good way to start the day, seeing your pretty face."

Her chuckle sidestepped his casual flirt. "Thank you, but I think you're here for Auggie's food more than my face. Enjoy your breakfast."

"So, when is this *first date* happening?" Magda asked.

"Saturday."

"I have some new dresses that just came in. Wanna take a look?"

Vivienne's eyes glanced away, and she smiled, as if remembering a moment in time. "I think I already have the perfect dress."

***

During the brief time between the breakfast and lunch crowd, Vivienne retreated to the kitchen to make a salad for herself. In the background, the quick, repetitive *thunk* of Auggie's knife hit the chopping block. She dug into her salad and reached for her phone, stopping mid-chew as she saw a text from Will.

*Almost turned around twice thinking about U. Dinner will B at Slow Hand Luke, Saturday, 8:00. If U think I can wait until then, U R wrong. I picked up some things for dinner. After a long day at the restaurant, I would love to cook for U and yes, I can cook.*

She put her fork down and sent a quick reply. *I'd love it. I'll leave the key under the mat.*

"Auggie, I need to attend to something at home." With her salad safe in the fridge, she stopped at the kitchen door. "I'll be back in half an hour."

Without a skip in his chopping, Auggie responded, "No problem, Vivienne."

She spotted Brendan clearing a table. "Brendan, I need you to move to the counter until I return."

"Sure, Vivienne." He stacked the last of the dirty dishes on his tray.

***

With the house ready for Will, Vivienne returned to work alongside the staff until closing. She walked past the darkened windows of Magda's store and hoped that Owen was home with her. In the distance, she could see the hurricane lamps glowing on either side of her front door. Excitement made her steps quicker, imagining Will busy cooking in her kitchen and what the hours after dinner would be like. In the time before Nate passed, it was Vivienne who waited at home, dreading when he would stumble in. Tonight, it was Will who was waiting to greet her after a long day. Her heart began to race as she opened the door.

"Dinner will be ready in half an hour."

"Something smells delicious." On her way to the kitchen, she glanced at two glasses of wine on the coffee table. Will was at the stove, looked up from the skillet, and smiled. Behind him, the remains of green and red peppers, mushrooms, and discarded onion skins lay on Vivienne's well-used chopping block.

"I'm just about to put this in the oven."

Her curiosity brought her to stand beside him. Thin pieces of chicken were surrounded in everything he had put together, all sautéing in a delectable sauce. The aroma rose from the skillet, and she hummed. "Mmmm... It's making my mouth water."

They both stepped back so he could open the oven and transfer the skillet. "I'm glad." He took her hand and led her to the couch. "Welcome home, baby," he whispered. His voice warmed her like a fire cackling in the cold winter months.

She closed her eyes as his lips drew near. The pleasure of seeing him tonight made his kiss so sweet. "I didn't think I would see you before Saturday."

"I didn't want to sleep without you."

"You'll have to get on the road early tomorrow."

"It's a small price to pay for another night next to you."

Vivienne picked up her glass and enjoyed the delicate taste of cherry in the red wine he chose. "So, *Slow Hand Luke.* Tell me about it."

"Southern cooking in the city of Bawstin? You can bet it has people talking."

"And it has my interest, but not above the aroma coming from the kitchen."

Will picked up his glass and the bottle of wine and rose from the couch. "Should be done now."

***

Will was smiling at her clean plate. "Did you like it?"

"Very funny."

"There's a little left. I'll put it in a container for you."

"I'll take that for lunch." When she reached for the plates, he stopped her. "I got this."

"Are you sure?"

"Absolutely. I always clean up after myself."

"Okay. I'll be upstairs."

With the kitchen officially closed for the night, Will climbed the stairs and leaned against the entrance to her bedroom. She was wrapped in a terry towel and smiled at him as she rubbed the excess water from her hair with a smaller towel. "I left fresh towels for you."

"Be right back."

After showering, Will slipped the towel from his waist and climbed into bed. Vivienne faced him, and her fingers began to gently play with his soft beard.

He sensed her thoughts that were keeping her silent. "What is it, baby?"

"You know," she whispered, "I've managed to shut this entire part of myself away. The wanting, the vulnerability, I thought I was done with it. But you brought it all back."

Will began to speak, but she placed a gentle finger on his lips.

"I don't think either of us knows where this is leading us. But I need you to know one thing. If you ever find a reason not to stay, if this becomes too much, or just not enough, I won't be the woman who tries to keep you from leaving."

"I'm not waiting for a reason to leave. I'm here because there's not a single reason to be anywhere else. If it becomes too much, we'll carry it together. And, as for it being not enough, baby you're everything."

Vivienne felt every word in the tenderness of his kiss. Unable to deny what her heart wanted, she closed her eyes, safe in his arms.

# Chapter 11

Will met up with some of his friends at a local bar Friday night. Holding an ice-cold bottle of Budweiser, he asked his friend, Gavin, "How's the new job going?"

"I've been wanting to get into this architectural firm for a long time. Now that I'm there, I come to find out there's an inside pecking order, so I got a shit job nobody wanted. I'm revising specs for a waste management company."

"Yeah, but if you want a spot in that pecking order, take the shit job they gave you and make them a ton of money."

"Will's right," Tom said. "Money talks."

"So, what's up with Alex, Will?" Silas asked. "I heard you broke up with her."

Will sighed. "It's been brewing for some time. I took her to a restaurant review. Big mistake. She had something bad to say about the wait staff, the food. The whole night was a disaster, and it was the last straw. I ended it that night."

"She hangs out with the same group of friends my girl, Bridget, does," Silas added. "She said that Alex is devastated you broke up with her. Apparently, that's all she talks about, and they're all tired of hearing it."

Will put his empty bottle on the bar and raised his hand to the bartender for another. "I am, too. I should have never hooked up with someone at work. She's hovering around my desk all the time. I come back from the bathroom, and she's there."

"If she's like this now, what are you gonna do when you start seeing someone else?"

A roguish grin slowly appeared on Will's lips. "Alex won't know, because the woman I'm seeing doesn't live in Bawstin."

And the questions began.

"Where did you meet her, Will?" Tom asked.

Remembering their first argument, and Vivienne not wanting to be a *laugh at their expense*, he kept his answers a shadowy version of the truth. "At a restaurant. She's in the food industry, too. I couldn't take my eyes off her."

"Was it at one of the restaurants you reviewed?"

"No. Like I said, she doesn't live in Bawstin, but she'll be here when I have dinner at *Slow Hand Luke* tomorrow night."

"Have you been seeing her long?" Silas asked.

"No, but long enough to know I'm ready to make a commitment."

His friends stood speechless, with three pair of eyes staring at him in shock, until Tom broke the silence. "Are you serious? Okay. Now you gotta tell us who this mystery woman is?"

A hint of a smile pulled at his lips as he thought of her. "Her name is Vivienne, and I've never met anyone like her. The first two times we were together ended in arguments. She's feisty, but she has a soft side no other woman has ever showed me."

"Feisty, but gentle...a provocative combination," Gavin put in.

"You have no idea."

***

Vivienne didn't expect the steady, pelting rain that hit the streets and sidewalks on Saturday. Even the steadfast tourists hunkered down in their hotel rooms, waiting out the storm while they occupied their restless children with iPhones and iPads.

Today, Vivienne took her car to the restaurant and grabbed a parking spot two stores down. The umbrella kept her head dry, but her feet were soaked and squished in her deck shoes as she ran to the restaurant.

The wait staff were prepping the tables, but not at their usual hurried pace. "Good morning, Vivienne." Their voices broke the sound of the pummeling rain.

"Morning, everyone." She put her drenched umbrella in the pail near the hostess station. "Wow, this is one heck of a storm."

"We got soaked."

"Did you grab the extra t-shirts and shorts in the back?"

"We did, Vivienne. Thank you."

"The weather may break, so let's be ready if and when it does." She walked quickly toward the kitchen, knowing she would have to dry the water trail she was leaving on the floor. The pots of chowder were already on the stove, and she looked to Esty. "I see the storm didn't keep you away."

"Brendan picked me up."

Vivienne leaned toward her mother, concerned. "You're a little pale, Mom. How are you feeling?"

"Like the weather." She pointed to a cup and dish on the table near her chair. "I'm having a muffin from the first batch out of the oven, and Auggie made me a cup of tea."

Vivienne and Auggie shared a glance before she made her way to the back of the kitchen where she changed into a pair of old sneakers. After reaching for a clean apron, she continued the conversation with her mother. "You know, Mom, you could have stayed home today."

"Honestly, Vivienne, you talk like I have one foot in the grave. I don't like staying home alone. Being here makes me feel useful."

Seeing Esty's *I'm not budging* look in her eyes, Vivienne rolled her own. "Okay, Mom, I can see it's useless to push the issue, but will you consider staying home tomorrow if you don't feel better?"

Esty just smiled. "Tomorrow's another day, Vivienne."

Before going out to the counter, she pulled Auggie aside. "I want to remind you that I'm leaving early today."

"I put it on the calendar when you told me."

"I'm excited to see Will's side of the business." She sighed. "But with Mom not feeling well, maybe I should cancel."

"She's stubborn, Vivienne, and she'll push you out the door if you even suggest it. At her age, she'll have good and bad days. You know we'll keep an eye on her."

"Evan and Grace said they'd check on her, too."

"You've covered all the bases. Enjoy the dinner and quit worrying about everyone else."

"Thank you, Auggie." Feeling relieved, she pushed through the kitchen door and quickly gathered the wait staff. "Some people may want a late breakfast, so use the breakfast and lunch menus today."

Tables in the dining area were set with utensils, waiting for hungry customers. The sound of the rain brought down everyone's spirits as they looked out at the gray, dreary day. She dreaded the rainy drive to Boston for dinner with Will.

***

She stood at the window, nursing a cup of coffee and imagined Magda doing the same, waiting for the rain to let up. After a few hours, nature had replenished the thirsty flora from the scorching summer sun. Through the fading clouds, arose a glorious double rainbow. From the window, she saw people flocking to the streets and went out to join them. Many were using their phones to capture the vibrant colors of the spectrum. Vivienne simply stared at its magnificence and felt as if the heavens heard her silent wish for the rain to stop.

It wasn't long before people began trickling in. Vivienne didn't have to check the kitchen. Whatever the weather, Auggie was ready.

At the end of the counter sat her first two customers. "If you're still in the mood for breakfast, we have everything available on the menu. Can I start you off with something to drink?"

"My wife and I heard about the chowder, but we haven't had breakfast yet, so we'll share. I'll have coffee, the pancakes and a side of hashbrowns."

"An iced tea, and a bowl of chowder for me," the woman added.

Vivienne smiled as she wrote the slip. "Good choice."

She took orders from two more customers before putting the tickets on the wheel. Despite the change in weather, there wasn't the usual line outside, but Vivienne knew it was just the ebb and flow of the restaurant business.

It was late afternoon, and people were back in town, walking the streets, and stopping in for dinner. Without missing a beat, the wait staff collectively took over Brendan's tables so he could move to the counter.

Vivienne grabbed her bag from the back of the kitchen. Esty put her fork down on the plate of seared scallops and fresh spinach that Auggie made for her. "Enjoy your evening in Boston. You could use a night out, Vivienne."

She bent down and kissed her mom's cheek. Feeling it warm against her lips, she stepped back. "You have color in your face again, Mom."

"I told you I would be fine. You worry too much, Vivienne. Be careful driving."

"I will, and I'll see everyone tomorrow." With her bag on her shoulder, she left the restaurant and picked up her pace to her car. As she drove home, her thoughts turned to the next few hours. *Magda was right. It is our first date, but it's still work for him. Focus on that.*

She spritzed a light scent of *spring rain* on her freshly showered shoulders and packed a small bag with incidentals and a change of clothes. The bohemian maxi dress that Will first saw her in hung on the closet door, ready to make its second appearance tonight. At the bathroom mirror, she pulled her hair up into a casual bun, darkened her lashes with mascara, and added a dab of blush to her cheeks. A light swipe of gloss was all Vivienne's lips needed.

Instead of carrying her shawl, she simply draped it across her shoulders. With her overnight bag and a clutch in her hand, she stepped out of the house and into her car. Will's apartment had already been programmed into her phone, which she placed in its holder on the dashboard.

The map appeared on her phone, and as she drove through town, the pleasant voice of the *App woman* spoke to her from her phone. *"Take US-6W and MA-3N toward Boston."*

# Chapter 12

Will stripped to his boxers and scrolled to Vivienne's number as he ambled down the hall for a shower.

Vivienne hit speaker as she kept pace with the moving traffic. "Hi, Will."

"Hey, baby. Where are you?"

"Route 3 North. Should be there soon."

"I've been thinking about this all week."

"Me, too, but it's still work for you."

"I know, but it feels like our first date. Be careful driving."

"I will. Bye."

Knowing he felt the same way about tonight, Vivienne's excitement rose a notch down to her foot, which took some careful time off her trip. She wasn't expecting another call, and her brows rose, when she saw Audrey's name.

"Hi, Audrey. Is everything okay?"

"Everything's fine. Is tonight the night you're going with Will on his restaurant review?"

"Yes. I'm on my way now. Auggie made me promise to take mental notes for him."

Audrey chuckled. "It was nice of Will to invite you. I know you're gonna enjoy it, Mom."

A twinge of guilt silenced her for a second, prompting her to switch the subject in her reply. "I'm just glad I'm not driving in the rain. We had a doozy of a storm today."

"Well, enjoy dinner. Hugo and I want to hear all about it."

"Okay, bye for now."

"Bye, Mom."

Her excitement grew with every glance at her phone, watching the miles go by, waiting for the friendly app woman to speak again. *"At the next light, turn left onto Longfellow Place."* She slowed down and focused on her surroundings. *"Your destination is on the right, The Towers at Longfellow."* In the parking garage below Will's building, she entered the security code he gave her, and pulled into a guest spot, then quickly checked herself in the small visor mirror. She reached for her clutch on the passenger seat, but paused for a moment, and decided to leave her small overnight bag on the back seat. *Will can get it, if I'm going to stay.*

*Third floor, last door on the left,* Will had told her. She pressed the button for his floor. The door slid open, and she looked down the hall, the warm lights leading her way. Her fingers brushed over the smooth leather of her clutch, as she approached Will's door. She focused on her breathing, trying to keep calm, as the prospect of kissing him was moments away. Her knuckles gave his door three sensible knocks, but in her anxiousness, she thought, *maybe I didn't knock hard enough.*

She was just about to raise her hand again, when the door opened. Will's broad grin greeted her while he tucked his white shirt into his pants and stepped aside. "You're early."

"I was just moving with the traffic. Maybe there were people as eager to get to their destinations as I was."

Vivienne took her first peek into his life. She envisioned him relaxing on his modest couch while he pointed the remote at the sensible-sized flatscreen TV. But her focus shifted as he stood behind her and wrapped his arms around her waist.

"You're wearing the dress I love," he whispered. "I still think about slipping the straps from your shoulders and letting it fall at your feet."

Vivienne smiled and lowered her eyes at the thought. "Maybe you'll get a chance later. Dinner first."

He turned her around, and his arms pulled her in close and tight. "This is the first time I've ever wanted to pass on a restaurant opening."

"I wouldn't want you to do that, Will."

"Can I kiss you first, before we leave?"

His kiss was becoming familiar. The subtle way he would begin, touching his lips to hers as if to say, *hello sweetheart.* They moved ever so softly, and Vivienne felt herself relaxing in his arms, aroused by the slow, tender kiss of his tongue.

"I'm glad you're here with me, baby," he whispered.

"I am, too."

"The restaurant is only a few blocks away. We'll be walking by some cool shops on the way. We can check them out on the way back."

"I'd love that."

He reached for her hand, looking forward to the evening ahead, as they made their way toward the elevator.

***

Stepping out of his building into the warm evening, Vivienne kept his slow pace, walking beside him.

"How long have you and Audrey been friends?" she asked.

"We started at the Tribune at the same time. I guess because we were both the new kids on the block, we gravitated toward each other, but we were looking for different things. She was looking for love, and I was looking to avoid it. The mix made for a perfect friendship."

"When did she tell you about her and your father?"

"Actually, it was my dad who broke the news to me. My mother had been gone for a while, but Audrey still felt it would be better coming from him. I respected the boundaries she made for herself. I knew my dad missed my mom. I did too, but I didn't want him to be alone for the rest of his life. Having listened to Audrey pine for that one man who would lay his heart before her, made me happy she found that in my dad."

"I am, too, although the age gap took a bit of getting used to."

Will stopped and turned to Vivienne. People were walking by, but, to Will, she was the only person on the street. "And what changed *your* mind?"

His gaze and provocative tone captivated her. "I think you already know, but I'll be happy to show you after dinner."

At the restaurant, they navigated the crowded entrance and, once inside, were met by a young woman. She looked up from her reservation book and greeted them with a manufactured smile of perfect veneers. "Welcome to *Slow Hand Luke.* Do y'all have a reservation?"

"Yes, Michael Connors, table for two."

"Your table is ready, if y'all will follow me."

Will rolled his eyes as they walked behind her. Conversation was low, as was the distinct voice of Alicia Keys filling the modest-sized space with her music.

The hostess stopped at a table, centrally located in the room, with full view of the chefs behind a windowed wall. "Your server will be by shortly."

Will held the chair out for Vivienne, who looked up at him, and gave him a sly wink, as she slipped the shawl from her shoulders. "Thank you, *Mr. Connors*."

"Having a southern restaurant in Bawstin draws enough attention," Will began. "It's overkill to have the Bawstin staff butchering a drawl."

"Like someone from the south, working in a New York Italian restaurant."

"Exactly." He leaned toward her and whispered, "By the way, you're not driving tonight, so feel free to drink whatever you're in the mood for."

They weren't waiting long when a lanky guy, sporting two detailed tattoo sleeves with warriors and dragons, stopped at their table. "I'm Tyler, and I'll be serving you tonight. Can I get y'all something from the bar?"

"I'll have a Cosmo," Vivienne said.

"A Budweiser, and hold the glass, please."

They shared a chuckle after the server left. "I bet the only requirement for the staff is to say y'all," Will commented. "I hope the owner holds the food to a higher standard."

Vivienne couldn't remember the last time she felt this relaxed. Knowing that Will wanted her to stay the night, she leaned toward him. "I packed an overnight bag before I left, but I wasn't sure about telling you."

He reached for her hand, holding it with care in his. "Why?" he whispered. "Did you think I wouldn't want you to stay?"

"We've only been together a couple of times, Will. I didn't want to assume."

"A Cosmo for the lovely lady," the server said, interrupting them.

Will released her hand and watched the server place the martini glass in front of Vivienne, careful not to spill a drop of the light-pink cocktail.

"And a Budweiser for the gentleman. I'll give y'all some time to look at the menu."

Despite the annoying overkill of the southern drawl, Will made a mental note of their server's quick return with their drinks.

Will then turned his focus back to Vivienne. "I know the restaurant keeps you busy. Can we talk about you coming to Bawstin more often?"

A sly smile pulled at her lips as her gaze held his. "I don't have to punch a clock."

"I would love to have some of your things next to mine in my dresser."

Everyone knew where she was, no looking over her shoulder for someone to come out of the woodwork. She never would have thought the woodwork had other ideas.

"Well, if it isn't Will Lawson. What are you doing here?"

They were pulled from the moment to discover two women at their table. Vivienne recognized Sivila immediately but only had to wait a mere second before she knew it wasn't Sivila she would be dealing with.

Will's nostrils flared with every angered breath, but his silence only served to provoke her. "What's the matter, Will, cat got your tongue?" She wore her confidence in the little black dress that could have been taken off the hanger in Magda's window. Vivienne could feel Will's discomfort in his refusal to respond, while she sat quiet in the middle of the silent battle ensuing between them.

Aware of the people around him, Will bottled his anger as he mumbled his curt answer. "I'm working, Alex, so don't blow my cover."

"Don't tell me what to do. And *who is that* anyway?" she snapped, pointing her manicured finger at Vivienne.

*Alex.* As Will spoke her name, a memory suddenly surfaced in Vivienne's mind, remembering Nate saying women who wore dresses that short were looking for trouble. Her skin suddenly felt uncomfortably warm, but it wasn't the lack of air in the room. Trouble in the black dress was looking to start a war.

"It's none of your business," Will replied under his breath.

"That's Vivienne, Audrey's mom." Sivila's arms were crossed, and she looked down her nose at Vivienne, gloating as if she'd just opened some secret can of worms. "I noticed them standing a little too close at Audrey's engagement party. Later, I saw her getting into Will's car."

Alex didn't waste a minute, directing her sexual sarcasm at Vivienne. "His car is a bit tight but makes for some steamy sex, don't you think?"

It was a place Vivienne didn't want to be, backed into a corner. She had no choice but to come out swinging. "You're Alex, right? I don't care about your *Fifty Shades* scene in the car with Will, but Sivila seems to think there's a law against accepting an unassuming ride home."

"While we're at it, Sivila," Will added, "would you like me to explain to Alex that it was more than my tie you wanted to touch at Audrey's party?"

Alex's medically enhanced lips parted as she looked with outrage at Sivila.

Will chuckled. "Some friend you got there, Alex."

She fired back: "Maybe Audrey would like to know about your little tryst at dinner with her mother."

"Audrey knows that I invited her mother for dinner." Will's eyes narrowed, his focus intent on delivering each threatening word under his breath. "Don't fuck with me, Alex. If you spread any insinuating gossip, I'll turn your reputation to shit in this town. If you don't want to flip burgers at Pete's Patties, keep your mouth shut."

On the outskirts, their waiter was watching with intense concern. He notified the manager, who approached with purpose in each step and ushered the two women along. "If you ladies will follow me, your table is ready."

When Will was certain the manager had done his job, he turned to Vivienne. "Let's get outta here."

"What about the review?"

"I've walked out on restaurant reviews before. I'll chalk this one up to *classless clientele.*" He paid for their untouched drinks, and they walked back to his apartment, taking time to browse the shops and bring back dinner from a local Chinese restaurant.

As they opened the containers, Vivienne's empty stomach began to groan, bringing an amused smile to Will's lips. "Hungry?"

She clasped her stomach, tying to silence it. "I haven't eaten anything since breakfast."

"I guess we better do something about that."

She put a sample from each container on her plate and dove in with her chopsticks, picking up a swirl of Lo Mein. Conversation naturally gravitated to the hours before.

"I'm sorry you had to deal with that woman," Will began.

"You have nothing to be sorry for. It wasn't your fault."

"I can't guarantee that Alex won't try to stir the pot of gossip, but I promise you, she'll regret it."

Vivienne put her chopsticks down. "It's not worth it, Will."

Her words felt like they had punched the air from his stomach. "Is what we have not worth it?"

"Of course it is. That's not what I meant." She reached for his hands. "I've lived in boundaries all my life, never going beyond what my family expected of me, as a wife and mother. I'm no longer a wife, and I won't live in the boundaries my family still have in their minds for me, if you're not in my life."

Will rose from his chair and took Vivienne in his arms. "I always avoided those strings that would tie me to a life I didn't want. I only know I want those strings around me, tied to you."

There was no fanfare, no fireworks. Just the acceptance of each other, becoming stronger as their kisses deepened. He slipped the straps of her dress off her shoulders. A moan left her, as he brushed his fingers over her aroused nipples. "I'm not hungry anymore," he whispered.

Vivienne's own thoughts turned from food to his body pressed against her.

The urge to touch him aroused every erogenous place she wanted to be touched. She saw the wanting in his eyes and placed her hand on him. "I'm not either, at least not for Chinese food."

***

Awakened suddenly by the ringing of her phone, time stopped as Vivienne stared at Evan's number. She swung her legs out of bed, dreading the words she had to say. "Evan, what's wrong?"

Will immediately sat up, waiting, as Vivienne listened in silence.

"I called the house, Mom, but you didn't pick up. I was worried, so I drove over. I thought you would have been home already from that restaurant thing. Where are you, Mom?"

Evan's rambling only made Vivienne's anxiety worsen, and she snapped at him. "Just tell me what's wrong, Evan."

"Gram hit her life alert button at home. The EMTs believe she had a stroke and rushed her to the hospital in Hyannis. I called Audrey. She's on her way with Hugo. It's 2:30 in the morning, Mom. Are you going to tell me where you are?"

Vivienne didn't imagine she would have to tell Evan or Audrey this way. "I'm with Will, and we're leaving now." She hit *END*, before Evan had a chance to reply.

Will was already out of bed and getting dressed. "Leave your overnight bag."

Vivienne quickly put on her jeans and t-shirt.

"Just take your phone, wallet, and your keys."

They ran to Will's car. It took only minutes for him to get them on the road. "There won't be many people on the highway this time of night." When Vivienne didn't respond, he reached for her hand. "She's in good hands. Try not to worry."

She couldn't speak the words that were terrifying her thoughts. She could live with Audrey and Evan not speaking to her, but she wasn't ready to live with only the memory of her mother's voice.

# Chapter 13

In the quiet hospital hallway, Vivienne and Will were met with scowls from Evan and Audrey, who had turned toward the soft *ding,* as the elevator door opened. Vivienne felt as if she were walking into a hornet's nest, but her focus went to the doctor standing with them.

"Doctor, Bellam, I'm Vivienne Callane, Estelle's daughter. How is she?"

"Yes, Mrs. Callane. I was just telling Audrey and Evan that, when Estelle arrived, the EMTs gave me an overview of what she was experiencing. She was confused and couldn't remember how she got in the ambulance. She mentioned feeling dizzy and a numbness in her right hand. She must have hit her life alert button before she passed out. I ordered a CT scan and MRI. The tests showed definitive proof that she had a TIA, which is a transient ischemic attack. She was immediately given Activase. It's a clot-busting medication, given through an IV, to restore blood flow to the brain. The good news is the EMTs got her here in time for the medication to be most effective."

For all the talking the doctor did, Vivienne knew her mind wouldn't rest until she saw her mother. "Can I see her?"

"You can, but one person at a time and only for a few minutes. At this juncture, we want to keep her as calm as possible."

"I understand. Thank you."

"We'll need to keep her here for a few days, to see how she progresses. She might need to go to rehab for OT and PT."

"She's living in a small retirement community," Vivienne said. "I'm sure I can arrange whatever therapy she needs."

"We can schedule that when she's ready to be discharged. In the meantime, any of the nurses on-call can give you an update on Estelle."

As the doctor disappeared down the corridor, the brooding stares of Evan and Audrey reappeared. Without a word to anyone, Vivienne took the initiative and entered her mother's room first.

Vivienne's worst thoughts were washed away with relief when she saw the attending nurse holding a juice box to her mom's lips. "Estelle, you have a visitor."

Her words were slow but clear. "My daughter, Vivienne."

"That's a beautiful name," the nurse said.

"Thank you. I see she's sitting up."

"Oh, yes. Estelle's a fighter. Nothing's keeping her down, isn't that right, Estelle? I'll let you have a little time with her. Not too long."

When Vivienne took Esty's hands, she noticed the lack of strength in her mother's right hand. Remembering the doctor mentioning that she had felt numbness, Vivienne gave her a gentle squeeze of encouragement. "You're going to be okay, Mom. One day at a time."

"The restaurant. How will I stir the chowder?"

"I don't want you worrying about that. Auggie's in charge for now. He'll take care of the chowder."

Raised voices from Evan and Will came from the hall. She kissed her mom's forehead. "Try to get some sleep. I'll be back tomorrow."

The scene Vivienne walked into in the hallway was not cordial.

"You've got balls, showing your face here," Evan said to Will.

"I didn't want Vivienne driving here by herself."

Evan's brows rose, deepening the lines on his forehead. "Oh! So, it's Vivienne, is it? I guess you think it's okay to be so personal because you're fucking her."

Vivienne gasped, and Hugo then attempted to give Evan's arm a calming touch, but his eyes narrowed in a hostile glare, as he swatted Hugo's hand away. "I'm warning you, old man. Don't you lay your hands on me."

That unmistakable expletive perked the ears of the attending nurse, who glanced down the hall at the quarreling group of men. As the voices rose in a heated exchange of words, she stepped from behind the desk and approached them with caution. "Excuse me," she said with care in her voice. "I have to ask you to please move to the family room where it's more private."

Hugo said, "Let's all go outside, get some air, and calm down."

"I don't need the air outside." Evan's retort bit right through Hugo's request. "I need to clear the air *in here*. Right now!"

The nurse focused her response on Evan. "Please move to the family room, sir, or take your argument outside. I won't have you disrupting the hospital and upsetting the patients. Don't make me call security."

Evan's boots stomped on the linoleum as he headed to the family room while the others followed. After he closed the door, Evan turned his rage toward his mother. "Have you lost your fucking mind? Do you remember who you just buried?"

"Don't you dare speak to me like that, Evan! I do remember. Every single day! But I won't discuss your father in this room."

"Okay. What would you like to discuss? That you're sleeping with someone young enough to be your son?" Evan then moved closer, within inches of Vivienne. "Tell me, Mom. Do you think about Dad when this guy's about to please you?"

"Evan!" Grace yelled.

The flat palm of Vivienne's hand slapped his face. The sharp, percussive crack rendered his cheek red, with the imprint of Vivienne's hand, a stark reminder of his foul disrespect.

Grace gasped, witnessing a moment that would sear itself in her memory.

Audrey shouted, "Mom!"

Evan touched his throbbing cheek as he glared at Vivienne. Her eyes were brimming with tears, clasping her hand that had never once disciplined him.

"I guess I deserved that," Evan said. "I'm done here." He paused as he put his hand on the door handle and turned to Vivienne. "Is this what you want? To give up your family for a few fleeting moments of pleasure? Because that's what you're doing."

Vivienne stepped toward him, her voice quivering as she pleaded. "Don't say that. Evan, please..."

He put up his hands to stop her. "Don't. Just...don't."

She brushed away her tears. Tears shed from the piece of her heart that belonged to Evan, when he was born. The pain of his words paralyzed her, leaving her helpless to stop him as he left the room with Grace.

Vivienne turned to Audrey, and found her stepping toward Will, her shoulders squared and determined, as she lashed out at him. "Is this how you repay my friendship? To assume that it entitles you to make my mother your next conquest?"

"What's in my past is in the past," Will replied, "but your mother is the woman who changed that."

"And you expect me to believe you?"

"Yes. Yes, I do. We're friends, Audrey. I've never lied to you. Why wouldn't you believe me now?"

"You've got to see how this looks from the outside, Will," Hugo added. "It's your lifestyle, and it gives me a serious reason for pause." Hugo's own despairing uncertainty looked for an answer in Will's eyes. "Hearts are not meant to be tossed around. How will you make amends when Vivienne's heart is left in pieces in your hands?"

"If anyone's heart is broken, it will be mine." Will stood his ground, calling his father's love for Audrey into question. "I know how this looks, but you would still be with Audrey, regardless of what people thought. Tell me I'm wrong."

"I can't."

"Then why should it be different for me?"

Will's persistent argument paired Hugo against Audrey. Hugo's hand instinctively went to the back of his neck, rubbing at the tension. "I don't know, Will. This came out of left field. Emotions are stretched tight right now."

"You can't question Will's intentions, without putting me under the same scrutiny," Vivienne said. Turning from Hugo to Audrey, she added, "We wouldn't be having this conversation if I didn't accept his advances. You and Evan deserve an explanation...when you both decide you're going to listen. Have we all forgotten what brought us here tonight?"

"No, Mom, we didn't," Audrey replied. "But finding out about all this put *you* in the spotlight. Are you happy?"

"Do you remember when you asked me to keep an open mind?"

Audrey's jaw dropped, hearing her mother's preposterous comparison. "You mean to compare what you're doing with *him*, to Hugo and I? He's a bachelor, Mom. *A bachelor!* He's gonna have his jollies and move on before your sheets are cold." Her eyes rolled in disgust. "Ugh! I can't believe I just said that."

"You're wrong, Audrey," Will said.

"Your track record says I'm right. I can't talk about this anymore. I'm going to see my grandmother, and then I'm putting all this out of my head."

Hugo, Vivienne, and Will were the last three standing, and Hugo released a deep sigh. "Audrey holds on to grudges."

"Long after their expiration date," Vivienne added. "But what happened here tonight is different, Hugo. I think it's best if Will and I leave before she comes back."

"Do you believe me, Dad?" The words rose inside Will like a river rising in a storm.

"I want to, but it's not me you need to convince."

***

Will's elbow rested against the car door with his hand cradling his head, and the other hand on the wheel, as he drove Vivienne back to Wellfleet. Vivienne's altercations with Evan and Audrey were only hours old, but he knew the words spoken would never age, living forever in their hearts. Her silence made him worry that she was thinking, *we shouldn't have done this.*

"I wish I could undo this," he murmured. "Not us, but the way it hurt Evan and Audrey."

Vivienne didn't look at him but kept her gaze out the window. "I don't want to talk about this anymore, Will."

"I'm sorry I brought it up. I'll let you get a few hours of sleep and take you back tomorrow, to see your mother."

"You need the rest, too, but I think it's best if you drive back to Boston tomorrow."

"I can't. Not when you need me."

"I'll be fine, I just can't think straight. The distraction of the restaurant, and my mother, is what I need right now."

Vivienne's mind couldn't hold another thought, and her heart couldn't bear any more pain. She trudged up the stairs, with Will behind her. In the quiet darkness, only their unspoken thoughts lay between them when Vivienne turned off the table lamp. Evan and Audrey's unconscionable words settled in Vivienne's heart, and the thought of losing Will over this made her shift toward him.

"Are you sorry about us?" Will asked.

She saw his heart laid bare before her, looking through eyes waiting, as if with bated breath, for her answer. "No. I'm sorry for what it did to Evan and Audrey. I don't know if they'll ever look at me the way they used to, but here, with you, my heart is telling me to look closely."

"What do you see?" he whispered.

"Myself, in your eyes. The way I am. The way I want to be. With you."

***

Vivienne listened to Will's quiet breathing, but it wasn't enough to lull her to sleep. The events of the last few hours spun like a torrent in her mind. Will's arm lay in slumber on her waist, but even her careful movement to slip out of bed, stirred him.

"What's wrong, baby? Where are you going?"

She leaned down to kiss away his worry. "Nothing's wrong. I just need to clear my head. Go back to sleep."

Will rolled over, and Vivienne quietly left the house. The sun hadn't risen yet, and the cool air from the bay felt good against her skin. The stone pillars marked the end of the street and the entrance to the cemetery, along with the sign, *Dead End.* The town board members were oblivious to the obvious pun that flew over their heads, when they voted to put it there. She opened the rusted iron gates, and their high-pitched groan announced her early morning visit. Her sneakers made no sound as she walked the dirt path that sprouted occasional patches of grass and weeds. When she came to Nate's headstone, she stood for a moment before she began to speak.

"What happened to my mother made me face the inevitable, that I could lose her, too. I can hear you taunting me, *you shouldn't have put that guy before your mother,* guilting me when I couldn't have known this would happen to her. Now I'm facing disownment from Evan and Audrey, and the words we said to each other can never be taken back. I don't know if they'll ever speak to me again. They're angry at me for this. They don't understand it, and you and I know why. They don't know the years I existed in a loveless marriage. I can just imagine you squirming in your green skin, never admitting, even to yourself, that it's not my mother, but your jealousy of Will that's your issue. You stopped being intimate with me long before you passed away, so you can't be jealous over something you denied me. I didn't realize how much I missed being with a man, loving him and being loved by him, until I met Will. I don't know what the future holds. I don't even think you have an inside glimpse into that. What I do know, is that my heart is moving me forward, and who can deny what the heart wants? Sleep on that, Nate."

The iron gates groaned again when she closed them, keeping guard of her words left within the hallowed grounds.

***

Will heard the door and came out from the kitchen to greet her. "Where'd you go? I was worried."

"Nowhere special. I was too restless to sleep, and didn't want to wake you."

Will held up a mug. "Want some coffee?"

"I'd love a cup." She sat at the counter and watched him pour the caffeine she would need to compensate for her lack of sleep.

Will made a cup for himself and sat across from Vivienne. "Are you sure you don't want me to take you to Hyannis?"

The coffee tasted as good as the aroma rising from the mug. "I have things to take care of at the restaurant, and you must have a ton of emails waiting for you...and restaurants to consider for review. Besides, you don't want to get on your father's bad side."

"Maybe not, but I could feel him caving when Audrey went to see her grandmother. How will you get to Hyannis?"

"Magda or Owen."

Will rose from the chair at the counter and went to Vivienne. He took her in his arms, and hers settled around his waist. "When am I going to see you again?"

"I don't know, Will. It's not like I live five minutes away. My priority is my mother now, and I may need to stay at her place for a while...when she comes home."

His lips gave hers a soft kiss. "Can I drive down and take you to dinner, somewhere local?"

She returned his kiss. "I'd like that."

He kissed her again, lingering a little more. "If you'll be staying with your mom, we won't have any privacy. Can I take you here where we can love each other until the sun comes up?"

Her lips pressed against his, urging his mouth to open. As she pulled her lips away from his, she gave his bottom lip a gentle bite. "Yes, please," she whispered.

He pulled up her sundress and moved aside her panties. "I can feel what all this seductive talk has done to you. Can we go upstairs now?" he whispered, as he slowly began to love her.

Vivienne tilted her head back, and a soft drawn-out moan left her as she closed her eyes. "I thought you'd never ask."

# Chapter 14

Their kiss was one of hopeful anticipation, embracing each other behind the safety of Vivienne's front door. Safe from local curiosity.

"So, I'm taking you to dinner?" Will asked.

"Yes. I'll know how much free time I'll have after I see her doctor today. We can talk about dinner plans then."

Vivienne's spirits were given a boost when she opened the door and waved at Magda, who waved back, as she walked toward Vivienne's house.

When she stopped at his car, Will greeted her. "Morning, Magda."

"Leaving early, Will?"

"Viv's got things to do, and I like driving in the morning. Less cars." He then turned to Vivienne, standing by his car door. "I'll text you when I'm home. Let me know how your mom is doing."

"I will. Please drive safe."

His gaze said *I want to kiss you,* but he clasped her hand before slipping into the car. Vivienne stood with Magda, watching him drive up the street until he disappeared, making the turn into town.

"Evan called me last night and asked if I would watch Tory," Magda said as she followed Vivienne into the house. "He was speaking quickly and said EMTs took your mother to the hospital. Is she alright?"

"So far." Vivienne instinctively went to put on a pot of coffee. "Did he say anything about me?"

"No. I assumed you were on your way to the hospital, too. It was when they got back that Evan told me your mom suffered a stroke of some kind, but I could see that something else was very wrong. His cheek was red and swollen."

As she placed the cup in front of Magda, she lifted her eyes to her, revealing what her soul would never forget.

"Don't tell me you slapped him?"

Vivienne then repeated Evan's phone call to her. "This wasn't the way I wanted him and Audrey to learn about Will and I, and it only got worse when we got to the hospital. I've never seen Evan like this, Magda. It was like watching someone I didn't know. He asked me if I *lost my fucking mind*, but in that moment, I knew *he* had snapped because he said the most repulsive things to me."

Magda reached for Vivienne's hands, urging her on with a gentle squeeze. "Tell me," she said, and took on the storm that Vivienne could not weather alone.

"He's grieving," Magda finally said. "I'm sure he didn't mean it, Viv."

"I would like to believe you, but I can't. He sees this as me dishonoring his father's memory."

But Magda gently reminded Vivienne: "Lord knows you didn't dishonor Nate."

"Audrey is livid with Will. She accused him of taking advantage of my situation and has severed their friendship. I should have said no to Will."

"And who would have that appeased? Evan and Audrey? They'd be singing a different tune if they knew what you've kept from them about Nate."

"Trying to make my case with either of them now, would be like throwing shit into the wind. No matter what I do or say, I'll never come out of this smelling like a rose."

"I'm partial to peonies, myself. And so what, if you don't? I can't imagine your children denying you access to their lives because of your involvement with Will. Emotions are stinging their already prickled skin. They need time. And so do you."

"What could I ever do to repay your friendship?"

Magda smiled. "Be happy, Viv. You haven't been happy in a long time."

Vivienne sighed, feeling a bit of relief resonating with the hug they shared.

"Can Esty receive visitors?" Magda asked.

"Yes, but only one at a time."

"I'll call Owen, and you can hitch a ride with us. I didn't see your car in the driveway when Will left, so I assume it's in Boston."

"He didn't want me driving with all this on my mind. I've got to stop at Brendan's house before he leaves to pick up mom."

"I'll walk with you." Magda waited while Vivienne quickly showered and pulled her damp hair up.

Brendan's mother was out early, watering the plants and paused to greet Vivienne and Magda. "Good morning. Brendan is just about ready to pick up your mother."

"Morning, Penny. I wanted to stop by before he left. My mother suffered a stroke last night and is—"

"Oh, God!" The water bucket slipped from Penny's hand. "Is she alright?"

"Thankfully, the EMTs got there in time. She's in the hospital in Hyannis."

Brendan stepped out of the house. "Who's in the hospital?"

"Esty. She had a stroke."

"Is there anything I can do?" He blinked to hold back tears. "I'll work extra shifts, if you need me."

"We'll all have extra work while Esty's recovering, and I know she'll love to see you when she comes home."

"Can I drive you to the restaurant?"

"I'd appreciate that, Brendan."

"Call me when you're ready to go," Magda said. "I'll close the store, and Owen and I will pick you up."

***

A few of the wait staff were already prepping the tables when they paused to give their attention to Vivienne and Brendan walking in.

"Where's Esty?" Ryan asked.

"Just a minute, Ryan," Vivienne headed for the kitchen.

Auggie was deveining shrimp. "Auggie, can you and the chefs please come out to the dining area?"

The ominous sound of her voice made his cheeks pale, and he slowly put down his paring knife. "Okay, chefs, let's take a moment to step out of the kitchen."

Gathered around Vivienne were the furrowed brows and concerned eyes already anticipating bad news. "Esty had a stroke last night." It brought gasps from some, and shocked others, who covered their mouths. "The EMTs got her to the hospital in Hyannis quickly."

"How bad is it?" Auggie asked.

"She has numbness on her right side, but the doctors are giving her a good chance for recovery." She then turned her attention to the staff. "I'm putting Auggie in charge of the restaurant until further notice, so I can be at the hospital when I'm needed and focus on bringing her home and getting her well."

Carol, one of the permanent staff asked, "Can she have visitors?"

"Her doctor is limiting visitors to one person at a time, so it may be best to wait until she comes home. She'll enjoy seeing you more without all the hospital machines beeping and blinking around her."

Vivienne could feel her throat tightening, as she collected her feelings for the people around her, some of whom were dabbing their eyes. "We're a family, and we keep the heart of this restaurant beating every day. I'd appreciate any additional help you can give while Esty is recovering."

Auggie cleared his throat and quickly passed his hand over his teary eyes. "Tell her...Auggie says not to worry about her chowder. Just focus on getting better."

"I'll know more about her prognosis when I talk to the doctor today. Thank you all, again. Please keep Esty in your thoughts, and let's get started for the day."

The dining staff picked up where they were, but their pace was now a little slower, mindful that one of their own was missing. The kitchen had its own quiet sadness. Around the clatter of pans and the rhythmic chopping of knives against cutting boards, they worked in silence, aware of Esty's empty chair, and the absence of her bubbly voice. It was the profound impact of Esty's frail, unassuming presence on everyone that Vivienne took with her as she left the restaurant.

***

Magda shifted in her seat, turning to Vivienne in the back as Owen drove toward the hospital. "How did the staff take the news?"

"There were tears, and the kitchen staff took it especially hard."

"I can only imagine," Owen said. "She's with them every day."

"My people are a tight bunch, I can tell you that. They didn't bat an eye when I left the restaurant in Auggie's hands. Nate would have said that's what they should do, but I know my people, they rally together when one of their own needs them."

Magda shifted forward again. "You know they love you, and especially Esty." Expecting Vivienne to reply, Magda received only silence. "You okay, Viv?"

"Yes...No. I don't know. How can I keep what happened between me, Evan, and Audrey from my mother? If she doesn't see it in my face, she'll hear it in my voice. There's no getting around her."

"Maybe not, but are you forgetting how you kept that dark time with Nate from Evan and Audrey? You can keep this from your mother...until you decide to tell her."

"That's my Magda," Owen said, exuding the pride he felt. "She can see through a thicket of troubles and make sense out of it all like no one I've ever met."

"It's easy, because my heart is in the same place," Magda said.

"And this is why I love you." Owen chuckled.

Magda smiled and reached to touch Owen's cheek. "I love you, too, sweetheart."

Vivienne knew that Magda hadn't said those words to any man since Griffin had passed away. Hearing them both acknowledge this to each other was a turning point in their relationship.

"That makes two of us, Owen," Vivienne said and leaned her head against the back seat. She closed her eyes for the remainder of the trip.

***

The soft *ding* of the elevator announced their arrival on Esty's floor. The nurse smiled as they approached the desk. "How can I help you?"

"I'm Vivienne Callane. I'm here to see Estelle Atwood."

She glanced at her book. "Room 3105. One person at a time."

"Will Dr. Bellam be available to speak with me?"

"He's in the hospital. I'll page him after your visit."

"Thank you."

"It'll be okay. We'll be waiting here." Magda pointed to the bench in the hall.

Vivienne took in a breath and let it out as she opened the door.

"You have a visitor, Estelle," the nurse announced. "Can you tell me who this is?"

"Vivienne, my daughter."

"Very good, Estelle! Her speech is good. We're working on her motor skills."

Vivienne glanced at the nurse's badge. "Thank you, Frances."

"She's doing much better, which is what we like to see."

"This is such good news, Mom," Vivienne said.

"I'll be back later, Estelle," Frances said.

When Frances had left, Esty looked to Vivienne. "Audrey was crying the other night."

*I'll tell her, when the time is right.* "Of course she was crying, Mom. She was upset about what happened to you, and that she had to go back to Boston. She didn't want to, but I told her I would keep in touch. I'm sure she'll be down this weekend to see you."

But Esty shook her head. "No. Evan was here this morning. His face was red, and he wouldn't tell me why."

Vivienne felt Esty's pressure and began to straighten her blanket, killing some time while she scrambled for a reply. She avoided Esty's eyes, knowing every deceiving word she said would show in her own. "They're upset with me, because I wasn't back in time from the restaurant review in Boston. I got here as soon as I could."

Vivienne's excuse was as close to the truth as she wanted to get, but seeing Audrey and Evan told Esty otherwise. She fixed her gaze on Vivienne, who tried to skirt around it and forced a smile.

"I brought someone with me that I know will cheer you up. She'll spend some time with you while I speak with your doctor." She leaned to kiss Esty's cheek and felt her left hand grip her arm, to keep her from leaving. Vivienne had no choice but to look into her mother's eyes.

"Evan's face."

"That was me," she stated. "We were all worried about you, and no one was thinking straight. Evan said something disrespectful to me, and that was my reaction. But it's not my priority now. You are. Your doctor is waiting to speak with me."

Esty released her hand, but her eyes were still searching for something more in Vivienne's.

"Everything's okay, Mom. I promise." She felt the lie stick in her throat.

She left Esty's room feeling the weight of that lie on her heart and on her face, as shown in the shock of Magda's gaze.

"Geez, Viv, what happened in there?"

"She knows something's not right. I got around Audrey crying, but Evan's red face was a big red flag."

"You told her?"

"I had to, Magda. The one thing I've never done is lie to her, and it's already boring a hole in my conscience. I just told her everything is okay, and I put my promise on it...when I'm not even sure my children will ever speak to me again."

Magda rose from the chair. "Let me talk to her."

Vivienne touched her arm, stopping her for a moment. Magda's gaze softened, trying to calm Vivienne's worry. "She won't get anything from me."

Vivienne let out a sigh. "Thank you."

***

Vivienne's encouraging news from the doctor had to wait. Magda came back too soon and was sitting next to Owen. Vivienne's anxiety surged, but Magda stood up and held out her hands for Vivienne to grasp.

"It's okay, Viv. Yes, she's upset about Audrey and Evan, but more so about you. I repeated that what happened to her had an emotional toll on everyone, but she shook her head. The way you knew Audrey wasn't telling you everything about Hugo, Esty can sense you're holding something from her."

"I won't tell her about Will until I have this mess settled with Evan and Audrey...if that's even possible. Her doctor is discharging her tomorrow, along with a script for PT. This is what I need to concentrate on."

"You'll need your car," Owen said. "We'll drive you to Will's place, and I'll follow you and Magda back in your car."

After a moment, Magda turned to Owen. "You know, sweetie, Viv's been under a lot of stress. With Esty coming home tomorrow, she could use a little time to herself."

That was code Owen didn't need to decipher. "You're right. We'll drive back together."

"Let me text Will," Vivienne said, and was happy to see the message he promised her he would send when he arrived home.

*Back in Bawstin without U. Not happy.*

*Sorry for the delay. Just leaving the hospital. Mom coming home tomorrow. Magda and Owen R driving me to your place.*

*Do U still have the access code to the garage?*

*Yes.*

*Do U have to drive back today?*

*I'll stay after they leave.*

*I was hoping U would say that. Inviting everyone to lunch at my place.*

"He would like you both to stop for lunch at his place," Vivienne said.

"My stomach's already rumbling," Owen replied.

Vivienne smiled as she texted her reply. *Just a heads up. Owen has a hefty appetite. I'll text you when we're a half hour away.*

*Leaving the office now.*

Vivienne placed the phone on her lap. "He wants me to drive back tomorrow."

Magda shifted toward Vivienne and shared a sly smile with her. "Did you think he wouldn't?" She then left Vivienne to her own thoughts.

Vivienne's mind returned to that traumatic night in the hospital, and her thoughts found a voice. "I never expected Audrey and Evan to react with such intense hostility. If you could have seen the coldness in Audrey's eyes and the way Evan's jaw tightened before he said those detestable things to me. Some lines crossed, can never be uncrossed."

Magda turned back to Vivienne, concern deepening the lines between her brows. "Remember the circumstances. Everyone's emotions were already at the limit. It wasn't the best time to hear about you and Will."

"They're siding with their father, a man who has no say, but is speaking volumes from the grave. In their mind, I've tarnished his memory."

"As their father, Viv. They didn't know him as a husband."

"I've bruised my relationship with them. I don't know if the mark I put on Evan's face and Audrey's heart will ever heal."

"They will. When they're ready to listen to you."

***

Will's broad smile greeted them at his door. "This was a pleasant surprise!" he said as he stepped aside. "I hope you brought your appetites."

"I could eat a horse," Owen said.

"Well, you're at the right place. I had time to do some shopping while you were on the way."

They followed Will into the living room where he placed a quick kiss on Vivienne's lips.

Vivienne pulled him back and pressed her lips to his. "That's better."

He then turned to Owen and Magda. "Thank you for bringing my girl to pick up her car."

"Viv's been under a lot of stress," Magda said. "Owen and I suspected that seeing you would help."

Owen looked at the table Will had put out for lunch. "If I'd known there was going to be this spread, I would have driven faster." Minutes later, he was biting into a fresh, warm Cubano sandwich.

"Was it an inconvenience for you to leave the office?" Vivienne asked.

"No. My dad knew your car was here, so I left after our weekly meeting to discuss my next review."

"Can you tell us?" Magda asked, as she stabbed her fork into her salad.

"Actually, it's a food truck. Gourmet Mobile Bistro has been drawing crowds outside Fenway Park and TD Garden. They offer several interesting twists on the classic baseball hotdog, but I really want to try their grand slam nachos."

Owen's brows rose, and he put his sandwich down, eager to talk to Will. "A lot of chefs are taking their culinary talents on the road. Man, those food trucks pop up all over the place, and I swear, each one is better than the last."

"I don't know how the other fast-food places are still open," Magda added.

"How were things at the office when you got back?" Vivienne asked.

"With Audrey? After the hospital scene, not better. I almost bumped into her on my way out of my dad's office. I acknowledged her, but she just brushed by me."

"I've known Audrey all her life," Magda added. "If Vivienne didn't give her a toy or something she wanted, she'd sulk and hold a grudge even after she no longer wanted it."

"This is more than a grudge," Will said. "She had to pass my desk the other day. I tried to talk to her, but it's like talking to a wall. It's a complete shutout."

"In her eyes, you overstepped your bounds, but it was me who let you," Vivienne said. "It's on me to fix this."

"She may be able to ignore Will," Magda said, "but she has to listen to you, Viv. Even if you think your words have no impact, you're as much a part of her, as she is of you."

***

Magda's voice lingered in Vivienne's mind after they left, and when she climbed into bed next to Will that evening.

"Magda's right," Vivienne said as they faced each other. "Audrey can't ignore me forever and neither can Evan. What happened between us isn't bigger than my love for them, or their love for me."

Will's hand found hers and brought it to his lips. "I've had knockdown drag-out fights with my parents, but not once did my love for them ever come into question. I know it's the same for Audrey and Evan."

She let herself believe the quiet hopefulness of his words. "I'll try again tomorrow, and the next day. As many days as it takes, I won't give up."

"I know what it's like to lose a parent," Will said, "but a spouse? You plan a future together and share dreams. I can't imagine walking that road alone. You're a strong woman, Vivienne. Don't ever question where Audrey and Evan got their fortitude."

Her finger gently touched the soft hair above his top lip. "Do you know how much I wanted to kiss your lips the night you walked into the restaurant?"

"Can you show me?"

She leaned in and pressed her mouth to his, and her fingers tangled in the soft waves of his hair. Her kiss became more fervent, with every pass of her tongue on his, telling him, *I want you.* Slowly, their language of love found its place in the quiet. A sigh, a breathless moan, quickened voices urging for their pleasure to find completion.

***

Vivienne listened to Will's sleeping breaths, and every fiber in her told her that she loved him. She knew he was worth fighting for, and who to battle with. *Who will I lose in the end?* She fell asleep before she could answer her heart.

# Chapter 15

Esty's PT appointments over the last few weeks had gone well enough for Vivienne to return to work, so she was up early, eager to get back to her regular routine. Before she left the house, she sat at the kitchen counter and sent yet another text to Audrey and Evan.

*Morning. U won't answer my calls, so I'll keep texting. Can't we talk about this?*

She stared at her phone and sighed again, seeing that her message was read, but with no response. Their silence since that infamous night in the hospital was her punishment, and every unanswered message was grinding it a little deeper into her heart.

Vivienne tossed her phone in her bag and walked the few blocks to her mother's apartment. "Morning, Mom."

As Esty made her way from the kitchen with the help of her cane, her steps were slow and deliberate. "Mornin', Viv."

Vivienne's brows rose. "Where's your walker?"

Esty's pride lit up her face. "Helen has been helping me every day to surprise you."

"Let me help you to your chair."

The offer only prickled Esty's feisty side. "I'm not an invalid."

When Esty was finally settled in her chair, Vivienne sat across from her. "I couldn't be happier to see the progress you're making, but your stamina hasn't yet caught up to your determination."

For the first time, Esty used her right hand to brush off Vivienne's concern. "Oh, fiddlesticks! I'm fine. But something's bothering you."

"Evan won't answer my calls. I'm going down to the dock to meet him when he pulls in today."

"Stubborn...like his father was."

Before Vivienne could reply, their attention shifted to the door. Esty's therapist, Helen, was punctual, and a whirlwind of energy in a well-worn pair of sneakers and standard navy-blue scrubs. "Esty! I see you surprised Vivienne, like we planned." At five-foot-four, her athletic build was softened by her cheerful voice that encouraged every small victory a patient won. She was a welcome change from where the conversation about Evan was headed.

"She certainly did." Vivienne closed the door behind her. "Since I brought her home from the hospital, she's made slow, but steady progress, but this blew me away. I'm curious. How long have you been working on this surprise?"

"We began last week. Because Esty's stroke wasn't severe, her paralysis is responding well to therapy."

"I agree with you," Vivienne added. "And seeing this surprise today, I feel good about my decision to return to work."

"And me?" Esty asked.

"That's something Helen is more able to answer."

"Not just yet, Esty, but you're moving in the right direction."

Esty's pursed lips left no debate on her mood.

"I know it wasn't what you wanted to hear," Helen said, "but your health is my priority, and we'll work together toward your goal." Helen smiled, knowing the dismissive flit of Esty's hand was more disappointment than a reflection on her.

"What would you like for lunch, Mom?"

"My chowder."

Vivienne held down her chuckle. "Always the skeptic. Auggie isn't messing up your recipe. Anything else?"

"Crab cakes."

"And what would you like, Helen?"

"I appreciate anything from your menu, Vivienne."

Vivienne leaned down and kissed her mother's forehead. "I'm proud of you, and I *am happy* that you're doing so well. I'll be back with lunch."

Helen placed her chair, and folding table, in front of Esty and spread out the toothpicks. "Let's get started."

The last thing Vivienne heard before she left was Helen's voice saying clearly, "Pick up one at a time with your right hand."

***

Heidi's smile proudly showed her beautiful teeth, minus the braces. Her face glowed, full of the promise and potential of her age, as she greeted Vivienne at the door. "Good morning, Vivienne. It's good to have you back."

"Morning, Heidi. I see your braces came off while I was away. The boys will be buzzing around you soon."

The notion warmed her cheeks as she lowered her eyes. "I hope so, Vivienne."

She waved to the wait staff as she passed the dining area and Brendan, who was busy talking with customers at the counter. As Vivienne pushed open the kitchen door, Auggie was barking concise orders like a drill sergeant. "We don't serve flabby bacon, Marty. Six orders on the wheel, people. Let's go." His broad smile warmed her heart as he welcomed her. "Chefs, our boss is back!"

Vivienne knew they wouldn't stop, but she saw their smiles, nonetheless.

Chance watched his eggs sizzle on the griddle. "Welcome back, Vivienne."

"When will Esty be back?" Crystal asked as she worked on the pancake orders.

"Not for a while, but if she had it her way, it would be today. It's good to be back." Vivienne was proud of the blueberry muffins Devon pulled from the oven, baked to glorious, golden perfection.

"Did she ask for chowder again?" Auggie asked.

Vivienne shrugged. "What can I say? Old habits die hard."

"Esty may not be here, but she's making sure I get it right every day," Auggie said.

Vivienne then placed Esty and Helen's lunch requests on the kitchen tackboard and grabbed an apron from the shelf in the back.

"It's good to have you back, Vivienne," Brendan said as she joined him at the counter.

"It's good to be back. I see we have a full counter."

"Liam just walked in. Caleb hasn't decided yet."

Vivienne went to the opposite end of the counter. "Morning, gentlemen. What's your pleasure today?"

"You, Vivienne," Caleb replied. "My eggs weren't as *sunny* while you were away."

Vivienne's head tilted, her smile and her eyes full of amused skepticism. "Are you trying to schmooze the owner for an extra egg?"

Caleb chuckled. "Just missin' your smile, Vivienne."

"How is Esty?" Liam asked. "A lot of us in town...uh...I was worried when I heard the news."

Vivienne sensed where Liam was going and kept the focus on Esty. "She's a feisty one, I can tell you. If it were up to her, she'd be with me today, but she's up against her therapist, who's just as determined to keep her right where she is until she's ready." She then turned to Caleb. "Ready for your sunnyside eggs and corned beef hash?"

"You know me like a book."

Vivienne smiled. "Only your breakfast, Caleb."

She put his order, with an *extra egg*, on the wheel and then turned her attention to Liam. "How about you, Liam? Anything spark your appetite?"

She knew his answer wouldn't be about the menu. His eyes were *all over her*. "How are you, Vivienne? I doubt you've had much time to yourself."

"I'm fine. I take one day at a time."

"It helps to have someone to talk to. Share a dinner, grab an ice cream in town."

It was a pass she couldn't ignore or accept. "We've been friends a long time. That would only complicate things. I wouldn't want to jeopardize our friendship."

The light dimmed in his eyes, and a frown replaced his brief moment of hope. "You don't need to explain." He slid the menu on the counter toward her. "I'll have a short stack and a cup of coffee."

When Liam left, she cleared his place and welcomed a new customer, yet their conversation lingered in her mind. *If I were with someone my own age, someone like Liam, my situation with Audrey and Evan would be different.* She thought of Will and knew it didn't matter.

***

Vivienne left the restaurant in Auggie's capable hands for the rest of the day. There was a purpose in her step, and one thing on her mind as she walked through town, toward the docks. She didn't even stop to browse at the new clothes in Magda's window. Her mind was on Evan and the knot tightening in her stomach.

She was still a good distance away but could see the boats pulling into their docks with the day's catch. She knew where Evan docked his boat. When she saw him stacking lobster traps with his crew, adrenaline rushed to her heart, making it pound like a gavel against her chest. She prepared herself for the confrontation that could no longer be avoided, but when he finally noticed her, she only received his dismissive glance and continued to stack the traps.

She stood there as he conversed with his crew, deliberately ignoring her. She felt more like a stranger than his mother, and more awkward with every minute of silence that passed between them...until he finally addressed her.

"Is there a reason you're here? I'm busy getting the catch off the boat."

"Let the crew handle it. You know why I'm here, Evan. We need to talk."

He jumped off the boat, onto the dock, and walked toward her. "I don't see the need to. It's pretty clear how I feel. And I'm not in the mood for another slap."

She reached to touch his arm, only to have him pull away. "I apologize, Evan, but I didn't think I would ever hear words so detestable from you."

He leaned toward her and mumbled under his breath. "They're not nearly as repulsive as the image of my mother with that guy, that I can't get out of my fucking head." In his anger, he turned his back on her and began to walk away.

Vivienne called out to him. "Don't walk away from me, Evan. Tell me. What's so repulsive? That I still have love to give and want to receive? If you were gone, would you want Grace to live out her life alone?"

It was as if Vivienne had reached in and touched the most vulnerable part of his heart. He turned to face her. His eyes were as cold and unforgiving as a turbulent ocean. "Don't pull my wife into this. What we discuss in private is none of your business."

"I only hope you love her enough to give her what you're denying me."

"I went to see Dad the other night after I docked the boat. He worked long hours, put Audrey through college, and made me the fisherman I always admired in him. You disgraced all that."

"Do you hear yourself, Evan? Yes, your father did all those things, but not once did you mention what he did for me. I can't fault you for that. You and Audrey were busy making a life for yourselves, but we wouldn't be having this conversation if you knew..." Vivienne caught herself before she said what was too soon for him to hear.

"Knew what? So, now you're gonna drum up some random fight

you had with Dad eons ago to try and sway me? That guy will never be invited into my life. I don't even want to see him in the vicinity of my house. The choice is yours."

As he climbed back on the boat she called to him, "Memories have no flaws, Evan. Remember that."

He disappeared under the hull, leaving her with an ultimatum that was undebatable. It was late afternoon when Vivienne walked back through town again. Finally home, she leaned against the locked door and felt a heaviness on her shoulders, like she had lost the fight before the first-round bell was rung.

# Chapter 16

*That guy will never be invited into my life. The choice is yours.*

"Evan?" Vivienne's eyes opened as she said his name. Despite her decision to let sleeping dogs lie, her unresolved talk with him had become a recurring dream for several days. Rather than dwell on it, she swung her legs over the side of the bed and headed for the shower. She was towel-drying her hair when her phone on the night table announced a morning call from Will.

"Morning, baby. I miss you."

"I miss you, too."

"How is your mom doing?"

"Better each day, and more insistent on returning to the restaurant."

"Any word from Audrey or Evan?"

"After that disastrous talk with Evan on the dock? I'm beginning to think I may hear from Audrey before him. Has she softened up to you at all at the office?"

"Put it this way, my cold shoulder is now packed in ice."

"I'm sorry you have to work under these conditions."

"It's actually better this way. She doesn't bother with me. I get my work done, no drama. So how about I take you to dinner tomorrow night? I'll drive down to you."

The thought made Vivienne smile. "I'd like that. I'll ask Auggie to close for me."

"Great. I'll finish up my review and call it a day."

***

Every morning, Vivienne looked forward to seeing her mother's progress from day to day. She used her key and was met with a sight that gladdened her heart. "Mom, you made breakfast yourself?"

Esty was sitting in her chair with a cup of cereal on her folding table. "Helen said no cooking, only cereal."

Vivienne couldn't praise her enough. "This is great, Mom. Look at how far you've come. You get out of bed on your own, you get around with your cane."

It wasn't praise Esty was looking for in her determined gaze. "Bring me back to the restaurant."

Vivienne could no longer ignore that the cards were starting to stack in Esty's favor. "Okay, Mom. Let's talk to Helen."

Before she left, she kissed her mother's forehead. "I'll be back with lunch. We can talk about it then."

***

Vivienne stopped inside the door of the restaurant for a moment and glanced around, her eyes proudly taking in what she saw. The tables were immaculate, and the morning sun shone through the window, spreading its rays across the gleaming counter. The clang of pots and voices already resonated from the kitchen. Vivienne pushed open the kitchen door to find Auggie pacing.

"If you're agitated this early, it can't be good."

"I need to start another two pots of chowder for tomorrow," he replied. "I don't have enough quahogs to satisfy two more recipes."

Vivienne already had her hand on the kitchen door. "What do we need from Grace at the fish market?"

"Another 7 pounds."

"I'm on it." She pushed through the door.

"Okay, people," Auggie barked. "The boss has it covered. Everyone is on breakfast."

Vivienne knew Auggie was back on his game.

***

In her worn-in deck shoes, she was able to quick-walk the two blocks to the fish market. Grace was placing fresh catch and shellfish on ice in the glass case and looked up when she heard the door creak. Her eyes widened, showing her surprise. "Morning, Vivienne. I didn't expect to see you this early."

"We're going through Esty's chowder faster than we can make it. Auggie needs 7 pounds of quahogs."

"Sure."

Vivienne noticed an obvious shift in Grace, who was normally not at a loss for words whenever Vivienne would stop by the market. Today, her silence spoke volumes as she began filling the bag. Still, it didn't deter Vivienne into sparking a conversation. "Are you doing anything for Tory's birthday?"

Grace's eyes connected with Vivienne's for a fleeting moment, before she looked away. But it was long enough for Vivienne to see Evan's influence on Grace.

She kept her focus on the bag of shellfish. "Oh, we're not sure yet. We may just have a kid's party for him with some of his friends from pre-k."

Grace's message was clear, but so was Vivienne's as she put the cash on top of the glass case. "You're really doing this, Grace? I've been part of Tory's life all along. You think I can't read the signs?"

Grace couldn't skirt around the truth. "I'm in the middle, Vivienne, and I've been arguing with Evan since that horrible scene at the hospital. I told him he should apologize, and he almost cut my head off."

Vivienne's brows rose. "Evan apologize? Not in this lifetime. He's just as stubborn as his father was."

"You know what he said? 'When you decide to act your age.' Your slap left your handprint on his face. The next day it was red and swollen. The guys on the boat got a few laughs at his expense. Believe me, it hasn't been easy living with him. Don't take this the wrong way, Vivienne, but wouldn't it be easier if...if you..."

"What, Grace? Appease Evan and remain faithful to a man six feet under? Oh, and by the way, Audrey isn't speaking to me either."

"I've heard Evan talking to Audrey on the phone about Will. Evan said she didn't paint a picture of faithfulness."

Vivienne could feel her dander rising. "So, you believe what Audrey and Evan are saying, without knowing anything about Will? I know what Audrey said at the hospital, but neither she, nor Evan, have the right to make decisions for me. I'm a grown woman."

Grace couldn't hold her tongue. "They think you're making a fool of yourself."

"Are you *'they,' too,* Grace?"

She fell silent, but her answer lay bare in her eyes.

"I guess there's nothing more to say." Vivienne reached for the bag. "Let me know when I can stop by to give Tory his gift."

"I will, but Evan probably won't be at home. Things got worse with him...since your conversation on the dock."

"I won't be visiting my son. Right now, my grandson is the only one whose innocence won't allow him to pass judgment."

Vivienne left with 7 pounds of shellfish in her arms. *Tory was 7 pounds when he was born, and I was there with Nate when we held him for the first time. I realized then that mothers have second hearts that only grandchildren can touch.* Her thoughts were laden with worry that she feared was a foreshadowing of lonely times ahead.

***

Morning shifted seamlessly into the lunch crowd. Vivienne stopped Brendan as he was bringing in dishes from his table. "Are you serving any other tables?"

"Not in my section right now."

"Please cover the counter. I'll have the others split your tables until I get back."

"Sure thing, Vivienne." His keen eyes took only seconds to see who was waiting to be served.

In the kitchen, Vivienne shared the counter with Crystal, who was putting the finishing garnishes on a lobster, while she prepared quick lunches for Esty and Helen.

"Do you know when Esty will be back?" Crystal asked.

"That's been a big bone of contention for some time, between Esty and her doctor. She's never been one to sit at home and nurse an illness, and he wants her to use this time to recover. Her therapist has her hands full, to say the least."

"Well, we sure do miss her here in the kitchen."

"I know you do, and I would love to tell her, but it would only make her more determined to whittle away at the doctor's decision." With that, Vivienne packed the lunches and left the restaurant.

***

Over fish filet and crab salad, the path to Esty's return to the restaurant began to become clear.

"The last several weeks, I've been speaking with Esty's doctor about her determination, and reporting on her progress," Helen began. "He agrees with my decision and has cleared her to return to the restaurant starting with one half-day a week. Given the fast-paced environment, it's important not to expose her to too much stimulation."

"That's a conservative decision I feel comfortable with," Vivienne replied.

"She'll stay on this schedule for 4 weeks, and I'll monitor her to see how she does."

"I stir the chowder," Esty added.

"That's perfect," Helen replied. "There's not much exertion needed for that. Are you happy about this?"

"About time."

Helen closed her eyes for a fleeting moment, sighing as if she were throwing in the towel. "Okay, Esty. When would you like to start?"

"Tomorrow."

"I've cared for many people, but you are one for the books, Esty. I'll remember you, when others I care for want to give up. I'll tell them about your persistence to work with me every day to overcome this setback in your life. I feel confident enough to recommend your therapy for two days a week, from now on."

A sheen of tears showed in Esty's eyes. "Thank you, Helen."

Relief flooded Vivienne, seeing her mother clasp Helen's hands. "You know, there were moments in the hospital when I thought..."

"Bah! Not yet. I still got steam in my kettle."

Helen joined Vivienne as they began to laugh. "Yes, Mom, and both oars in the water."

Before she left, she tossed the throwaway plates in the trash and kissed Esty's forehead. "I'll let you two get back to therapy. I won't pick you up too early, Mom. I know you need time to get ready."

It was news she knew would burst from her and reached for her phone in her bag to text the two people she wanted to share it with.

*Evan and Audrey. I hope this will touch your hearts enough to put aside our differences and come together as a family. Gram's doctor has decided she's well enough to return to the restaurant for a few hours, one day a week. If I don't hear from U, please call Gram and show her some love.*

She pressed *SEND* and tossed the phone in her bag.

Back at the restaurant, she was unable to pull the staff from the busy dining area, so she went straight to the kitchen.

Auggie was shucking quahogs and glanced up. "Don't tell me. She complained that I didn't send a sample of her chowder to taste."

"Actually," Vivienne began in a casual, matter-of-fact manner, "there was no reason for her to complain...when she can taste it for herself here...tomorrow."

The kitchen fell silent, and all eyes were on Vivienne, before Auggie spoke. "Did I hear you right?"

"She's coming back?" Crystal said.

It brought a smile to Vivienne's face to finally be able to say it again. "Tomorrow."

The other chefs threw up their hands, broad smiles showing their happiness as they shouted in unison, "Yeah!"

"It's only a few hours to start, one day a week."

Auggie took Vivienne's hands, his voice cracking as he held them. "Her absence was felt by all of us in the kitchen and out front. We need her back."

"And *she needs* to come back. What helped her recovery was the support she felt from everyone. It gave her the courage not to give up."

Out front, Vivienne began to tell the staff, beginning with Brendan at the counter. "Esty's back tomorrow."

The wrinkled ears of a local, with expert hearing, perked up as he sat at the counter. "Esty's coming back?"

"Who's Esty?" the woman next to him asked.

"She's the owner's mother. Had a stroke a while back."

"A permanent fixture in the restaurant," the man on the other side of her added.

The staff waiting tables began to clap at the news and soon, the applause became infectious, even pulling in folks who didn't know Esty. Vivienne was moved to tears. *If you could only hear this, Mom.*

Though the counter kept her busy, Vivienne would occasionally glance at the door, watching Heidi greet and seat new customers. What caught her attention was Emma, who she met at Audrey's engagement party. Vivienne came out from behind the counter to greet her and the young man she was with.

"Emma, it's good to see you."

"You, too, Vivienne. This is Lucas."

He offered his hand to Vivienne while greeting her with a warm smile. "It's nice to meet you."

His hearty handshake put Vivienne at ease. "Thank you. I'm always happy to see Audrey's friends enjoying the Cape. Are you two celebrating something special?"

"Just a weekend getaway." Lucas shared a sly glance with Emma, who lowered her eyes. A smile tugged at the corner of her mouth, knowing it wasn't just a weekend getaway but their first true escape together.

"Well, you've come to the right place for dinner." Vivienne turned to Heidi. "Would you please seat them at table 16?"

It was an unexpected opportunity that Vivienne couldn't pass up. *Maybe I can sneak in a word or two about Audrey.* After their waiter had cleared their plates, she seized the moment and approached their table. "Did you enjoy dinner?"

"The swordfish was awesome," Lucas replied.

"Thank you. I'll be happy to tell the chef."

Emma added, "Audrey told us about the family restaurant months ago, so we wanted to be sure to stop here before we headed home."

It was the invitation Vivienne was hoping for. "I'm not surprised. Audrey and her brother, Evan, have been praising the restaurant since they were in grade school."

"Me and the other girls in her wedding party are so happy for her. Oh! And aren't her invitations beautiful? I love the tiny seashells she had drawn into the corners."

Vivienne's heart felt the pierce of the knife. Emma had unknowingly revealed that Audrey had excluded Vivienne, but her smile gave away nothing. "They are. I knew she would find a way to show her love of the bay and the ocean. We have some fabulous desserts on the menu. It's on me."

"Thank you, Vivienne," Emma replied.

"My pleasure. Have a safe trip back."

She continued the charade for her customers, hiding behind a smile and chuckle, when the reality of what lay ahead was wearing down her resolve with every beat of her broken heart.

***

Vivienne scanned the immaculate tables ready for tomorrow, before she turned the lights off and locked the door. She reached for her phone, her emotions now like a bubbling cauldron as she called Magda.

"Vivienne. Owen and I were just talking about how far Esty's come. Any update from her therapist?"

"Things couldn't be better for Mom. I'm not so sure about me."

Vivienne's somber tone struck a chord of worry in Magda's gut. "What's going on?"

"Something I didn't see coming."

"The door is open," Magda said.

Vivienne let herself in and went into Magda's outstretched arms. "I can't do this, Magda," she said between sobs.

"Owen," Magda said, "can you please open the bottle of wine in the fridge?"

He joined them in the living room but poured only two glasses. "I'm going to give you both some time alone."

"I'll call you in the morning," Magda said. When she heard the click of the front door, she sat next to Vivienne, who tried to steady her trembling voice.

"I couldn't have asked for a better day, today. Mom's doctor, and Helen, decided that she could handle a few hours at the restaurant, one day a week."

"That's wonderful news! It must have made her happy."

Vivienne broke to take a sip of wine. "More than you know. Mom didn't hesitate to say she wanted to go back tomorrow. I texted Evan and Audrey to give them the news, but I'm not surprised that I still haven't heard from them. Everyone at the restaurant was elated. The chefs and the wait staff began to applaud and soon the customers, some who didn't even know Esty, joined in. I hadn't been that happy in a long time."

"So, why the tears, Viv?"

When she had finished replaying her conversation with Emma, she looked at Magda through red and swollen eyes. "I thought Evan's anger would subside. I was wrong. But Audrey...to exclude me from her wedding, it's a blow to my heart I will never recover from. I'm in love with Will, but they're leaving me no choice."

"You have a choice," Magda said. "Do you think for a minute, that Audrey and Evan would want to live their lives without you in it? They may be angry now, but you're still their mother. Their relationship with you is equally at risk."

"You make a good argument..." Vivienne sniffled, "but if I were a betting woman, this is one with shitty odds. Will wants to take me to dinner tomorrow, but I think it's best if I tell him he doesn't have to make the drive." She rose from the couch. "Walk me home."

"Don't do this, Viv." Magda put on her sandals. "There are many emotions in play. Don't forget yours. We'll find a way. Together."

On her way home, Vivienne slipped her arm into Magda's and her pace slowed, as she shared a time not too long ago.

"I remember the first night Will walked into the restaurant, the feeling that rushed through me when I saw him, that powerful, instant crush. Not even Nate roused in me an emotion that intense."

"I watched the two of you at Audrey's engagement party, and again at Will's apartment. He couldn't take his eyes off you. Like Owen and I weren't even there. He's in love with you, Vivienne. I'm sure of it. If he hasn't said it, he will soon."

"When we're together, it's more than just sex. It's a shared understanding that we were meant to be together."

Magda released her arm from Vivienne and came to an abrupt halt. "And you're going to give this up? I won't allow you to do that. If I have to talk to those two brickheads myself and risk alienating them, so be it."

Vivienne slipped her arm inside Magda's again and urged her forward. "Please don't. It will only make things worse. I'll talk to Will tonight."

Magda waited on the path until Vivienne unlocked the door and then called to her, "Let him take you to dinner."

"I will," she replied, and topped it with a convincing smile.

The moment she was alone, a wave of sadness washed the smile from her face. She glanced in the kitchen and envisioned herself slipping her arms around Will's waist as she stood behind him at the stove while he made breakfast. "That was the first meal you cooked for me," she said.

Her feet slowly took her to the slider, and she stepped out onto the patio. She wrapped her arms around herself, wanting to bring back the feeling of Will's arms around her. Her eyes closed, as they did on that night, and her mind repeated the words he whispered. 'Will you let me kiss you?'

"Only if you let me kiss you back," she whispered as if he could hear her.

She made her way upstairs and lingered at the doorway of her bedroom. She saw herself tossing with him on the bed, and her heart responded, remembering the passion that left them breathless as their bodies tangled in a night of feverish love. She sat on the bed and began to cry. "It's more than love I'm giving up. I've given you a piece of my soul."

She pressed his number, and wondered where he was, as she listened to the rings reaching his phone.

His upbeat voice greeted her. "Hey, baby. I just whipped up a quick dinner for myself, but I'll put you on speaker and won't have to eat alone."

"Will, I'll have to cancel dinner tomorrow."

"Hey," he said, trying to sooth her, "Take a breath, baby. Tell me what's wrong? Is your mom okay?"

"She's fine."

"Then why are you crying?"

She sniffled. "It's Audrey." Vivienne listened to the silence; a moment felt like an eternity until he spoke.

"You heard from her?"

"No, Will." She then recounted her conversation with Emma. "I played the part of the excited mother, keeping inside how heartbroken I was that she didn't include me."

"I can't believe she's doing this to you."

"But *I can,* Will. What's next? Picking her wedding dress without me? I thought I was strong enough for us, but not in the face of losing my family."

"I know you're upset—"

"Upset?" Her voice rose to the level of her emotion. "I'm totally coming unglued."

Will began to mirror her panic. "I won't let you go through this alone. I'll talk to Audrey—"

"No you won't! You'll only be adding fuel to the fire."

"Baby, please let's talk about this. I'll get in the car right now."

"There's nothing to say that will change the outcome. I have to end this."

"We c-can fix this. Together. I can feel what you're about to tell me. Don't leave me, Vivienne."

She heard his voice crack and, in that moment, felt the indelible imprint of his words on her heart.

She began to sob in earnest. "I have to do this alone. It's over. In time, you'll see I was right."

***

Vivienne lay awake for hours before she finally fell asleep. The knocking she heard came from deep in her subconscious as she slept, until it became loud enough to rouse her from sleep. She sat up and listened intently. Hearing it again, along with Will's voice, she made her way downstairs.

"Vivienne? Vivienne, I need to talk to you. Open the door."

A sheen of sweat on his forehead glistened in the darkness. His eyes held the shock and disbelief of Vivienne's words. "I'm not letting you do this."

"I have no choice. Why did you come here tonight?"

"I want to see it in your eyes when you tell me it's over."

She stood there, caught in his gaze, fighting within herself to make her words credible. "It's over, Will." Tears threatened to spill onto her cheeks. "There's nothing more to say."

She tried to close the door, but his hand stopped it. "I don't believe you." He pushed his way inside.

She headed for the patio, but he closed the distance between them. "Stop, Vivienne." He grabbed her around her waist.

"Look at me," he whispered.

She stood there and squeezed her eyes shut, fighting the desire to turn around and kiss him. "I can't."

"Then listen to me. I love you. I've never spoken those words to any woman before." And, suddenly, he moved in front of her. "Why are you giving up on us?"

"We never stood a chance, Will. God knows, I love you. I didn't think love this strong would ever find me, but it has. Those words have never meant more to me than they do now. I want this for us, but will it be enough when I can't see Tory opening his gifts at Christmas, or be there when Audrey puts on her wedding dress?"

"My love for you would be meaningless, if I asked you to give that up. You have a history with your family. Ours was just beginning."

Every tear on his face broke a piece of Vivienne's heart. She looked at his eyes, soulful and heartbroken, that once held the light of their newfound love. Her lips touched his wet cheeks, and he took her in his arms, moving his lips to hers, and the salt of their tears brought a sorrowful ending to their last kiss.

# Chapter 17

Hugo's 9:00AM meeting with some staff broke at 12:00PM. Walking back to his office, he noticed Will was just firing up his computer. He stood in front of Will's desk, becoming more annoyed with every minute that Will ignored his silent glare. Only when he cleared his throat, did Will acknowledge him, rolling his eyes before he looked up. "So what? I'm a little late."

Hugo was aware that others had noticed Will's disrespect and felt pressured to address it. "I'd like to see you in my office."

Will stood a ways back from Hugo's desk. Impatient and irritated, he spurted, "Is this going to take long?"

Hugo stopped where he was and turned toward Will, his shoulders squaring until they were a rigid line of muscle. His nostrils flared with every heated exhale. "You can't just show up whenever you want."

"Then fire me!" Will shot back, throwing his hands up.

"What's your problem, Will?"

"My problem? It's funny you asked that. I actually *do* have one you may be able to help me with. Vivienne called me last night. She said—"

A couple of taps on Hugo's door interrupted Will. His eyes settled on Audrey as she peaked her head in. "I'm sorry, Hugo. I'll come back later." She tried to duck out, but Will pounced, ready to sink his teeth into her.

"No, no, please. Come in. You couldn't have interrupted at a more perfect time. In fact, Audrey, I believe you'll be delighted to hear what I was about to say."

Audrey knew Will's sarcasm could slash through the toughest of skins. Walking in on the blind, left her feeling vulnerable and unprepared. She stepped with caution into Hugo's office, walking past Will to Hugo's desk.

"Where was I? Never mind. Now that Audrey's here, I'll start over. I wouldn't want her to miss a word. As I was saying, Vivienne called me last night. She said we couldn't see each other anymore. Needless to say, I was pretty upset, so I drove to her place." Will paused, this time addressing Audrey, with an accusatory point of his finger. "*You* couldn't see the heartbreak on your mother's face, but I did, when she told me how you and Evan are keeping her out of your lives for the choice she made. So, it's done. She gave up what she wanted, for you. I'm out of her life. Are you happy now?"

"What do you want me to say?" It was the first time Audrey spoke to Will since she saw him at the hospital. "I know the way you are with women. For that matter, so does your father. You're the last thing my mother needs."

"What your mother needs? Wow! I never realized how totally in the dark you are. She might as well be a stranger to you. Tell me, Audrey. When was the last time you talked to her, asked her what *she* wanted, now that she's alone, instead of monopolizing the conversation about yourself?"

The truth hit Audrey hard. Will's words stripped her of the cloak of self-righteousness she proudly wore. Her eyes narrowed as she lashed out. "What you know about my mother is nothing, Will. Evan and I have a history with her that your brief time can't compete with."

"She can't live in the past, Audrey. She wants her family to help her move into a new life for herself. What she wants. Don't you think she deserves that?"

Fired with anger, Audrey's eyes bore into Will. "I'll tell you what she *doesn't* deserve, no pretentious show of affection or love, which is right up your alley."

Being close to the door, Will turned and put his hand on the handle but paused to look back. "I'm in no mood to work today, so I'm going home. I'm taking a sick day, Dad. I think it's apropos in light of Audrey's heartfelt sentiments. And you don't get to ream me out for being late." He then turned his gaze to Audrey. "We've never had reason to argue until now. I can't say your feelings are conducive to fostering our friendship. You and Evan got what you wanted. Just do me a fucking favor. Don't punish her anymore."

The defensive cross of her arms was like an armor of protection surrounding her unwavering stance as Audrey watched Will leave.

"You know I'm right, Hugo," she said. "He's your son, and I know you love him, but my mother's just another stop on the way to his next conquest."

Hugo knew how to break through Audrey's obstinate wall. "Come here, baby." His voice softened. He uncrossed her arms and slipped them around his waist, then pulled her close to him. "Is this the way you want your mother to live out her life? Surrounded by you and Evan. Watching you move your lives forward while hers slips further behind?" His eyes were clouded with the uncertainty of his troubled heart.

She gazed up at him. "I'm just trying to protect her, Hugo."

"From whom or what? Will? A broken heart? Things are not always black or white, this or that. No one escapes having their heart broken. Neither you nor your brother can shield her from that possibility."

"We can try."

"What's the point if her heart won't let you? The heart wants what it wants, baby."

Audrey sensed Hugo's pressure to stand against her unyielding opinion. She released her arms from him and abruptly stepped away. "Are you siding with Will?"

"It's not a question of sides, Audrey." He stepped toward her and pulled her to him. "You haven't talked to your mother since the hospital."

"I want to see Gram first."

Hugo ran his fingers over her cheek. "Whenever you decide to go, it's a visit you should make without me." He leaned his head down and kissed her, and he felt her body relax in his arms.

After Audrey had left, Hugo's mind remained unsettled. *If anyone's heart is broken, it will be mine.* Those words from Will, that night in the hospital, returned to him and were matched by Vivienne's bold defense of Will. *We wouldn't be having this conversation if I didn't accept his advances.*

As he headed to another meeting, his mind kept drifting to what just took place in his office. In light of what he had heard from Will, after three long, tension-packed hours, discussing the release of headline-breaking news, he sent Audrey a text and grabbed his keys.

*Have to meet a client outside the office. I'll see U at home later.*

***

Though he had Will's apartment key, he rang the bell first. When a second ring produced no answer, he let himself in. The apartment was quiet, except for a barely audible voice coming from the TV. Hugo grimaced at the stale odor of liquor.

Will was sprawled on the couch in nothing but his boxers, pointing his remote at the TV, unaware that Hugo had even entered his apartment.

"Will," Hugo called.

He turned his head slowly, his glazed and bloodshot eyes focusing on his father. "Did you know there have been 6,504 wildfires in California in the current year?"

"Why are you doing this?"

"Why not? Since I have a whole lotta nothin' goin' on in my life, I thought I would have some friends over. Don Julio, Jim Beam, Johnny Walker. I wanted to celebrate my good news. Vivienne left me." Will picked up the closest bottle. "You wanna join us?"

Hugo put up his hand. "I'm good."

"Suit yourself." Will lifted the bottle to his lips to polish off what was left.

"Okay. You've had enough. Let's get you in the shower."

Too drunk to argue, Will stumbled into the bathroom with the help of his father's strong arm under his shoulders.

Hugo had already cleaned up the empty bottles by the time Will made a slow return after the shower.

He sat on the couch and rested his elbows on his thighs while holding his head in his hands.

"I made a pot of coffee," Hugo said.

Will raised his head, and his still-foggy eyes focused on his father. "Why did you come here?"

"Because I feel there's more to this than who's right or wrong for whom."

"I thought if I could be the man she needed, everything would work out. I know now that love wasn't in the cards for me. I was dealt a hand that I had to play for her happiness. I love her, Dad, but all the trying in the world can't make the pieces fit. Her heart is broken and mine is in a shambles."

Hugo lowered himself onto the armchair opposite Will. He let the words settle and contemplated the scope of everyone's emotions, all tangled in a fight to save love, or see it die. "When I decided to end my relationship with Audrey, she was devastated."

"I remember." Will rubbed his numb lips. "It was my shoulder she cried on, and that's what makes this so unfair. She wasn't a nun when you met her. I could have made a list of every man she slept with...as a reason to keep you apart, but I was glad when she found happiness with you, Dad. This wedding means a lot to the both of you, so I'll step aside as Best Man. If it's one thing weddings don't want, it's an unhappy bride."

"Let me handle Audrey. Make things right in your life, Will."

Will looked at his father with eyes questioning, hoping. "What are you saying?"

"Is Vivienne who your heart wants?"

"More than anything, Dad."

"So, what are you going to do about it? Sit here and wallow in self-pity?" Hugo went to Will's bathroom and came back with two aspirin. "Take these and get some sleep to clear your head."

"Why are you doing this?"

"Vivienne and I both share the heartbreak of losing someone and filling that loss with someone we never expected."

Before he left, Hugo stood at the door and looked back into the living room. Now that Will had fallen asleep, Hugo's thoughts shifted to Audrey's upcoming visit to see her grandmother. *Will she finally give in and talk to her mother?*

***

When Vivienne woke, her eyes burned from too little sleep and too many tears. Today was her mom's first day back, and it would have been Will that she shared it with. But she thought better and put her phone down, knowing how hard their last time together was for both of them.

She arrived at her mom's place, surprised to see her dressed and sitting in her chair in the living room.

"How long have you been up?"

"Six. I couldn't sleep."

Vivienne threw in a white lie for good measure. "I couldn't either. I'm excited, too. Have you had breakfast?"

"Cereal."

"I'll make you tea when we get there, and you can have one of Auggie's muffins."

People were standing in line when Vivienne double-parked out front. "Wait here. I'm getting someone to help you in."

Minutes later, Brendan was beside Vivienne, helping Esty out.

"Take your time, Esty," he urged. Locals, along with folks who frequented the restaurant, were watching and began to clap. Soon, the sound of whistling and cheering came from everyone as Esty slowly made her way to the door.

Vivienne held it open. "Welcome back, Mom."

Esty's eyes were filled with a million reasons why she needed to be there as she scanned the bustling restaurant. The wait staff took a moment in turn, from their tables, to welcome her back.

She looked at Vivienne and smiled. "Home."

"Yes, you are, Mom."

The last to welcome Esty were the kitchen staff, who bellowed in unison, "Welcome back, Esty!" The pots of chowder, and Esty's chair, were ready for her. As she promised, Vivienne took one of Auggie's muffins from the oven and set it on the counter to cool while she made her a cup of tea. With her mother settled, she grabbed an apron and went out front behind the counter.

Even with Esty's feisty determination, the couple of hours proved more than enough for her first day. After Brendan had helped her into Vivienne's car, Esty rested her head against the seatback. "I'm tired."

"I'm not surprised, Mom. Your mind may be ready for work, but your stamina has a long way to go before it catches up."

Esty's steps mirrored her fatigue, and Vivienne took each slow step with her until she had her resting comfortably in her living room. Feeling the vibration of an incoming call, Vivienne reached into her pocket and, seeing Will's name, turned to her mother. "Mom, I'll be right back. I have to take this call."

She stood outside, with the front door as a buffer. "I wasn't expecting to hear from you. This is only going to make the situation harder."

"For whom. You? Me?"

Questioning her feelings only served to get under her skin. "I can't believe you're saying that. Who do you think? For both of us. It upsets me that you have doubts about my feelings for you."

"I don't, baby. I'm upset, too. Can't we tackle this together?"

"I have to do this alone, Will. And that's if I can even get Evan and Audrey to talk to me."

"Well, I should feel special, then. Audrey spoke to me yesterday."

It wasn't that Audrey had finally ended her streak of silence, but how, as she listened to Will repeat Audrey's unwavering feelings about them.

He then drew on the conviction of his father's words. "I'm not giving up on us. This isn't over, Vivienne. I feel it, and I know you feel it, too."

"I do, Will, but this whole mess of a problem is the last thing you need. Soon, it will become too much jumping through hoops when you can just pick up the phone and ask another woman to dinner."

"I don't want to ask another woman to dinner. I'm asking my girl, and nothing is too much for you, baby."

"We can't talk about this now. It was my mom's first couple of hours back at the restaurant. I just brought her home and she's exhausted."

"That must have meant a lot to you."

"It did, and to her, too. I'll call you when I know more."

"Being apart doesn't mean I stopped loving you."

"I love you, too." When she ended the call, she feared that, in the face of a prolonged separation, the life expectancy of his words wouldn't be long. She took a moment to compose her emotions before going inside. She expected Esty to be asleep in her chair but found her alert with her eyes on the door.

"I thought you would be asleep by now."

"My mind is troubled."

Vivienne knelt down in front of her and took her hands, giving them a gentle, encouraging squeeze. "Please don't worry, Mom. You did well for your first day. Helen will be so proud when I tell her."

"Not me. You."

All her mother's prodding wasn't going to chip away at Vivienne's wall of secrecy. "The stress of Nate's funeral and running the restaurant—"

"I saw him."

Esty's words grabbed Vivienne's attention. "Who, Mom?"

"You're too old to play innocent with me. I saw him holding your hand at Audrey's party. Hugo's son, Will."

"You remembered his name?" Vivienne pulled one of Esty's chairs over and sat in front of her. "It's not what you're thinking, Mom. We were just having some fun, because he didn't bring a date and I am...well, a widow. Now that I think of it, maybe I should have asked Liam to escort me."

Esty flung her hand up in disgust. "Bah! He's an old coot."

Vivienne was pulled in by Esty's hearty laugh that jiggled her belly and shook her rounded shoulders.

"He's not an old coot, Mom. I think he's good-looking, and he's Nate's age. Did you think Nate was an old coot?"

"I had other words for him."

"I know, but Liam is just looking for companionship. Okay, maybe more. He took it hard when Charlotte left him."

That same hand then touched Vivienne's cheek. "He's not for you. You're too beautiful."

"And you're biased." She kissed her mother's forehead, just as the doorbell rang. "That must be Helen."

Over tea and cookies, Helen listened intently, her brows rising, and her broad smile showing her pride as Vivienne described Esty's first day at the restaurant.

"I feel as if I were there with you, Esty." She reached for her hand. "Remember. There are no barriers for one whose mind doesn't see any."

Those words may have been meant for Esty, yet Vivienne was energized by their power. She left Esty's house repeating them, becoming her silent mantra for the hurdles ahead.

# Chapter 18

The restaurant could be likened to an orchestra with no conductor: utensils clanging, people talking, an occasional dish hitting the floor. But these collective sounds all came together in one beautiful orchestral piece. Yet, they couldn't drown out Vivienne's thoughts that followed her from breakfast to dinner, thoughts of Audrey driving to see her grandmother tomorrow.

Caleb was among the first people to park his faded overalls at the counter. Vivienne knew to fill a mug of coffee and placed it before him with the dinner menu.

"How's Esty?" he asked, looking above his bifocals.

"Resting at home. The first couple of hours back were harder than she expected."

"You can't keep a good woman down."

"Surf n' turf!" Auggie called, sliding the order under the heat lamps.

Vivienne picked it up for a customer at the end of the counter, just as Evan walked in with his crew.

Getting Heidi's attention with a lift of her arm: "Table 8, Heidi."

She kept her focus on the counter customers, but couldn't help making eye contact with Evan, and the chilly glance he gave her as he passed by.

She found herself lifting her eyes toward their table for a quick second, every now and then, as they were eating. Behind Evan's smile and laughter, Vivienne wondered if he was feeling the same tension as she was. When Hannah finally brought their empty plates to the kitchen, she followed.

"Can I see their tab, please?" Vivienne asked and quickly ran down the receipt. "I'll take care of this, Hannah."

"Sure, Vivienne."

She approached Evan's table, feigning the confidence she didn't have inside, with a smile. "Did you all enjoy dinner?"

Beck, one of Evan's crew, leaned back and patted his stomach.

"Only thing better than catching lobsters is eating them at *Callane's*."

Vivienne chuckled. "I can tell from that empty carcass on your plate in the kitchen, and all your empty plates, for that matter."

Jaxon, another of Evan's crew, added, "No better place to eat after a long day on the water."

That Evan sat in silence, with his eyes on her, only made it more uncomfortable for Vivienne. "I'm glad Evan brought you all in for dinner. Hannah will be back with the dessert menus. Everything's on the house tonight."

"Thank you, Vivienne." "I'm gonna roll out of here, Vivienne." "Evan is one lucky guy."

Of all the compliments, the last one was like a stab to her heart. She looked directly at Evan and sent her words home. "I'm sure he knows that."

Vivienne was clearing empty plates and cleaning the counter, as Evan's crew headed out.

"Good night, Vivienne," each of them said in turn. Evan followed last and stopped at the counter for a moment.

"Tory liked the Spinosaurus you bought him for his birthday."

It was a shot in the dark, but Vivienne jumped on the chance to stall Evan for another minute of conversation. "Grace mentioned it was his favorite dinosaur." Vivienne paused for a moment to gage his reception to her comment, but not too long. "You know, it means a lot to your grandmother, that you make time to visit her. She realizes you have a lot on your plate."

When Evan lowered his eyes, Vivienne knew he felt pressured to keep up the conversation, as he looked at the green-speckled counter while he searched for words. "It's hard, being out on the water all day, getting the catch to the market, finding time for Grace and Tory. I do my best."

"I know you do, Evan, and I'm proud of you."

Vivienne's words struck a nerve between a mother and son. As he raised his eyes to her, she could see the internal struggle he was battling. Her heart ached for him, and she held her breath, hoping to hear him end the division between them. Yet, it was his father's obstinate nature that made his words take a different direction.

"Audrey called me. She's visiting Gram tomorrow. I'm having Beck handle the catch, so I can be there."

"Gram will be happy to see you both together. With your busy lives, that doesn't happen often anymore."

"She told me about you and Will."

She shrugged. "What can I say? What's done is done." She then pointed to his crew waiting at the door. "I think my time is up. It was good seeing you, Evan."

She turned and left him at the counter, taking her much-needed refuge in the kitchen.

***

Before Vivienne turned out the lights, she stood at the door and glanced once more into the quiet space that was bustling with noise just a few short hours ago. On the street, the lights from the other shops had gone out, as well. The town was asleep, but a warm glow shown from inside the houses as she walked by. The hurricane lamps, illuminated on either side of her front door, were a beacon guiding her home. But her troubled mind was steering her feet in a different direction. Once again, she pushed open the rusty iron gate that moaned in the quiet. It was a lonely place, but loneliness was already her closest companion. She found a strange comfort in the silent solitude among the dead; they, at least, asked nothing of her. Only the chirping of the crickets and an occasional *ribbit* broke the silence. Her dockers settled slightly with each step on the damp grass as she made her way to Nate's resting place.

She stood there, gathering her thoughts, and feeling as if the inhabitants under all the headstones were saying *hurry up, already!*

"I'm in love. With Will. I thought it was only right that I tell you. But before you go rolling over in your grave, we're not together. You have Audrey and Evan to thank for that. They still have you on this pedestal, Nate, but I suspect your ratings would have hit the skids if they knew what I hid from them. How you kept your illness from me, trading the support I would have given you for a barstool at the Fore N' Aft. But don't worry, I'm not in the business of retaliation. Your secret's safe with me. I don't know if I'm meant to be with Will, but what I do know is that I've been able to love with such passion in the short time I had with him to erase the memory of those years you left me alone. And for that, he will always have my heart. There weren't many times when I asked you for something that was important to me. I'm going to ask now. Whatever capabilities this next plain of life has afforded you, I hope you can give Audrey and Evan the insight to let me live my life and accept the love you denied me for so long."

Vivienne paused for a moment and scanned some of the gray chipped headstones of the other folks. "I hope I didn't keep you awake," she whispered.

When she turned to leave, it was Magda she saw standing in the distance, holding a bottle of wine. With slow steps, Vivienne trudged up the path toward her.

"I went to your house after dinner, thought you might want to share this," Magda began. "When you didn't answer the bell, I had a feeling you would be here. But don't worry, I wasn't eavesdropping."

"I didn't say anything you don't already know, except that Evan initiated a conversation with me at the restaurant today."

When they reached Vivienne's house, she had walked Magda through everything that happened.

"You've had a day, Viv. You could use this." Magda held up the bottle of wine.

On Vivienne's patio were two chaise lounges and a table between them made of teak that had aged to a silvery-gray patina from years of exposure to the Cape's weather. She set the wine glasses down while Magda popped the cork and then poured the wine.

"I guess Evan felt obligated to thank me for Tory's birthday gift," Vivienne said. "By the way, this is an excellent bottle of wine."

"Owen brought over this one...and a nice Malbec, which we had last night with dinner."

"This is the longest you've been with someone, since Griff," Vivienne commented. "What's different about you and Owen?"

"We accept what each of us has to give, nothing more, and that works for us. He has his place, and I have mine. We see each other when it suits us both. Do we love each other? Yes, and neither of us are shy about showing it. Where this is going is where it takes us each day. But it's not Owen and I that we were talking about. So, Evan will be with Audrey when she visits Esty tomorrow. Should make for an interesting visit, to say the least."

"I get the feeling I'll be the main topic of conversation."

"Your mother's a sly one." Magda poured a little more wine into both their glasses. "She knew something was up at the hospital, and she's been prodding you ever since. Mark my words, before her visit with Audrey and Evan is over, she'll have pieced everything together."

"I don't know whether to be relieved or terrified." The wine gave

Vivienne the courage to admit her deepest fear. "If she sides with them, she may be the next person that cuts me off."

"Esty? Not a chance in hell. If anyone has your back, it's your mom and me. Are you forgetting, we're the only two who know what you went through with Nate? You're overdue for some love in your life, Viv. As far as Will is concerned, your mom may be old, but the heart's memory of falling in love never grows old. And then there's this. Your mom likes him."

"All this talk, and the wine, makes me want to call him. I know sex doesn't solve problems, but I want him here, in my arms, in bed with me."

"It sure can make for one hell of a good time trying. You know this is far from over. If Will didn't love you, he would have thrown his hands up at the first sign of trouble."

"Well, he's got a shit load of that now."

Magda's laugh brought a lightness to the conversation. "He sure has." She held up her glass one last time. Vivienne followed, and the tiny *tink* their glasses made as they touched was carried away by the evening breeze, along with Magda's words. "And all in the name of love."

# Chapter 19

*Emma, the Maid of Honor, had tears in her eyes as Audrey entered the church.*

*"What's wrong, Emma?"*

*"You can't get married, Audrey."*

*"Why are you saying that? What's wrong?"*

*"There are no wedding rings."*

*Even through Audrey's blusher, Emma could see relief wash over her face. "That's silly. Will has the rings."*

*But Audrey's response only increased Emma's tears. "You never included your mother in the wedding. She's not here, so neither is Will."*

*Her heart shattered as she stood in the vestibule, her tearful eyes focused on Hugo waiting for her at the altar, alone, without Will as his Best Man. As the organist began playing the wedding march, Hugo turned and left the altar.*

Audrey's eyes flew open as she sat up. Like bullets, they darted around the room, searching for something familiar to calm her racing heart. But it was Hugo's arm around her shoulder, and his voice, that pulled her from the lingering images of her night terror.

He held her close but could feel her shaking in his arms. "It's okay, Audrey. You just had a bad dream."

"This was literally my worst nightmare, Hugo. We couldn't get married because there were no wedding rings. When I told Emma that Will had them, she said he wasn't there because Mom wasn't invited. It was all my fault."

"It's just reflective of what's going on right now. This conflict with your mother is clearly bothering you. It isn't something you can just push under the rug. You're seeing your grandmother today. Won't you consider making time to talk to your mother?"

Audrey leaned back on the bed and closed her eyes. "Right now, I won't consider anything that doesn't relieve the splitting headache I have."

Hugo sighed at Audrey's resistance and swung his legs out of bed. He returned with two aspirin and offered them to her. "You'll feel better in a few minutes."

She lay there, listening to Hugo's puttering in the kitchen while the aspirin slowly made its way to her throbbing head. Finally feeling better, she decided to drown the lingering pain with a good dose of caffeine. Taking Hugo's fresh brewed coffee with her into the bathroom, she stepped out of the shower refreshed and ready to finish packing her bag for the weekend.

Audrey's duffle was at her feet as she stood at the door in Hugo's arms. Her eyes lifted to his, eyes that held the future he promised her in the tenderness of his kiss.

"Any plans for the weekend?" she asked, wiping the bit of her red lipstick from his lips.

"Let's see. Catch up on some reading, do laundry, watch the ballgame at *The Pru* while I have dinner at the bar, and dream of you, baby."

"Makes me a little jealous. Your weekend sounds much better. Any chance I can persuade you to switch with me?"

"I'm just killing time until you get back. I can't do this for you. Call me when you get there."

"I will." She kissed him once more before she left.

With the faint swish of the washer in the background, Hugo settled in the living room with a cup of coffee and the latest espionage novel on the bestseller list. He was enjoying the first few chapters, when his mind began to wander. He reached for his phone and called Will, listening to the rings until he picked up.

"Hey, Dad. This is a surprise. What prompted this call?"

"You, actually. Audrey will be in Wellfleet for the weekend."

"She's seeing her grandmother. Vivienne mentioned it."

"I know you're not scheduled for a review tonight, and I was going to have dinner at *The Pru.* You wanna join me?"

"You sure you want me around, Dad? I'm missing Vivienne and not in the best frame of mind."

"All the more reason to get out of the house. Come by around eight, and we'll walk over."

"In that case, there's something I want to discuss with you. I'll see you then."

Will's comment made him pause in thought when he ended the call. *Could it be about him and Vivienne?* He put the coffee to his lips and grimaced, finding that it was now lukewarm. Switching to the novel, he was about to reach an intriguing part of the story when his phone announced an incoming call from Audrey. "Hey, baby. How was the drive?"

"Smooth sailing until I got onto the Cape. I hit some traffic. Saturday is check-in day for vacationers. I should have booked a suite. They have me in one of their *cozy* rooms. Cozy as a broom closet."

Hugo chuckled. "It can't be that bad. I think you can handle one night. What time are you meeting Evan?"

"I texted him when I got here. Gram is expecting us soon. He's picking me up."

"I'm sure your grandmother will be happy to see you. Don't worry about calling. Just enjoy the time with your family."

"Are you still going to *The Pru*?"

"That's the plan."

"Keep your eyes off the pulchritude."

Hugo chuckled. "I only have eyes for you, baby."

He rested the book on his lap and rubbed his forehead. *Would Audrey try to end the division with her mother? Can Will and Vivienne find a place in each other's lives?* Having no answer for either thought, he decided to wash his worries down the shower drain, for now.

When the bell rang, Hugo looked at the time while he was putting his wallet in the back pocket of his jeans. He rushed to open the door.

Will smiled as he looked down at his own faded jeans. "Wow! Audrey lets you wear those?" He stepped into the foyer while his dad turned on the table lamp near the couch.

"Not when she's around. She likes the more fitted jeans I have. I prefer these because they're relaxed. She thinks they make me look old."

Will chuckled. "You are old, Dad, but the jeans? They look ready for a night at *The Pru*."

***

*The Pru* was a gold mine. During the week, locals would flock there to wind down after work and catch the latest sports on the bar's numerous screens or get in a game of pool. Weekends brought in tourists looking to grab a table and sample their famous Shepherd's Pie.

Hugo put his name down for a table before they made their way through the crowd. Standing two-deep at the bar, he raised up his hand, getting the attention of the owner, Declan O'Sullivan. "Two Buds, Dec," he shouted above the din of conversations.

Some of Will's friends acknowledged him as they were heading out. "Haven't seen you in a dog's age, Will. Still off the market?" one of them called out.

Not to battle the noise, he just answered with a *thumbs up*.

Hugo held up his bottle, and Will followed. "Cheers."

Will downed the first sip. "Nothing beats an ice-cold Bud."

"Have you talked to Vivienne?"

"I did, but not much has changed. Her kids won't talk to her, she's worried about her mom, she has the restaurant to run. Doesn't leave much room for us."

Hugo tread carefully with his next words. "Maybe it's not just Vivienne that needs room."

"Actually, that's what I want to talk to you about. Do you remember last year, one of my professors at the Culinary Institute of America called and asked if I would be interested in teaching a semester on restaurant reviews?"

"I do remember that."

"He mentioned that the faculty was considering adding a course on that. I told him the timing was off, and that I'd just started working at The Tribune. Yesterday, just on a fly, I called him back."

Will's unexpected news was interrupted by a text on Hugo's phone, notifying them their table was ready. Once seated, Hugo's brows arched high, deepening the lines in his forehead. "When I said it's not just Vivienne that needs room, I wasn't thinking about that much room! You want to leave The Tribune and move to New York?"

"It's not permanent, Dad, just a sabbatical. I don't see her situation getting any better. Maybe some space will give everyone's emotions a chance to calm down. Anyway, my professor was very interested in starting up this conversation between us again."

"Welcome to *The Pru*," the waitress announced, unaware that she had interrupted their conversation. "I'm Fiona, and I'll be your server tonight." She wore a black t-shirt with *The Pru* in white lettering across her chest. Her flaming red hair was twisted in a lazy braid that flowed down her breast, almost to her waist. Not a stitch of makeup was needed to enhance the deep blue of her eyes, or her youthful skin, dotted with a sprinkling of freckles across her nose and cheeks.

"I see you both have Budweisers that look almost finished. Can

I get you refills while you look at the menu or start you off with some appetizers?"

"Yes, on the refills, and yes, we'll start with the loaded nachos," Hugo replied. "And can you put us down for a game of pool?"

Her smile puffed her cheeks. "Of course! I'll be right back."

"You have to admit, Dad, it's not the best scenario at work. People are noticing the tension between me and Audrey. I'm sure the *breakroom gang* have their own suspicions. Don't get me wrong, I can play the silent treatment game with her until hell freezes over, but you have a wedding in a few months."

Will's comment brought Audrey's nightmare that morning to Hugo's mind. "She hasn't been herself since that blowup at the hospital."

Will held up his palms. "I rest my case. You wanna live with *Bridezilla?*"

So involved in their talk, they didn't notice how quickly Fiona returned with their appetizer, beers, and slot for pool. "I can put in your dinner orders, if you're ready."

"I'll have the Reuben," Hugo said.

"The Shepherd's Pie for me," Will added.

"I appreciate that you're willing to remove yourself from this equation, Will, but have you thought about what your leaving will mean to Vivienne? From the things she's said, I know she loves you."

"I love her, too, Dad, but if my being in her life isn't settled with Audrey and Evan, there's no difference with us being apart, whether I live in Bawstin or New York."

"Your argument could win over a jury." Hugo downed a slug of beer. "When will you hear from your professor?"

"He has to discuss it with the faculty. Believe me, it's not a conversation I'm looking forward to having with her."

"I asked Audrey to see her mother while she's in Wellfleet. I hope she does. This is one grudge she's going to regret holding for so long."

"Evan has a part in this, too, Dad. Neither of them can see beyond their own feelings."

Hugo's thoughts silenced him, taking his gaze somewhere distant for a moment. "I know you want Vivienne to be happy," he finally said. "I admit, I had doubts about your intentions in the beginning, but the choice you're considering is not about what you want. You thought about Vivienne first and bringing her and her family together. That's a selfless act of love."

Will managed a small, grateful smile. "Thanks, Dad. It means a lot to hear you say that."

"Just promise me you'll keep in touch." Hugo reached over the table to squeeze Will's shoulder.

"I promise, Dad, but I'm not going anywhere yet."

***

With one leg crossed over the other, Audrey's sandaled foot gently pushed her in the rocker while she waited for Evan on the front porch of the Inn. She was scanning the emails on her phone when the approaching sound of a bad muffler lifted her eyes to see Evan's black flatbed up ahead. When he pulled up in front, she picked up the small giftbag next to the rocker and noticed Evan peering through the windshield at Hugo's sportscar.

"That's some set of wheels. Is that your car?"

She climbed in. "It's Hugo's. I could hear you all the way up the street."

"I need a muffler."

"Where's the seatbelt buckle?" She fumbled around to find it.

Evan huffed, as he took the seatbelt from her hands. "I'll do it." When he heard the click, he put his hand on the shifter and made his way toward Main Street. "What's in the bag?"

"A framed picture of me, Hugo and Gram, taken at our engagement party. I thought she might like it."

When Evan turned onto Main Street, Audrey's stomach began to feel the jitters of tension, knowing the restaurant was up ahead.

Her eyes darted to Evan, as he pulled the truck toward the curb. "Why are we stopping here?"

"Gram likes this bakery, so I'm getting some of her favorite pastries." He left the engine running.

Audrey looked straight ahead, not daring to turn her head toward the left, fearing she would see someone she knew in front of the restaurant. She glanced at the pastry shop window and huffed, watching the woman behind the counter fill a box large enough to feed a party of ten while Evan pointed here and there at the glass case. She wanted to reach over and hit the horn, but thought again, knowing it would only attract attention. Her eyes rolled when Evan exited the shop.

"How many pastries can one little woman eat, Evan? Are you looking to make diabetes her next illness?"

He shot her a quick, annoyed glance. "Don't go getting all Dr. Oz on me, Audrey. I saw you bringing Gram a plate full of desserts at your engagement party. Besides, these won't go to waste. Her PT nurse, Helen, sees her a couple of times a week, and Mom stops by, too."

"Fine." She quickly eyed the clothes in Magda's store window as they passed by.

Evan pulled his eyes off the road for a second. "What crawled up your ass?"

As quick as he asked, she turned her gaze to him. "I'm just not in the mood to run into Mom, okay?"

When they approached Esty's retirement community, Evan lowered his window and pressed the code for the entry gate. He lowered his speed to the pace of the residents and parked in front of Esty's door.

Audrey stepped out of the truck and ran her hand down the front of her sundress to smooth the non-existent winkles. She stood next to Evan as he rang the bell, suddenly feeling worried, a little too late, at not visiting her grandmother sooner.

"Just a minute," they finally heard, followed by Esty's smile greeting them.

Audrey immediately went from worried to an overcompensating smile. She stepped toward Esty first and kissed her cheek. "Gram! It's so good to see you."

Having visited his grandmother often, Evan let Audrey have her moment in the spotlight. "Hi, Gram," he finally said, taking note to kiss her other cheek.

"Take these." Evan handed Audrey the box of pastries. He then took over, walking next to Esty to be a support to her as she headed to her chair with the help of her cane.

With the giftbag dangling on her arm, and the box in her hands, Audrey walked at a snail's pace behind them, rolling her eyes while she listened to Evan boast. "I brought your favorite pastries, Gram. You want one?"

"Not now," Esty said.

Evan made her comfortable in her chair.

"Sit with me. You and Audrey."

They each took one of the kitchen chairs to sit in front of her. "How was your first day back at the restaurant?" Audrey asked.

"I was tired, but happy to get back."

"I know you're gonna make a stink," Evan said, "but I'm gonna say it anyway. Maybe it's too soon, Gram."

A flit of her hand dismissed Evan's feeling. "Agh! I'm no China doll. I'm fine."

Audrey then showed her the giftbag and removed the frame for her. "I thought you would like this."

Esty's eyes didn't move from the photo, becoming teary as the memory of that day resurfaced. "You look beautiful, Audrey, but I always said there's no one more beautiful than my granddaughter."

"And Mom bought you a new dress from Magda's store. You look so nice, Gram."

"Tell me about the wedding."

"It's going to be on the beach, Gram. We just got the invitations back from the printer. I had the designer draw seashells in the corners."

"Seashells! You love the beach." But then the light in her eyes dimmed, and a frown replaced her smile.

Audrey reached to touch her hand. "Gram, what's wrong?"

"I told your mother you were visiting me today and asked her if she wanted to stop by. She said the restaurant was too busy. Why didn't she want to be here?"

The moment arrived sooner than Audrey and Evan expected. They shared a glance before Audrey said, "We know why, Gram. Evan and I want to talk to you about something."

Esty listened as each word they spoke resurrected that dreadful night in the hospital. Like a blank page, her face was unreadable, until they ended with the disastrous results that were now placed before her.

"Audrey, can you please make some tea for us?"

"Sure, Gram. Evan, please bring Gram to the kitchen when it's ready." Rising quickly, she found little refuge there to gather her thoughts, only the five or ten minutes it took for the water to boil in the kettle.

To their surprise, it was Esty who began the conversation as they sat around her small kitchen table.

"Why are you both angry?"

Her question took the first stab at Evan's perception of what happened, putting him on the defensive. "Why? Did Mom tell you about all this already?"

"No. Your mother has too much integrity."

Evan wasn't convinced. "She didn't say anything?"

"Not a word, Evan."

"Mom should have been here that night. Not gallivanting in Boston."

"Did you think I would have a stroke?"

"No, but—"

"Then how could your mother have known?"

Evan's anger rose. "She could have come home, Gram. She dishonored her husband by sleeping with that guy."

"No!" Esty slammed her hand on the table, making Audrey and Evan jump in their chairs. "Things are not always what they seem."

"Huh?" Evan winced.

Esty's fierce defense of Vivienne held them captive. They listened in stunned silence as she revealed a chapter in their mother's life that Evan and Audrey knew nothing about.

"Life was good. You were both settled in your lives. The restaurant was thriving. It was what your mother and father envisioned, until the steady rhythm of life began to break. It started with your father stopping occasionally at the Fore N Aft with his crew at the end of the day. Your mother grew concerned when it became more frequent."

"Didn't she try to talk to him?" Audrey asked.

"He called it *bonding* with his crew. Soon, your mother began to dread the end of every day. The smell of stale beer and smoke clung to his clothes and forced her to hold her breath as he slurred his anger at her frustration."

Evan ran his hand through his hair. "I'd see him there when I was out with my friends. I had no idea it was every night."

"By the time he stopped his incoherent shouting, and passed out wherever he landed, your mother faced the cold reality that the man she would wait for at the end of the day was gone, long before he stumbled in the front door. She didn't lose your father the morning he died in the living room. She lost him in increments, one drink at a time, until there was nothing left but the hollow shell of a man she didn't recognize."

Audrey gasped and covered her mouth. She felt her eyes beginning to sting with the rise of tears. "When we were all together, she was always smiling and happy. Why didn't she tell us?"

"It was her burden, not yours. She didn't know he was ill until he passed away. The doctors told her he didn't want anyone in his family to know about his illness."

"I need a little air." Evan rose from his chair and walked out.

Audrey's voice quivered with emotion. "He's always had our father on a pedestal, Gram. This is a different man you showed us."

"It's your mother who should be on that pedestal. And tell me, why she shouldn't be with Will?"

"I know him. He's going to break her heart."

Esty lifted her knotted index finger. "You've already done that, telling me you've kept her from your wedding plans, and how do you know what Will's feelings are for her? Only your mother can tell you. She's a grown woman who has earned the right to make her own decisions, good or bad. Leave her be and apologize to her."

If Audrey couldn't abide by Hugo's wishes and speak to her mother, as he'd asked, he would have been disappointed, but she knew that he would still marry her. Looking into her grandmother's pleading eyes, and breaking that same promise, was something she wouldn't dare do. Audrey lifted her grandmother's hand and kissed it. "I promise to apologize to her, Gram."

"I'd like to sit in the living room now."

Audrey took each slow step with Esty, then adjusted the pillow on her chair.

Evan returned. "I'm sorry I left, Gram. This isn't who I thought my father was."

"Come sit by me." Revealing these harsh truths left Esty feeling drained, yet her relentless disapproval of Nate's treatment of Vivienne gave her enough gumption to chastise Evan. "Remember what I told you today! Let it remind you to put Grace and Tory before everything. Your father's gone, but your mother is still here. Repair this division you and Audrey have with her. Don't force her to live the life *you* see for her. Let her live the life *she wants* for herself."

"We need to talk to her, Evan," Audrey added.

"I'll never be able to take back those words I said to her," he muttered. "Yet, she spoke to me the last time I was in the restaurant."

Esty touched his arm. "Because she loves you, Evan. Love doesn't hold grudges."

"I can't promise I won't stew over the next *issue* in my life,"

Audrey said, "but I can promise her that I'm letting this one go."

Tears filled Esty's eyes. Tears that finally released the silent burden she carried with her daughter.

"The truth is finally out. The secret can no longer hurt your mother. It has no more power over her."

Evan caught her tears with his handkerchief. "We'll make things right, Gram."

Before their quiet exit, they turned to look at their grandmother. Time had rushed by like a time-lapsed camera that showed the once vibrant woman, now frail and hunched over in slumber, her hands resting on the blanket Audrey placed on her legs.

The revelation of their mother's life, revealed to them over the last couple of hours, left them silent, each wondering what the other was thinking as they climbed in the truck. Evan reached over to clip Audrey's seatbelt. "We need to go to the cemetery."

Audrey's sandals sank along the soggy path, and dirt collected, like clay, in the grooves on the bottom of Evan's boots.

Evan read aloud the inscription of his father's headstone. "Nathaniel Callane. Fisherman. Beloved husband and father. How could Mom write that, knowing he wasn't what she needed him to be?"

"Because it was easier to live a lie." Audrey sobbed. "We just didn't know."

"You really fucked things up, Dad," Evan said to the tombstone. "I can't change what happened between you and Mom, but I can make things easier for her. I accused her of dishonoring you, but keeping your illness from her, you broke your vow, *in sickness and in health.* I'll never again presume to know what she needs in her life."

When it began to rain, they ran across the damp grass and found refuge in the truck, but not before the heavens opened on them.

"I'm leaving tomorrow morning," Audrey said. "Let's go to the restaurant tonight...before it closes. We can sit down and talk to her with no one around."

"How about I take you to the hotel," Evan suggested, "and you change out of those wet clothes. I'll pick you up, and you can have dinner at my house. Grace and I wouldn't want you eating alone, and Tory would love to see his Aunt Audrey. We can see Mom after."

"I'd love that. Thanks, Evan."

***

The dinner crowd began to lighten toward the end of the day. The kitchen wasn't cooking at warp speed, and the wait staff downshifted their pace to accommodate fewer customers. Vivienne took a minute to pour herself a cup of coffee. Will's number lit up her phone. With the counter customers well into their dinners, she quickly headed to the back of the kitchen, which afforded her a little privacy. "This is a pleasant surprise."

"I thought I would call to see if you heard some good news. Wasn't Audrey supposed to visit her grandmother today?"

"Yes, and I haven't heard a word from her, or my mother. It doesn't look promising."

"I'm sorry, baby. I think it would have made things worse if I tried to help. Maybe your idea to work this out without me wasn't such a bad idea."

The sudden switch in his eagerness to help her sat in her stomach like a bitter pill she was forced to swallow. "What do you mean?"

"Last year, my professor at the Culinary Institute called and asked if I would be interested in teaching a new course they wanted to offer on restaurant reviews. At the time, I had just started my job at The Tribune, but I think this is a good time to take him up on his offer."

Vivienne's heart sank, but she revealed not an ounce of emotion. "It's been a year. Are you sure the position is still available?"

"I spoke to him the other day. It's mine, if I want it."

She kept her voice from trembling. "Do you?"

"I leave tomorrow. It's only a semester, Viv. Maybe things will have calmed down by then."

A lump began to form in her throat, yet she wouldn't let her feelings compromise his decision. "I'm relieved that you can see this situation with a clear head," she heard herself reply, though every bit of her wanted to hold him to the promise he made, *'I only know I want those strings around me, tied to you.'* "This is an opportunity that I wouldn't want you to pass up. I'm happy for you."

"New York is not that far away. We can still see each other. I love you, baby."

He'd finally found a reason not to stay, but she wouldn't be the woman who would try to keep him from leaving. Vivienne recognized the script. New York wasn't far, but the distance he was creating in that moment was immeasurable. 'I love you, baby,' felt like the necessary period at the end of their sentence. The finality settled into her chest, heavier than any goodbye could have been.

She heard herself say, "I love you, too," as tears pooled in her eyes.

She slipped her phone in the pocket of her apron and knew the life expectancy of the words 'I love you, baby,' had just expired.

***

The remnants of fresh-shucked corn, red snapper filets, and baked clams littered their farmhouse table.

Grace said, "Tory made me promise to leave his building blocks on the floor before going to bed."

"I was happy to see that he like them," Audrey replied. "Keen's Toy Store hasn't changed much since I was a kid. And thanks for this luscious dinner. I know this was spur-of-the-moment for both of you."

"Not at all. It's what we were having for dinner tonight. Evan wanted the corn, so he made a run to the grocer for it."

Evan glanced at his watch. "We should head over to the restaurant."

"Let me help Grace first." Audrey stood and began to collect the dishes.

"Leave them, Audrey. It won't take me but a few minutes to clear the table. You and Evan should get to the restaurant before Vivienne closes it."

***

Evan parked across the street from *Callane's*. "The lights are still on."

"I'm a bunch of jitters inside," Audrey said as they crossed the street. "I've said so many hurtful things to her."

"Excuse me?" Evan huffed. "But I believe I've got you beat on *hurtful*." He reached for the door handle but pulled back when the door suddenly opened.

"Hi, Evan," Brendan said. "Are you looking for your mom?"

"Is she still here?"

"She's inside."

Crystal pushed open the kitchen door and, seeing Evan and Audrey, held it open. "Vivienne, you have company."

*Company is another word for paying Auggie overtime. It's the last thing I need right now.* "You should have locked the door and turned the lights out," she said to Crystal, before she brushed past her. "I'm sorry, but the kitchen is..."

Her gasp filled the empty dining room. Her feet were like anchors, keeping her in place, though she wanted to move toward Audrey and Evan.

Auggie stepped out from the kitchen and quickly ushered Crystal toward the door with him. "Good night, Vivienne."

"I wish I knew you were coming. Is Gram alright?"

"She's fine," Evan said, "but we would have risked the chance of you saying no."

"No? Never. Why *are* you here? If it's about Will, you've both been very articulate about your feelings."

"That was Audrey. I was vulgar, Mom, and I'm sorry."

"All of a sudden you're sorry? What's going on?"

"Gram told us everything," Audrey said. "We know about Dad."

Vivienne often wondered how she would feel when or if this time would come. She turned her eyes toward the window and the view of the bay. Floating on calm water, boats had dropped their anchors and lowered their sails for the evening. And Nate came to her mind. "What about your dad?"

"Those years in Hell you kept from us. I can't believe you stayed with him when most women would have walked out. Why didn't you leave, Mom?"

"I'm glad I didn't, Audrey. Your father knew he was ill, but for whatever reason that made sense only to him, he kept it from me. After he passed away, the doctors told me of his demand to keep silent. I'll never know why he didn't put his trust in me. I would have carried that burden with him. His choice to escape the reality of his illness, instead of leaning on me, was a betrayal of the promises we made to each other. *In sickness and in health.* Did he doubt that I was strong enough? Was I ever enough in his eyes? They're hard questions to live with, knowing I'll never receive an answer. I'll never forget the years *before* your father's illness, the *good years.* Now that you both know, it's easier for me to leave the *hard years* behind."

Evan's shoulders heaved with broken sobs, his tears a visible outpouring of his soul's profound sorrow. "I can never take back the horrible things I said to you. Will you ever be able to look at me and not hear those words?"

Vivienne touched his wet cheek, the same cheek that felt the palm of her hand in a moment that seemed impossible to mend, until now. "Not a day goes by that I don't regret what happened between us, but we can forgive each other, Evan, and put this behind us." Vivienne grabbed each of their hands. "I love my family, but when our connection broke, it felt like I had lost both of you."

"Where do I begin?" Audrey said. "I've been wrong about so many things. I thought I had all the answers, but the truth is I didn't have a clue. I've known Will a long time. It's always been *no strings* with any woman he's been with. I couldn't imagine that this time, with you, it would be different."

"It *is*, Audrey, and you can't place blame on him when I wanted his love as much as he did mine." Only hours earlier, her dream of a life with Will had been shattered. Yet, every word she spoke defended him. "I won't tell you the intimate things we talked about, but I'll share with you what he said to me one night over dinner. 'I've always avoided those strings that would tie me to a life I didn't want. I only know I want those strings around me, tied to you.'"

Vivienne's words tore through Audrey's perception of Will. They toppled the bricks of her self-assurance, leaving her with nothing but profound self-doubt. "I was so caught up in my own problems, that I couldn't see past the barrier Will put between himself and any woman who tried to get close to him. You changed that for him, and I'm sorry that I fought you both with such vengeance. I questioned your love for him and failed to trust in his love for you. I've hurt you in ways that are difficult to forgive, but I hope you can because I don't want to get married without you. Will you be there for me, Mom?"

"How could I not?" Vivienne's voice cracked, her emotion palpable. "A wedding is a dream every mother has when their daughter is born."

***

Evening fell on the small town of Wellfleet. Shades were drawn, and *CLOSED* signs hung on the doors, but one light shown through the window at *Callane's*. Vivienne kept the sadness of losing Will to herself, as she, Audrey and Evan found their life together restored again, talking well into the morning hours.

# Chapter 20

The next morning, Vivienne opened her eyes and felt the shift in her life. The division with Audrey and Evan was over, as if the strife had drifted away quietly with yesterday's evening tide. When she rolled over and looked at the pillow where Will had lain his head, she knew the tide had pulled him out, too, leaving her standing on the loveless shore alone. But life would continue as sure as the morning sun rises.

***

She put herself on autopilot and focused on the day ahead of her, the first stop being her mother's. "Mom, I'm here."

Dressed and ready, Esty's pace from her bedroom raised Vivienne's brows. "You're walking much better. How do you feel today?"

"Better than yesterday." Esty headed for the couch. "Audrey and Evan's visit wasn't casual, to say the least, but before we go, I want to talk to you."

"They came to the restaurant last night..." Vivienne began, but the touch of Esty's hand on her arm silenced her.

"Why didn't you tell me?" Esty asked.

"I didn't want to worry you over what happened between us."

"No, Vivienne. Why didn't you tell me you're in love?"

"I couldn't risk losing you over Will, too."

"Risk losing me?" Esty threw up her hands. "Agh! Who you choose to let into your life is none of their business, or mine, and I gave them a good dose of my advice. You're a part of me, Vivienne. I knew something was wrong when I was in the hospital."

"Don't worry yourself, Mom. I talked with them. We settled everything, but our reconciliation came too late for me and Will. He took a position in New York to give me some space. The damage was already done."

Esty's eyes searched Vivienne's. "He left you?"

"It was the only thing left for him to do. He didn't want me to choose a life with him over a life with my family."

"What did Audrey and Evan say?"

"I didn't see any sense in telling them."

"Do you want it to be over with Will?"

"It doesn't matter what I want, Mom."

"Nonsense. Of course it does."

"He has a life, too. He can't just up and leave his job...not that he'd even want to consider that at this point." She took Esty's hand. "Thank you for telling them about Nate. If it had come from me, they would have thought I was trying to smear his memory."

"He did that by himself, Vivienne. They can choose to remember him whatever way they want, but what I told them will always be the truth."

***

The lunch crowd was a loud mix of locals, families taking a beach break with their kids, and tourists checking *Callane's* off their list of places to eat on the Cape. Vivienne's arrival with Esty was later than expected, but the timing couldn't have been better. She had to speak above the clattering of dishes, as she stopped at the counter stool where Magda was sitting. "What brings you in for lunch?"

"A pesky customer. I needed a little air."

"You've had them before."

"This one had the audacity to tell me how to pair my items."

Esty added a special touch to her own two cents. "You should have kicked her out the door."

Magda laughed at the suggestion. "Oh, I did, but with a little more finesse."

Brendan placed a cobb salad in front of her.

"Bah!" Esty replied with a flit of her hand. "Who needs finesse?"

"Let Magda eat her lunch," Vivienne said and ushered Esty to the kitchen. She then grabbed a clean apron from the back shelf and headed out front.

Brendan had become adept at handling the counter crowd and gave her a quick rundown before he took over his tables in the dining area. "The kitchen is working on a fish taco for seat six, a burger and onion rings, and a grilled fish sandwich for the couple at seats eight and nine."

"Mom!" Audrey called, waving her hand.

It was pure joy that captured Vivienne's face. Nothing left between them but the love of a mother and daughter. She raised her hand, signaling the just-vacated seat next to Magda.

"Hi, Magda." Audrey hung her purse on one of the hooks under the counter.

More than her casual greeting, was the shock of seeing Audrey in the restaurant, actually *speaking* to Vivienne, but Magda kept her surprise in check. "You look wonderful, Audrey. How are the wedding plans going?"

"Great. You'll be receiving an invitation soon."

"What can I get you?" Vivienne asked.

"Just a coffee and one of Auggie's muffins. I'm running late."

"I'm sorry I kept you and Evan talking so long last night."

"There was a lot that needed to be said. I didn't get much sleep, but it was the best I've had in a long time."

Vivienne returned with Audrey's coffee and cranberry muffin. "Gram's in the back. I told her you were here."

Moments later, Chance, one of the chefs, held the kitchen door open for Esty. "Where's my granddaughter?"

Audrey rose from her seat and rushed around the counter to meet Esty with a hug. "I'm glad I got to see you before I left, Gram."

"Promise me you'll come back soon...and bring Hugo."

"I promise. We'll take you and Mom out for dinner, if I can pull you both away from the restaurant."

Vivienne hugged Audrey. "No problem with that."

***

The last remaining emotions in Vivienne found their way to her teary eyes as she stood with Audrey in front of the restaurant. "I didn't think this weekend would end on such a happy note."

"I see you in a whole different light, Mom. I just wish I had known about Dad sooner."

"Maybe this was the time for you and Evan to know. What matters is that you understand now."

"And we have Gram to thank for that."

"She only wants your happiness, as do I, for you and Evan."

Standing at Audrey's car, Vivienne looped her arms around

Audrey and pulled her close.

Audrey pressed her face into her mother's shoulder and began to cry. "I never stopped loving you, Mom."

For a moment, Vivienne felt as if Audrey were not a grown woman, but the child she would sooth in her arms. "I know, sweetheart, I know. There are so many wonderful things ahead for you, and I'll be there to share them all with you."

"I'll keep in touch." She placed her purse on the passenger seat and climbed in behind the wheel. "I'll let you know when I want to go shopping for a dress. You can put it on your calendar."

"I'm looking forward to it." When Audrey's car was no longer in view, Vivienne turned toward the restaurant door.

Magda was holding a container with her leftover salad and stepped up next to her. "If you don't tell me what happened, I may burst at the seams."

Vivienne took in a breath and felt the freedom that came when she released it. "Mom told Audrey and Evan everything. They came to the restaurant last night, and we talked and cried until this whole mess was behind us."

"I'm so happy! This is what you've wanted, Viv. Now you can be part of every detail of Audrey's wedding. Have you told Will?"

"There doesn't seem to be a point, now."

"What are you saying?" Magda asked with curious caution.

"He decided to give me some *space,* time to work things out, and accepted a position at the Culinary Institute of America, in New York, of all places. Not that he needed my approval. He made it perfectly clear. By giving me this much space, he was telling me, *we're done.*"

"After you take Esty home and close the restaurant, have dinner at my house. Owen won't mind taking a rain check."

"No, I couldn't let you send Owen home. I'm the one intruding, but if he wouldn't mind me joining you two for dinner, I could use a man's take on my situation."

***

Magda left her door unlocked for Vivienne, as usual, who arrived with fresh-cut flowers for the table. The rich, savory aroma of seared beef drifted down the hall from the kitchen and made her mouth water.

Owen was standing in front of the oven and smiled as he glanced up at Vivienne. "I hope you brought your appetite, Viv. London Broil is my specialty." He then glanced at Magda. "Are the green beans ready, hon?"

She turned to meet his gaze. "Ready when you are."

It was a moment that Vivienne felt privileged to see. In that simple exchange, she witnessed their shared contentment. Her happiness for Magda overflowed as she struggled with her own disappointment in Will.

After rehashing her situation over dinner, Owen gave his assessment. "Yes, he could have been upfront with you, but I think he would regret leaving if he knew that your life's path was finally your own to choose."

"Or maybe the distance is his way of saying he's moved on. I won't be that woman, making him feel guilty for a decision that was his to make. I'm glad I didn't tell Audrey and Evan he'd left, especially Audrey. After finally admitting she'd been wrong about Will's sincerity this time, what an absolute fool I would look in her eyes if she knew that she was right all along."

***

Hugo was enjoying a beer while watching the newest mystery movie on Netflix when his cell announced a call from Audrey.

He checked the time on his watch. "Hey, baby. It's 4:00. Where are you?"

"I slept late. I'm on the highway, about a half hour away."

"I'll order our usual from the Thai place. We'll have an early dinner."

The thought made Audrey's mouth water. "Great. I'm starving. Don't forget my Tom Yum soup."

Thirty minutes later, Audrey snuck by the delivery guy while Hugo was tipping him. She dropped her duffle and purse in the foyer and inhaled the familiar spices rising from the fat paper bag Hugo set on the table. Only then, did she go to his open arms. The intense, emotional weekend had followed her home from Wellfleet. As their lips met, she didn't just realize, she *felt* how brutally fleeting life could be. A terrifying fear seized her heart, and she held him tight, burying the thought of losing him deep in her mind where her heart couldn't hear the words. She pressed against him, molding her body to his, and the gentle rhythm of their kiss quickened into something more demanding. When she reached down to touch him, his strong arms swept her up.

Between urgent kisses they shed their clothes. The strong muscles of his chest lay soft against her breasts, as he leaned her down on the bed. She weaved her hands through his hair, pressing her mouth to his, wanting to make up for the hours she'd been away from him.

When he pulled his lips from hers, her breath hitched in her throat, and her stomach quivered with anticipation. "Touch me," she pleaded.

"I don't want this to be over too soon."

His lips brushed the tips of her breasts, before he took each one into his mouth, feeling them rise with the playfulness of his tongue. She touched him and felt herself throb. "I want you inside me," she pleaded, but he gently moved her hand from him.

"I missed loving you, baby," he whispered.

Her heart raced as his lips kissed the flushed skin between her thighs. Beneath her soft mound of hair, he found her aroused, waiting for his love.

With each pass of his tongue her breath increased, giving in to the rising, intoxicating bliss that left her with no thought but the release that was moments away. She squeezed her eyes shut and cried out as she let go, consumed in an orgasm that pulsed with exquisite, decadent pleasure.

Hugo slipped deep inside her, feeling her warmth and lingering pulses that pushed him closer to the edge with every thrust. He arched his back as he climaxed, sending his love into the very core of her.

Audrey could hear his heart beating for her as she laid her head on his chest. "What we just shared is something I didn't know my mother had been missing in her life."

Hugo shifted on his side, his brows raised in astonishment. "Your grandmother told you that?"

"Yes, *and* my mother confirmed it."

"Tell me everything."

Nestled close to him, her tears wet his shoulder as she shared every detail of that heart-wrenching visit. "I've been wrong about so many things, but mom let them go as if I'd never uttered a word."

"Love doesn't hold grudges, baby. I admire your mother. Losing a spouse isn't easy, but neither was the life she hid from you and Evan."

"Will has a right to be angry with me. I raked him over the coals, and I wouldn't blame him if he won't accept my apology, but he, at least, has to listen to me if I stand in front of his desk."

"That may be a little difficult."

Audrey turned her quizzical face to him. "What do mean?"

"The day you left, I asked him to join me for dinner at *The Pru*. He was upset about the way things were headed for him and your mom, so he decided to give her space to work this out with you and Evan. He took leave from the paper, and accepted a teaching position for a semester, at The Culinary Institute of America, in New York."

"It's odd that my mom didn't mention it to me and Evan."

"Maybe he hadn't told her yet."

"If all of this has taught me anything, it's that some things are not what they seem on the surface. I'm done interfering. They should work this out together."

"Don't you think he deserves to know you and Evan have patched things up with your mom?"

"Yes, but he needs to hear it from her."

# Chapter 21

Will was fresh from a shower when his cell rang. "Hey, Dad. You're calling early. What's up?"

"I wanted to catch you before you left for class. This is something I should ask face-to-face, but as you're in New York, I hope you will reconsider being my Best Man."

Flabbergasted, he sat at his table. "Dad, we already talked about this. Audrey's gonna blow a gasket."

"Did you receive the invitation?" Hugo asked.

Among the pile of mail lay an envelope with tiny painted seashells in the top left corner. "Yeah."

"Please open it."

Will pulled it from the envelope, and his jaw dropped while reading Audrey's handwritten note on the bottom.

*There are no words to make up for the words I said. But I hope a simple I'm sorry will bring back the friend you were to me.*

"Did you read it?"

"Read it? I almost fell off the chair. You must have lost your shirt to get her to write this. Come on, I gotta know. What'd it set you back? A year's salary for some diamond earrings from E. B. Horn?"

Hugo's laugh bellowed through the phone. "It's not what you're thinking, but she knows what it means to me for you to be my Best Man."

Will smiled. "I'd be honored, Dad."

"Thank you. So, when should we expect you at the Cape?"

"I'm leaving right after class. Oh, and I'm bringing Sam."

"Who's Sam?"

"Samantha, Dad. She's a colleague whose never been to the Cape. The Bayview was full, so we're staying in Chatham, close to the restaurant."

Hugo had a sinking feeling that daggers would surely fly when Vivienne and Will saw each other, but he masked the apprehension he felt. "Okay. I've missed you, Will."

"Same here, Dad."

When Will ended the call, he picked up the invitation and read Audrey's note again. His fingers idly toyed with his beard, mulling the abrupt shift in her attitude. *If it wasn't Dad, I wonder what made her suddenly flip the switch from enemies to friends again.*

***

Vivienne tried to convince herself that she was over Will, but after three months apart, her sadness hadn't faded—it deepened. The news of Audrey and Evan, once so significant, felt trivial now, mirroring the hollow connection they seemed to share.

Audrey's early morning call had reached panic level. "Mom. Can you please call *the Wicked Seashell?* The email I received from them said they didn't have the Prosecco I asked for."

"You're going to give yourself, and the owner, an ulcer, Audrey."

"I just want everything to be perfect."

"And it will be, I promise. I'll call Cane and go over the bar and dinner menu...to ease your mind."

"Thanks, Mom. That's one less thing I have to worry about."

"You shouldn't be worrying about anything, Audrey. Everything will be fine."

"It's really happening, Mom."

"Yes, it is. You're getting married tomorrow."

"I have to finish packing. I'll call you when we arrive."

When Vivienne hung up, she took a steadying breath and grabbed a light sweater. Before she left, she paused at the door. The house felt different this morning. The anticipation of joy lifted the sadness that had darkened the rooms.

Esty being home today was one less worry for Vivienne, who managed to get her own list of things before tonight, done, in addition to the one added by Audrey's call. With the arrival of guests in Wellfleet today and tomorrow, Vivienne recalled that Will had stepped down as his father's Best Man. He'd surrendered an irreplaceable moment in time for her, which was a debt she couldn't repay.

***

Vivienne laid the ivory silk shawl over her shoulders and checked the time. *Evan is never late,* and, as sure as her thought, came a knock on the door.

"You look beautiful, Mom."

"Thank you, Evan. I've never seen you dressed in a linen shirt and pants."

"Grace chose what I'm wearing."

"She has a good eye. It's perfect for tonight and also for a night out with your wife. I know you and Grace don't have much opportunity to go out together. I'd be happy to watch Tory whenever you and Grace want a night to yourself, or even a weekend."

"I appreciate that, and I'm sure Grace would even more."

He opened the car door, and Vivienne carefully slipped into the back seat.

Grace shifted toward the back. "I love the full skirt of your dress. Is that vintage? It must be Magda, right?"

"She had something specific in mind," Vivienne replied.

"Even down to the Robin's egg blue. It certainly makes a statement."

***

Will and Sam had checked into the two rooms Will had reserved at The Chatham Crest Inn. "We have a few hours before the party," Will said as they walked up the stairs to the second floor.

"Great. I'll set my alarm and just chill for a while," Sam replied. "I'm sure this bed is way more comfortable than the one I'm currently sleeping on."

They parted ways across the hall, and Will proceeded to case out his room. He hung his garment bag in the closet and wheeled his suitcase into the corner. He checked his alarm and sprawled out in the middle of the bed. Despite their distance, Vivienne had never left his mind, or his heart. One thought troubled him. *If she didn't mend the division between Audrey and Evan, she won't be here. Her dream of seeing Audrey married will be lost forever. I'll be here to see it without her.*

Will met Sam in the lobby, and they walked the short distance to the restaurant.

"You were right, there are shops as far as I can see," Sam said, but stopped at a bakery window to admire the delectable display of pastries and cakes. "A pastry chef's dream."

"A *master* pastry chef," Will added.

"I'll still need to taste some of these before we leave."

They worked their way by several people who were gathered outside the restaurant entrance.

"Wow! *The Wicked Seashell*," Sam exclaimed, gazing at its place of honor above the reception area in the lobby. "That's one ominous conche!"

The celebratory *POP* of a cork in the room ahead led them to the party. Hugo's broad smile greeted them. "Will!" His arms wrapped Will in a papa-bear hug. "I've missed you."

"Me, too, Dad. I'd like you to meet Sam."

"Samantha," she cut in, "but Sam works just fine."

"She's a master pastry chef."

Hugo felt a knot tighten in his stomach, yet he managed to pull his lips into a calm, smooth grin. "Ah, pastries. My weakness, as my waistline can testify to."

"There are plenty of low-calorie desserts that are every bit as delicious as the traditional ones," Sam said.

"You're welcome to tackle that conversation with Audrey, but I warn you, it'll take a bit of convincing. Speaking of Audrey, let me introduce you."

Blindsided, Will's direct, unblinking stare threw the first daggers at Vivienne. *WTF! I was worried she would miss Audrey's wedding, and POOF! Here she is with a smile on her face!*

Beneath her calm demeanor, Vivienne was silently seething, sharpening her blade, as her eyes went to battle with Will's. *Don't even tell me he's angry! He steps out of my life, and VIOLA! Three months later, he shows up with some young babe on his arm. He hasn't met 'angry' yet.*

With slow definition, Hugo delivered the coded message to Audrey's blank face. "Audrey, *this*...is Sam. She's Will's *guest*...who'll be attending the wedding tomorrow."

Audrey's doubletake at Will dissolved into a warm smile for Sam. "I'm so glad to meet you." She held out her hand. "You must be one of Will's new friends. From the Culinary?"

"Yes, actually," Sam replied. "We both teach there."

"She's a pastry chef," Hugo added.

"Well, we have a delicious assortment tonight. I hope you enjoy them."

As a gentle interruption, Hugo placed his hand on Audrey's arm. "If everyone will excuse me, I want to make sure Cane has the bottle of Macallan I ordered for the reception tomorrow."

Trapped by three women, one of whom was eyeing his head for decapitation, Will swallowed hard. "I think I'll take Sam to the terrace."

When they were out of earshot, Audrey spun around, stunned, as she faced Vivienne. Her hushed voice began to tread in the stormy waters. "Mom, did you ever tell Will that Evan and I had resolved everything with you?"

Vivienne then relayed every detail of Will's call. "He deliberately called me at the restaurant to deliver the news that he was leaving, so I wouldn't be able to discuss his decision. You know exactly what a move like that means. Telling him about you and Evan would have been a waste of my breath, and pointless, as you can see. He's moved on. I have my family back. End of story."

"Is it, Mom?"

"I won't have you or Hugo wasting your time on this, especially tonight. We've survived rough waters. I intend to enjoy this party, and I'm starting by having Cane make me a cocktail."

A couple of Audrey's bridesmaids were at the small bar, so Vivienne chose a seat at the opposite end.

"Enjoying the party, Vivienne?" Cane asked.

"I apologize for calling you so many times."

His sympathetic smile put her at ease. "Bridal nerves. It's the first thing I write at the top of the menu, for each party I host. What can I get you?"

"Some emotional numbness. A dirty martini, three olives, please."

She put her lips to the glass, knowing each sip would give her that temporary boost of confidence to handle the situation she couldn't avoid.

"A phone call would have been the *considerate* thing to do." Will's voice wasn't a whisper, but a low rumble, as he stood behind her. "Instead, I got blindsided."

Vivienne felt the heat of his words crawl up her neck, each syllable a physical sting. Still, despite her rising anger, she kept her gaze fixed ahead and her jaw clenched tight, refusing to look at his face so close behind her.

"While we're on the definition of *considerate,* maybe, just maybe, I deserved to hear the news that you were leaving face-to-face," she hissed through gritted teeth.

Finishing off the remainder of her cocktail, she spun around.

Anger burned in the darkness of his brown eyes, but hers blazed just as hot. "Instead, I get a five-minute phone call and nothing but the dust from your car wheels as you got the hell out of Dodge!"

The girls at the other end of the bar shot them a wary glance. Sensing a tense standoff, they quickly paid their bar tab and rushed away to get out of the line of fire.

"I don't appreciate your sarcasm, Vivienne," Will said. "I wanted to give you space to focus on Audrey and Evan."

"Two hundred ninety-three miles of space? Now I know why. By the way, did *she* like the terrace? A nice place to take your new babe for drinks before dinner."

She slipped off the chair and moved around him, only to have him stop her with his grip on her arm. "She's a colleague, Vivienne."

"Colleague? Can't you at least be honest? She looks at you like the two of you are burning more than the midnight oil." Audrey's words came back to her like a cold dish of *I told you so.* "Audrey was right. I *was* just a novelty to you, an older woman to check off your list. But the thrill of 'new' became 'old' fast. I'm glad I didn't tell you about Audrey and Evan. I would have felt like such a fool with you flaunting Sam in my face. I feel bad for her. Does she know the clock is ticking?"

She glared down at his hand. "Let...go...of me, Will."

Vivienne breathed a sigh of relief as Evan approached, knowing one more minute would have resulted in another altercation with Will.

"Audrey sent me to get you. Is everything okay? You're a little flushed."

She put on her best smile and reached for his arm. "That would be Cane's dirty martini. I'm fine."

Moments later, Vivienne was enjoying dinner, laughing and appeared perfectly at ease. Suddenly, the ceremonious tapping of a champagne glass brought the room to silence.

Seated next to his father, Will stood and scanned the faces in the room. "To keep your food from getting cold, I'll use the centuries old proverb and make this *short and sweet.*" In the soft ambiance of the room, flutes of champagne glistened like gold as everyone raised their glasses. "To Audrey and Hugo. May happiness be your path ahead, and sorrow follow only as a shadow that fades in the sunlight of your love."

A lump formed in Vivienne's throat, imagining Will at his desk, penning the words he spoke. His voice brought the poignancy of his words to her broken heart.

***

It was after midnight when Vivienne and Audrey finally settled on Vivienne's couch with two cups of tea.

Audrey cradled the warm mug in her hands, and her thoughts drifted to a vivid memory. "Do you want to know the first time I recognized in Hugo's eyes the same love *I* felt for *him*? Most people's thoughts would go to sex, but it was on the anniversary of Emily's death. He was melancholy and didn't have much of an appetite at dinner. I reached for his hand and said, 'Never hide your grief from me. It's the part of your heart only for her that no one can touch. I'll always honor that.' He didn't say to me, 'I'm too old for you.' He said, 'I know what it is to love deeply and grieve just as deeply. The love I have has stood the test of time. I'm ready to begin again. With you.'"

Vivienne's eyes pooled with tears. "You're a lucky woman, Audrey. You're marrying a man who has lived the meaning of those words. So few of us are that fortunate."

"I'm sorry things didn't work out for you, Mom. Are you sure you'll be okay tomorrow?"

"Things *did* work out for me, Audrey. Tomorrow, I will see you walk down the stairs in your wedding dress and marry the man your heart yearned for. What more can I ask for?"

"What *your* heart wants, Mom."

"That ship has sailed, Audrey, but I wouldn't change a single minute of my time with Will. He took my insecurity in his hands and molded it into the woman I thought I could never be. The words Hugo spoke to you, resonated in the deepest part of my soul. I, too, have loved deeply and grieved just as deeply. And just when I thought I was ready to begin again, I'm back to being alone."

# Chapter 22

After the wedding: "Can I offer you something from my tray?" The young woman stood before Vivienne in a crisp white shirt and black bowtie. "I have a refreshing Mojito, a light Aperol Spritz, and a classic Gin and Tonic."

The vibrant effervescent called to her from the large-stemmed glass. "I love Prosecco," Vivienne said.

"Then the spritz is for you." The server handed Vivienne the glass. "Enjoy!"

Everywhere Vivienne looked, she saw a face that had touched Audrey's life in the small town of Wellfleet.

"This is crazy. It looks like Audrey invited half the town," Magda said to Vivienne as she and Owen gazed at the people taking up every inch of space in *The Wicked Seashell.*

"She wanted everyone to share this day with her, so Hugo gave her carte blanche."

"Including Stella and Camile," Magda replied. "I couldn't believe it when they came in the shop, boasting that they had been invited. Getting an invitation must have made an impression. They haven't walked through the door in years."

"I'm glad they did," Vivienne replied. "I expected to see them in some moth-eaten dress they pulled out of their closet, but I have to admit, they look terrific in flowy pants."

Owen chuckled under his breath.

"Believe me," Magda went on. "For what they're wearing, they opened their wallets as wide as their gossiping mouths."

"The wedding was beautiful, Viv. The sun setting over the water, the sound of the ocean. It was as if Audrey ordered the *perfect day.*"

"You don't have to dance around what's really on your mind," Vivienne said.

"Not tonight. Enjoy every minute of this, Viv, even with Stella and Camille."

"I'll need another cocktail for that." She chuckled.

They parted ways, and Vivienne was enjoying hors d'oeuvres when Hugo approached. "Vivienne, I'd like to speak with you for a moment."

The warmth instantly drained from her cheeks, leaving her face stiff and pale. "Of course."

She followed him to a small office behind the bar, where Cane was waiting. "Take all the time you need," he said to Hugo and closed the door.

Vivienne turned to Hugo. "What's wrong?"

"Please, sit down."

The ominous mix of Hugo's request, his tone, and their secluded location could only produce one disastrous outcome.

"Is everything okay with you and Audrey?"

Hugo placed his hand on Vivienne's, as he sat across from her. "You'll never have to worry about Audrey or our love for each other. It was Audrey who urged me to have this conversation with you. She mentioned how upset you were that Will took the position in New York without discussing it with you, and that being the reason why you didn't tell him you'd reconciled with Audrey and Evan."

"This isn't the time to be talking about that."

"Yes, it is." Hugo poured a glass of ice water for Vivienne.

"I had dinner with Will during the weekend Audrey visited her grandmother. It was then that he told me of his decision to remove himself from your situation, not to end what you both had, but to let you focus on what was important to you."

"He was just as important to me."

"Was he?" Hugo's gaze didn't waver. "Would you have chosen your life with him over Evan and Audrey? He loves you, Vivienne. Enough to see you happy, even if it meant losing you."

"And Sam? I didn't see her at the wedding."

"Will had told her about you. There was nothing between them, nothing more than just friendship. After seeing how the two of you reacted to each other at the rehearsal dinner, she knew there was something special between you. She didn't want to stick around and be a hindrance. I arranged for a car to take her back to New York."

Tears welled in Vivienne's eyes.

Hugo handed her his handkerchief to dab the tears from her cheeks. "You don't have to settle everything tonight."

"What can I say to him?"

"Whatever your heart wants."

The steady, pulsing beat of music broke the silence as Hugo opened the door. He offered Vivienne his arm and escorted her back through the guests to Audrey, who had been waiting on the outcome of their talk.

"Don't let this moment slip away, Mom. You've given Evan and me a good life. It's time to live yours. Remember, there are no perfect words. Just the truth."

"Thank you, sweetheart, and to your gracious husband."

"I'm a softie when it comes to love." Hugo wiped his eyes. "I think it's time for me to take my bride to the dancefloor."

***

Guests stood at their tables, as Hugo walked Audrey to the middle of the floor. Under the dim light, they moved in a slow sway to *All of Me.*

As couples joined them on the dancefloor, Vivienne stood alone. Her heart was brimming with words, like an unread love letter, until she caught her breath as Will's arms slipped around her waist. Standing behind her, he began to croon, "Give your all to me. I'll give my all to you."

She couldn't fight it. Every sleepless night her pillow caught her tears, vanished the instant she felt his body against hers and the subtle caress of his words. She turned and kissed him, and in that moment, they were alone, back in each other's arms.

The sound of applause broke their kiss. Surrounding them were faces, smiling with the joy of their reunion. Will then led her to the dance floor. Holding her close, their sway was a slow, gentle rhythm to the music.

His voice was a low, intimate rumble. "You're one provocative woman, Vivienne Callane. Who also has quite the feisty side."

"Well, what do you expect when the man I love shows up with another woman?"

"If there's anything that makes me love you more, it's your jealousy."

"What are you going to do about that?"

"I have all night to show you."

Stella and Camille's hungry eyes didn't blink, devouring every juicy detail they couldn't wait to splatter all over town.

Stella cupped her hand over Camille's ear and whispered, "I overheard someone say he's Hugo's son, a food critic."

Camille's eyes widened, her mind instantly churning the gossip mill. "Will Lawson! I read all his restaurant reviews." A tinge of jealousy colored her next words. "What's he doing with *Vivienne*?"

"Things that would make the two of you beg for more," Magda said to their faces, now aghast and horrified.

***

When everyone was seated for dinner, Will tapped his glass, and the room fell to a hush. Standing before eyes all focused on him, he began.

"You know, love is a very quirky thing. It won't be told how to love, or who to love. It stands firm when it needs to and lowers to one knee to profess itself. We all heard it, in the words that Audrey and Hugo danced to. Love does not hold to conventional views but will always embrace endless possibilities. And it surprised Audrey and Hugo with its unexpected, yet perfect, timing. Please raise your glasses as we celebrate them, and a love that defies expectations."

During dinner, Vivienne whispered to Will, "That was a very moving testament to the power of love. Do you believe love is all those things?"

"I was thinking about you when I wrote those words. Even lowering to one knee."

Her eyes said *yes, I will,* but she moved closer and whispered, "I know I'm a lot to handle."

Will leaned toward her, his breath warming her ear. "It's okay, baby. There's no one I'd rather steal the blankets from."

She looked at him and smiled. "You'll have all night to try."

***

Will's car motor hummed low as he drove slowly down Main Street in Wellfleet. Only his headlights shown on the darkened street ahead, giving a glimpse of the shops that had been closed for the wedding.

At Vivienne's house, the click of her key broke the silence. "Go in and make yourself comfortable. I'll be right back."

He knew where she was going. "Do you want me to wait by the

gate?"

She kissed him. "I'll be fine."

The iron gate felt cold in her hand as she pushed it open, and the dirt was hard under her feet, cold and unforgiving as the winds that would soon cover the town in a deep freeze. She pulled her shawl over her shoulders, gathering her thoughts, while she looked at Nate's headstone.

"Audrey married Hugo Lawson today. Evan gave her away. The path to this marriage wasn't an easy one, for everyone involved. But we walked it and came together at the other end. I brought you along on this journey by standing here, telling you things I felt you didn't deserve to know. So, here's one more. I'm crazy, mad, head-over-heels in love. This is where my journey ends with you and begins with Will. I'll still tell you what's going on in Audrey and Evan's life. You're their father, but my life is...well...my life again."

As Vivienne approached the crest of the path, she saw Will waiting by the gate.

"I couldn't let you go by yourself. Besides, it's cold and you only had this flimsy shawl to cover you, so I brought this from the house." The soft wool of Vivienne's plaid blanket warmed her shoulders as he laid it on her.

Into the morning hours, not a minute was wasted as they tossed and intertwined in the passionate frenzy of love.

# *Epilogue*

*ONE YEAR LATER...*

Vivienne reached over to shut off her alarm and looked at the time. *No more getting up at the crack of dawn.* She raised her arms over her head and stretched her legs, feeling her body waking up to the new day. After a quick shower, she left for the restaurant with a travel mug of coffee in her hand.

Magda was standing on her front porch, watching a moving truck pull into the space in front of her house. "Viv!" she called, waving her over.

Owen got out of the passenger seat. "Morning, ladies."

"Today's the day," Vivienne added.

"Owen and I decided it was time one of us gave up our place. His was smaller. Mine has the front porch he can't do without."

They stood aside as two movers carried a dresser up the porch steps.

"It goes up to the second floor," Magda said.

Seeing the moving truck brought back Vivienne's memory of packing up her mother's place.

She sat in one of the wicker chairs on Magda's porch, soothing her nostalgia as she rocked back and forth.

"I know what you're thinking, Viv, but it was Esty's time, and even she would have said *enough.*"

"She's probably chastising me for wasting tears on her." Vivienne wiped her eyes.

"Then don't. You know how she would get whenever someone got in her hair. I can see her throwing her hands up, yelling, 'Bah! Never waste tears on things you can't control.'"

The memory made Vivienne smile.

"Can we pick you up later for some ice cream?" Owen asked.

"Sure. Just come by the restaurant."

With calm confidence, Vivienne walked into the height of lunch hour. "Afternoon, Heidi," she said, passing Audrey at the busy counter and heading straight for the kitchen.

"Afternoon, everyone." She grabbed an apron from the back shelf.

There was a definite shift in the mood of the restaurant, especially at the counter, since Audrey began working there. Locals embraced her return, and visiting customers responded to her casual openness. But to Vivienne, it was more than that. The big city of Boston couldn't compete with the small town of Audrey's youth, which pulled her home to find a contented happiness that Vivienne thought she would never see. As if life had come full circle.

"What can I get you, Mrs. Schneider?" Vivienne asked, already knowing the answer.

"Two soft boiled eggs, Vivienne. Now, you know, I like to crack the eggs myself."

"Yes, Mrs. Schneider. I'll tell Auggie."

"Mom," Audrey said, "Will's here."

Vivienne glanced up to see Will talking to Heidi, and her heart swelled as she waved him over. "Any traffic?"

Will leaned over the counter to plant an unabashed kiss on Vivienne's lips. "No, I was over the bridge and up Route 6 in an hour."

"Are you hungry?"

"I could go for some of Esty's chowdah."

Vivienne placed a bowl in front of Will.

"Thanks, babe."

"Your father is building a jungle gym in our yard for Tory," Audrey said, picking up an order from under the warming lights.

"But you and I know him. His career was all about making headline news, so this is gonna be the talk of the town. Evan's been helping him in his spare time."

"You're right. It won't be your *average* jungle gym," Will replied then finished his second bowl while Audrey and Vivienne crossed paths behind the narrow counter, carrying their plates with expert precision.

"Viv!" Magda waved her hand. "We'll be waiting outside."

"Wanna take a walk down by the pier?" Vivienne asked Will.

"A stroll through town with my girl?" He smiled. "Let's go."

She placed her apron under the counter. "We're walking down to the pier, Audrey."

"Okay. You kids have fun."

Vivienne glanced at Audrey, who just smiled and sent a playful wink.

***

"Ready?" Owen said. "I hear the ice cream shop has a new flavor. Sunset sorbet."

The sights and sounds of the summer season had settled on the town: the laughter of children holding mounds of pink and blue cotton candy, tourists unwrapping taffy as they sat in front of the shop, local police directing cars that moved at a snail's pace on their way through town.

Everything was right in Vivienne's little corner of the world. She weaved her fingers through Will's as he took her hand. And, with the slow patience of time, she finally felt free.

Magda said, "We talked many times about your wish to see Audrey working in the restaurant."

"After Mom passed away, Hugo mentioned that Audrey's need to be close to her family became stronger than her desire to be in Boston. When he retired, there was only one decision for them."

Fishing boats were pulling in their day's catch at the pier. Evan spotted them walking down toward the pier and jumped off the boat to meet them. "Where are you all headed?"

"Just grabbing some ice cream," Owen replied.

"Hit any traffic, Will?" Evan asked.

"No. I left after the tourists who were rushing to get on the Cape."

"Audrey told me Hugo is building a jungle gym for Tory," Vivienne said.

Evan's broad smile crinkled the corners of his eyes. "He just started laying out the design. I've been helping him in my spare time. Grace and I won't even tell Tory about it until it's finished. You should take your ice cream and walk over there. It's going to be amazing."

Vivienne knew the way. Past the ice cream shop, a dirt road strewn with rocks and broken seashells led them to a two-story house set back from the shore of the bay.

"This house was vacant for so long. I didn't think it was salvageable," Magda said. "But look at it!" Two decks ran the length of the cedar shake house on each level, Adirondack chairs inviting anyone to relax and take in the panoramic view of the bay.

"Hugo and Audrey have been working on it for a year now," Vivienne said.

"Dad!" Will called, seeing his father rounding the back of the house.

Decked in a carpenter's belt, his broad smile preceded his welcome. "It's good to see everyone! And I see you stopped at the ice cream shop first."

"This is a new look for you, Dad," Will said. "Your life has been reading articles for the Tribune. Now you're reading plans for a jungle gym."

"What can I say when a little boy steals my heart by calling me Grandpa Hugo. Besides, Evan has been helping me lay out the plans."

"We saw him at the pier," Owen said. "He was boasting about it."

"Let me show you. It's around back."

Everyone followed, but Vivienne's eyes were drawn to the shore, watching the sailboats skimming over the calm waters of the Bay.

Suddenly, she felt Will behind her as he slipped his arms around her waist. "Penny for your thoughts."

"I was thinking of what my life would have been like if I hadn't met you."

He chuckled. "A lot less turbulent."

"It's true. I've weathered my share of storms." She looked down at the ring on her finger before she turned and kissed him. "But, oh how I love the calm."

**Judith Paolercio** was in the fifth grade when she received her first writing award. She can still remember the excitement when they handed her the prize: a dark-green Parker pen. She continued to write but also found another passion equal to that. Ballet.

She studied dance, though not professionally, and was taught by former professional dancers. Many years later, that experience became the inspiration for her dance trilogy: Pas De Deux, Curtain Call, and Final Bow.

Various sources, both fictional as well as personal, provided avenues to explore for new novels. "When It Comes to Love" has a perfect combination of both, making for a novel that has garnered the attention of MAK Entertainment, who secured the film rights, and it now has working script in place.

She currently lives in upstate New York, Dutchess County, in the small hamlet of New Hamburg, on the Hudson River. She and her husband raised two children who are now grown with families of their own. She works in New York City for a prominent law firm.

www.ingramcontent.com/pod-product-compliance
Lightning Source LLC
LaVergne TN
LVHW091147080826
845145LV00008B/2288

*9781967888184*